Dead Man on Campus

Dead Man on Campus

Larry A. Nielsen

1

Wednesday

He grimaced into the mirror as he struggled to knot his tie. After several unsuccessful attempts, he gave up. He couldn't care less about the tie. He was focused elsewhere.

"It all ends tonight."

Drew Robbins didn't often talk out loud to himself. It showed weakness and a lack of reality. Why make noises if you were the only one listening?

But this was different. He was determined that his mind and his heart both got the message. "Yep, it all ends tonight."

He stopped the soliloquy there, but his thoughts continued. *No more short-cuts on my research, now that I've reached the top of my profession. No more worrying about money, because the Wallace Prize comes with a cool three million. No more chasing after college girls, because I have the most wonderful woman in the world right here.*

Just then that most wonderful woman stepped out of the bathroom. Her hair was wrapped in a white towel. A white silk robe draped across her shoulders, covering little more than her arms.

"What ends tonight?" Gina asked as she walked across the bedroom to Drew.

"Oh, nothing. I was just thinking out loud."

"Come on, tell me what you are planning to end tonight. It better not be me!" Gina put her arms around his waist and pulled him into a tight embrace.

Drew smiled. No, he wasn't quitting Gina tonight. Or ever. "I was just thinking that all the stress of making it will end tonight. I can stop trying so hard to prove myself. Now I can relax a bit and start thinking about my legacy."

"Age forty-two is a little early to be thinking about legacy, isn't it?" Gina asked. "You have a lot left to accomplish before we start drafting your eulogy, don't you think?"

"Yeah, yeah, of course," Drew answered, "but the stress is going to go down, way down, I'm sure. That is, as soon as I get this stupid rag tied around my neck."

He hated ties. They represented just another one of the ridiculous conventions that people expected him to follow. If he had his way, tonight he would wear his most effective uniform when he dressed for show—a denim shirt topped by a blue blazer, well-worn jeans and brown leather walking shoes. Ties were for accountants, not field biologists.

But Drew loved manipulating people and situations even more than he hated convention. He rebelled when he could, went along when it served his purpose. From his earliest days he understood that people were easy to control, just like other animals. Give them what they need—food, money, romance, perhaps just a bit of attention—and you could get anything from them. Tonight he would succumb to tradition instead of fighting it. He had too much riding on this night to let a pin-striped suit get the better of him.

The tie, however, remained a problem.

Gina turned him around and took over. "Let me take care of this," she said and went to work on the new silk tie she had bought him for this occasion.

"Where did you learn to tie a tie?" he asked.

"When a girl grows up in boarding schools in England, she has to learn many things other than algebra and French. Important things, like which fork to use and making sure your upper-crust husband looks presentable. Now quit fidgeting." She flashed a provocative smile. "Don't you have something better to do with your hands?"

He took the hint and found a very good use for his hands. He lifted the robe from her shoulders, and she lowered her arms for a moment to let it slip to the floor. His hands traveled slowly across her shoulders and then down her back. This, he thought, must be how a sculptor felt when he caressed the marble forms he created.

"Easy, m'lord," Gina said, "that's far enough. You need to be focusing on your acceptance speech." She tightened the tie around his neck, and turned down the starched collar of his shirt. "Besides, I need to finish getting gussied up myself. You don't want me to look like I just came out of the field, do you?" She slapped him gently on the rear. "Now go downstairs and look over your notes while I get ready."

Drew did as she asked. He always did what she asked. When Gina Rahim was in view, everything else faded into the background. Many women had passed through his life, and his bed, and he had always been in charge. He controlled his lovers just like he controlled everyone else. But not Gina. Gina had been different, right from the beginning. He didn't believe in love—other animals got along without it, and so could he—but if there were such a thing, he thought, this was how it would feel.

As he walked down the stairs, he reviewed his plans for the evening and smiled. He spoke to himself one last time. "Well not everything ends tonight. Some things are just beginning."

At the bottom of the stairs, Drew turned right and stopped under the arched entrance to his study. Not just a study, but the kind of place a great scientist needed and deserved. He loved his home, mostly because of this room. Its intended purpose was as a living room, of course, the gathering place for a family of parents and kids, strewn with the artifacts of conventional life—toys, the daily mail, television, an X-box, and too many remote controls.

But Drew had no interest in a family. He didn't care all that much for the human species in general, and he certainly didn't want the responsibility and irritation of a family interfering with his ambitions. The 1930s-era stone house was unsuitable for a modern family anyhow. The kitchen was too small, there was no family room, the bedrooms had tiny closets, the old pipes were wrapped in asbestos insulation, and the basement leaked radon. It suited Robbins just fine, however. The stone and cedar-plank exterior had the look he coveted; it was the kind of place an explorer might have called home, a welcoming retreat for a few months between adventures. He had installed state-of-the-art electronics to assist in his work, and as long as the microwave could heat up a carry-out meal, the kitchen served him just fine.

When he moved in, he immediately converted the living room into his study. Robbins had visited the historic homes of many early naturalists, and each one had a study like this. The room was staged to bring an earlier age of field exploration to mind—in both Robbins' mind and those of his visitors. In his study, he felt kinship with the great scientific adventurers of earlier centuries—James Cook, Alexander von Humboldt, Charles Darwin and the name-sake of the award he was about to receive, Alfred Russel Wallace.

The room was the largest in the small house, stretching from front to rear. Windows at the front looked east across the street to the edge of the university. Windows in the back looked west onto a replica of an English cottage garden. The early explorers all had extensive gardens, so Robbins made sure his home had one, too. He was no gardener himself, but the previous residents had been. Wide flower beds lined the borders of the yard, interspersed with flowering shrubs. He hired a horticulture student every term to tend the plantings. Regardless of season, the yard was a living Thomas Kincaid painting.

He had replaced the windows overlooking the yard with French doors that led onto a slate patio. When the weather and his schedule permitted, Drew spent the hour just before sunset there, reading a book from the best-sellers list while enjoying his daily indulgence of single-malt scotch whiskey. He was sure that the great explorers sipped whiskey in their gardens and read the latest novels while imagining their next conquest.

Robbins had renovated the room into a 19th-Century man-cave. The original large brick fireplace occupied most of the south wall. It burned wood, of course, not gas; he would have burned coal if he could find a steady supply. The mantel was covered with remembrances of his field projects around the world. A carved wooden bowl from the Amazon anchored one end, a clay figure of a tiger stood at the other. In between were several photos of Robbins in the field, flanked by his long-time research associate, Russell Bronoski, and various groups of field assistants.

Above the mantel hung Robbins' pride and joy, two Maasai spears, one above the other and facing in opposite directions. The spears were gifts from the villagers where Robbins had done his doctoral work in east-central Africa. Each spear had a broad, razor-sharp blade on one end, connected by a wooden shaft to a pointed metal spike on the other. Both ends of a Maasai spear were intended for action, one for slashing and the other for stabbing. Robbins had learned how to use a spear skillfully from the Maasai warriors who lived around his first African study area in Tanzania. Displayed now over his mantel, the spears reminded him that he, too, was a warrior, fighting with whatever weapons he needed to achieve his goals.

He had placed his desk opposite the fireplace, so he could work while looking at the fire and spears. On the wall behind his desk hung a painting of three young dogs sitting outside a basket. The painting had hung in his grandmother's house as long as he could remember. He had inherited the painting, along with all her other belongings, when she died. The painting hung above his desk wherever he lived.

After his parents died in a car accident when he was a boy, he had lived with his grandmother. She had been his only family, really his only friend. He was painfully shy as a boy, freezing up when he was expected to speak to adults or even his classmates. But when his grandmother brought home a dog from the local animal shelter, Robbins' life began to change. The dog gave him unconditional affection, drawing out and developing his personality. As he grew to be tall, strong and handsome, shyness gave way to confidence and then confidence to dominance. Andrew Robbins had to be the alpha dog, regardless of the setting or circumstances. He rose to the top in the classroom, on the playing field, and in the back seat of the car.

His success convinced him that people were there to be manipulated. He felt only disdain and pity for the people he bested. And the painting reminded him that animals, not people, were his true friends. He understood animals. Animals had no hidden agendas to derail a plan, no feelings to tip-toe around, no inhibitions that prevented following through on a decision. From his childhood, he felt more comfortable in the company of animals than in the company of people. He was sure the early explorers had felt the same.

Shelves filled all the remaining spaces on the walls, with carefully arranged tableaus of books, photos, mementos and specimens. Like everything in his life, his study was carefully constructed theater to make the world see Drew Robbins as Drew Robbins wanted to be seen. No one could visit that room without understanding that the man who lived there was a great naturalist and a great scientist.

2

Drew sat down at his desk and picked up the letter he had received two months ago from the Wallace Foundation. He really didn't need to look at the words—he had read the letter so many times he knew it by heart:

Dear Professor Robbins:

On behalf of the Alfred Russel Wallace Foundation, we are honored to inform you that you are the recipient of this year's Wallace Prize for Conservation. Congratulations! You join a small list of the world's most important conservationists who share this distinguished honor.

Our directors chose you over a field of impressive nominees. However, your groundbreaking work on the behavior of hyenas, described in your book, "The Hyenas of Tanzania," has been so fundamental to conservation of this previously misunderstood and under-appreciated species that the directors voted unanimously for your recognition. Your many other studies of carnivore behavior around the world have added significantly to the global protection and recovery of these taxa.

Our staff will contact you soon about the details of the award process, but I wanted to congratulate you myself on your most worthy contributions and achievements. I look forward to meeting you at the award celebration.

Sincerely,

Sir Archibald Harmon, OBE

Chair, Board of Directors

The Wallace Prize had become known as the "Conservation Nobel" since its inception in the early 1990s. It was simply the highest honor one could achieve in the conservation profession. Some people compared it to the MacArthur Genius grant because it delivered a massive financial prize—three million US dollars—with no strings attached.

He put the letter back on his desk and reached for the book that had been responsible for the award. *The Hyenas of Tanzania* was based on his doctoral research. He turned the book over in his hands several times, caressing the cover and spine as though it were a beautiful woman. Most doctoral dissertations moldered obscurely in science libraries, read only by a few students hoping either to repeat the work or move it further along. But Drew Robbins had been lucky, extraordinarily lucky. What should have been just another specialized tome in the field of wildlife animal behavior had jumped a literary fence and transformed into a best-selling book.

He thought back to the day when a film crew for *Africa Wild*, the Canadian nature show, had broken down near his research camp in Tanzania's Mazarie National Park. He had been near the end of his third and final field season as a doctoral student at Virginia Western University. He had taken in the crew while they waited for a mechanic, providing shade and water, and they had discussed his research. The producer had asked many questions and instructed his videographers to record their conversation and then to take more video of Drew and the camp.

Several months later, when Drew was back on campus and writing the first draft of his dissertation, the phone had rung, the display showing an unfamiliar area code and number.

"Hello, this is Drew Robbins," he said.

A vaguely familiar voice spoke back. "Hello, Drew. I hope you remember me, Jamie Nelson, from *Africa Wild*."

Drew couldn't think why he would be calling. "Of course, Mr. Nelson. Great to hear from you."

"Super," said Jamie. "So, listen, Drew. Our folks have an idea. We'd like to do an episode of *Africa Wild* about your research."

Drew's heart started beating hard, and his voice cracked as he responded. "Wow. This is a surprise."

"I hope it's a good surprise," Jamie said. "Listen, Drew, we've had shows about all the obvious African animals, elephants, gorillas, rhinos and such. We think it's time to introduce some less likable species, animal anti-heroes we're calling them. Our marketing people think the world is ready for hyenas. I showed them the tapes we recorded when you rescued us..."

Drew interjected, "I hardly rescued you. Just gave you some water and a place to wait for the repair truck."

"Accept it," said Jamie, "you're a hero to my boss. Anyway, we think you are the right person to feature in a show about a pack of hyenas. Sounds cool, eh?"

Drew thought quickly. He had wondered when he met Jamie Nelson why he had been so interested in the work Robbins was doing, so much so that he had made his crew jump into action with cameras and microphones and all their other equipment. He had watched the show *Africa Wild* a few times since he had returned, just to see what it was all about. He hadn't liked it. He didn't like the way animals were portrayed with human emotions and values. All the talk about mothers and babies made him laugh out loud. How typical it was that humans had to justify their own actions by transferring them to animals. It was all a con, and Jamie Nelson was the chief con artist.

But this would be Drew's big break. He had exploited people and situations his whole life to suit his interests. He could tolerate anything if it was to his advantage, even an anthropomorphizing television series. The possibility of becoming the next Jane Goddall was more than he could resist.

"That sounds great," Drew said. "But one thing—hyenas aren't really the bad guys everyone thinks they are. They're just doing the job they were born to do. And they live in clans, not packs."

"Perfect," said Jamie, "Canadians love clans. Hey, maybe we can name the clans after Scottish ones, like Campbell and MacGregor. They'll love it. And there's nothing better than turning the anti-hero into the hero! Disney made hyenas evil in *The Lion King*, and we'll even the score. Look out Bambi, here come the hyenas!"

Drew had cringed at that sentiment, but he did the show nevertheless. He and Russell Bronoski had returned to Tanzania the following spring along with Jamie Nelson and his crew. They spent several weeks filming in Mazarie National Park and some other locations, adding footage of other hyena species, the aardwolf of southern Africa, and the striped hyena of northern African and central Asia.

And the episode had been a hit when it aired the year after Robbins finished his dissertation. Hyenas turned out to be fascinating creatures, and Drew was correct that their behavior wasn't any more evil than the other carnivores of the African savannah, the lions, cheetahs, and leopards that fascinated people. Hyenas were smart, not dumb. They were primarily predators, not scavengers. They were brave, not cowardly, more often than not winning in confrontations with the so-called king of the jungle. In fact, Drew knew, hyenas were the real animal royalty. He made sure that watching hyenas go about their daily business captured viewers around the world.

It also helped that Drew Robbins turned out to be a perfect fantasy of the rugged outdoor adventurer. He was a real-life Indiana Jones. He had as much charisma as the animals, and the camera loved him. He looked like everyone's All-American, tall, with a slim swimmer's build, but obviously strong. His sun-streaked brown hair would not obey a comb, lending a boyish, casual charm that made older women think of the young Robert Redford. Younger women didn't remember Robert Redford, but they swooned anyhow. And children wanted to grow up to be the next "Dr. Drew."

The success of the television episode enticed a publisher to contract Drew to convert his dissertation into a book for general readers. He was a great storyteller—one of the skills that made the television show so engaging—and was equally adept at putting his stories on paper. His cumbersomely titled dissertation, "An observational and statistical analysis of the behavior of *Crocuta crocuta* in east-central Africa," remained appropriately obscure, but the book he wrote based on the dissertation, *The Hyenas of Tanzania,* became a commercial and literary success.

His exceptional dissertation research earned him a faculty position at his alma mater, Virginia Western. And his continued research on hyenas and other predators around the world over the next fifteen years earned him early tenure and promotions, university awards, and a salary well above his peers. The university did everything it could to keep Robbins off the job market, so when the new biological sciences building went up five years earlier, he was allocated one entire floor for his Carnivore Research Center.

He put the book down and next fingered the third item on his desk, a contract for a new television program. The Canadian television network that aired *Africa Wild* had offered him his own series—*Robbins in the Wild*—with an initial schedule of six shows over the next two years. The contract required a two-year leave of absence from VWU, a move that the university had already informally endorsed.

Yes, he thought again, everything was going to change, starting tonight.

3

"Well, what do you think?" Drew looked up from his desk as Gina walked into the study. All he could do was stare, mesmerized by the vision before him.

Gina looked like an Egyptian goddess. If a dress could be both modest and alluring at the same time, this was it. The halter dress covered her from neck to feet, but left her shoulders and arms bare, her caramel skin glowing beside the pure white silk. She wore a necklace of black onyx stones that matched the color of her shoulder-length black hair. The platinum mounting of the stones sparkled like sunlight shimmering on water.

She paraded across the room for his approval. Despite the black patent high heels, she walked with the practiced grace of a runway model, no doubt something else she learned in boarding school. She stood next to the desk, facing away from Robbins and wiggled. "Eat your heart out, Pippa!" she said.

Drew eventually found words. "I hope you can sit down in that thing."

Gina turned around and lifted a foot onto his knee. The dress opened along one side, well up her thigh. "No problem," she smirked, "it has a little slit in it, see?"

Early evening in April was spectacular in Stone Valley, Virginia. Spring was well underway, the colorful blooms of dogwoods, redbuds and serviceberry dotting every yard and hillside. Patches of azaleas adorned the park-like campus, which was known for its gardens and green spaces, all overseen by nationally ranked departments of horticulture and landscape architecture. The banquet had been strategically set for a Wednesday evening, as far away as possible from weekend athletic contests and student frivolity. The university's public relations director wanted no distractions from this extravaganza.

The ballroom of Virginia Western University's convocation center was dressed for a party. The media team had erected a metal lattice along the sides and over the top of the raised platform that held the head table. Spotlights in green and gold—the school's colors—trained on the huge black-and-white mural of hyenas running across an African savanna, acacia trees in the background. Twin pillars of green and gold balloons framed the scene.

The room was gradually filling with the university's elite—the board of trustees, vice-presidents, deans, and the faculty senate. Even the football and basketball coaches had been coerced to attend. Two tables were reserved for Drew's research staff; at the one directly in front of the stage sat Russell Bronoski and other members of Robbins' research team. Two other tables were reserved for members of the biological sciences faculty, including the head of Robbins' home department, Ted Graham. Others from the university and community filled the rest of the tables, and an empty row of chairs snaked around the sides and back of the room; later the chairs would be open to students who couldn't afford dinner but still wanted to see their hero crowned.

The head table had four seats on each side of the center podium. To the right sat the university's president, Alice Crutchfield, and her husband. Next to them was Archibald Harmon, there to present the award from the Wallace Foundation, and finally the chair of the university's board of trustees. To the left of the podium sat Drew, next to him Gina, and then Jamie Nelson from *Africa Wild.* Last was Nelson's guest, Misty Stanhope, a B-list actress who couldn't disguise her boredom despite a heavily made-up face and a low-cut dress that had the attention of every male in the room.

The dinner menu was also styled for the purpose of the event, an emphasis on environmental sustainability, one of the university's avowed values. All ingredients were "local foods," grown within a short distance of campus, and organic. If the university's public relations staff had had their way, the entrée would have been vegetarian, but Drew insisted, since he studied predators, that meat be served. They compromised on farm-raised Atlantic salmon, certified as sustainable.

After dinner, the doors were opened and a throng of students scrambled to fill the chairs along the walls. Quickly loud chatter penetrated what had been a reserved occasion. Most students were from Robbins' home department or the horticulture department that supplied gardeners for his yard. As if on cue—and probably actually on cue—the students began chanting "V-W-U, we love Drew!" The guests seated at tables gradually joined in, and for a few minutes, the room rocked like a pep rally. Then

President Crutchfield rose to the podium, and the room quieted for the program to begin. Drew's fans were pleased when the president recited some banal words of introduction and quickly turned the program over to Harmon.

"Ladies and gentlemen," Harmon began, "it is my honor to be here representing the Alfred Russel Wallace Foundation. Wallace, as I'm sure many of you know, was the co-originator, with Charles Darwin, of the idea of natural selection. Wallace labored for decades in the wilds of South America and southeastern Asia, much longer than Darwin, and he came to the same conclusions as Darwin. Together their work established the basis for what became the science of ecology and, today, the effort to preserve the world's biodiversity. We call that effort conservation biology."

Most of the audience knew this already, and they began to fidget, worried that they might be in for the opening lecture of an introductory course in natural resources. Mercifully, Harmon got to the point. "You know," he said, "most of the world's major awards bring the recipients to them. Not the Wallace Foundation. We come to the recipient. We believe that we should give the award in the awardee's habitat, surrounded by his or her natural community of friends and family. That is, after all, what conservation is about—recognizing and protecting the ecosystem that supports a species and its community." The students responded with applause. Yes, they were part of Drew Robbins' ecosystem, sharing in his glory.

Harmon went on with a long description of Robbins' accomplishments. The audience knew all this, too, but they were patient. At least his rambling remarks were about their hero.

Students loved Drew Robbins. His lectures (when he gave them) were like television adventure shows, filled with stories, photographs and videos of encounters with wild animals and vistas of exotic places. There was always a waiting list to get into his seminar classes, where students could get up-close-and-personal with a celebrity. Horticulture students also competed for the chance to tend his garden. He was regularly asked to speak to student clubs, alumni groups, and other university events; he never disappointed an audience, and thus managed to keep the university's leadership in his debt.

Sir Harmon eventually stopped speaking and presented the Wallace Prize, placing a gold medal around Robbins' neck. The medal bore a profile of Wallace on one side and a hyena on the reverse, along with Drew Robbins' name and the year. Everyone stood and clapped and cheered for Robbins. But then they gasped as Harmon finished his presentation by holding up a small piece of paper. "And here, Dr. Robbins," he said, "is one small addition to the Wallace Medal—a check for three million dollars." This, at last, was something most of the guests hadn't expected. The student chant erupted again, "V-W-U, we love Drew!"

Drew walked to the microphone, running a hand through his unruly hair and capturing everyone's attention with his brilliant smile. He gave a surprisingly humble acceptance speech, causing his departmental colleagues to roll their eyes. They all knew, through personal experience or reputation, that Drew Robbins was anything but humble. Don't stand between Drew and the camera or microphone, they had learned, and don't expect him to share the credit when the spotlights go up. That bothered the other faculty members in his department, perhaps, but it didn't phase either students or university leaders. "V-W-U, we love Drew!"

But then he surprised everyone. "Let me finish by saying that although the Wallace Prize is the most important and wonderful thing to happen to me in my career, I hope that tonight can end with something even more important and more wonderful for my life as a whole."

The room was now on high alert. "As many of you know, my companion for the evening, Gina Rahim, has been a doctoral student in the Department of Renewable Resources, studying animal behavior of the Scottish wildcat as part of my research team. I'm delighted to announce that the graduate school affirmed last week that she has completed all requirements for her degree. So, please join me in congratulating Dr. Gina Rahim!"

The applause was long and appreciative. Gina was well liked on campus. Many students knew her from her participation in departmental events, and she had been active in the graduate student assembly, so many of the administrators knew her also. She was obviously embarrassed to be taking attention away from Drew, but her pleasure at being recognized was also obvious.

He continued, "Gina, if you would join me please, I have a question I would like to ask." She stood and walked unsteadily to his side, her usual control abandoning her. She thought her heart might leap from her chest.

He reached in his pocket and held up a ring. "Will you marry me?"

The room went wild. Everyone jumped to their feet, clapping and cheering. The students at the back tables and along the walls modified their chant: "Gina and Drew, we love you!" The outburst continued for some minutes, long enough for

Gina to regain her composure. She nodded her head and as the room quieted in anticipation of her answer, she said in a throaty whisper, "Yes. Of course, yes! I love you!" He slipped the ring on her finger, and the crowd resumed its raucous celebration.

Eventually, President Crutchfield called the evening to an end, a rather anti-climactic effort on her part. Half an hour later, when every hand had been shaken and every hug had been exchanged, Drew and Gina finally escaped the room and drove home.

They parked in their driveway, and Drew walked around the car to open the door for Gina. Gina was distracted momentarily as she got out of the car, but quickly grabbed Drew and kissed him. She held him tightly as they stumbled toward the door.

"Careful, Gina," Drew said, "you're going to make us fall."

"Sorry," she said. "I just always want to be so close that no one can tell where you leave off and I begin."

"You just about got your wish," Drew responded, laughing. "One big lump of lovers lying on the ground!"

On the doorstep, they kissed again and she whispered, "Now the real party can begin!"

Gina woke in the morning as the sun slanted through the bedroom skylights. She smiled as she relived the previous evening and how it ended. The room was a mess. Their clothes were scattered on the floor, just like the scene in a 1950s movie before the screen fades to black.

She reached over to find her fiancée, but she was alone in the bed. Drew had a habit of rising early, preferring to obey the rhythm of nature rather than that of the alarm clock.

Gina stretched and looked down at the ring on her finger.

Like the necklace she wore last night, the ring held a large onyx stone, mounted in platinum. Onyx was her favorite gemstone, and Drew had commissioned a local jeweler to fashion a ring that matched her pleasure, not society's convention. She thought about what he had said before the banquet, that it all ended tonight. Maybe, she thought, but whatever ended last night promised a new beginning today.

She rose, slipped into jogging clothes and tied her hair into a ponytail. Drew might have been able to get right back to work, but she needed to get in a run and burn off some of the emotion of the previous night.

When she reached the bottom of the stairs, she called to Drew. "Good morning, my darling! I'll make the coffee." She turned to the kitchen and busied herself with the task. When the coffee was ready, she filled two mugs and headed to the study.

As she turned into the room, both mugs fell from her hands and crashed to the floor. She screamed. And screamed again.

Drew Robbins lay hunched over his desk, a Maasai spear lodged firmly in his back.

4

Tanzania, Eighteen Years Earlier

The single-engine Cessna descended quickly, hit ground hard and bounced forward on the dirt landing strip. Drew Robbins tensed as he watched the plane head towards a thicket of acacia trees at the end of the runway. Just as he thought his adventure would end before it began, the pilot turned the small plane, heading towards a building that served as the "airport." To Drew, it looked like a picnic pavilion badly in need of maintenance.

"Welcome to South Camp," the pilot said, glancing over his shoulder at his only passenger and giving a salute.

Drew returned the gesture. He was a basket of emotions. Flying in a small plane was a new phenomenon, as exciting as it was unsettling. He had just touched down in the place that would be his home for the next six months, and he had no idea what to expect. It was late May, and the main rainy season was ending, to be followed by months of dry weather. He was beginning the field part of his doctoral research, a scary enough prospect if you were going to run experiments in a controlled laboratory, but he was going to collect his research data in the wilds of Tanzania.

All those emotions—fear, excitement, uncertainty—were overshadowed, however, by one feeling that made his heart pound like a jack hammer. He was going to live in the wilderness, studying the species he loved the best, the spotted hyena. He was going to live and work like the explorers who had come to Africa a century before, using their wits and powers of observation to thrive in a virtually unknown and probably hostile world.

This is what he had been waiting for. He had completed all required classes, in which he effortlessly, but grudgingly, impressed his professors, regurgitating information that didn't interest him. He had jumped through all the hoops of the institutional animal care and use committee and other university offices that had to approve his research plans. All those boxes had been checked and forgotten. He was here now. Finally. Here, where he belonged, to become the human who knew more about and lived closer to hyenas than anyone else in the world. He imagined that Darwin had felt the same when the *HMS Beagle* anchored for the first time along the coast of South America.

He unwound his lanky frame as he stepped from the plane's cabin, stretching muscles that had been cramped for the entire thirty hours of the journey. A commuter flight to Washington, then overnight to Amsterdam, another jet to Kilimanjaro, and finally this tiny plane to—well, to nowhere. He reckoned he was as far away from Stone Valley, Virginia, as a person could get.

He gathered his belongings as the pilot pulled them from the small compartment toward the back of the plane. There wasn't much. A back-pack held a few changes of field clothes and the requisite supply of anti-malaria pills. It also held a large supply of digestive remedies; his advisor had laughed when he handed Drew what he called "starters and stoppers."

Most of the bulk and weight was a heavily padded camera bag stuffed with a pair of digital single-lens reflex cameras, another pair of video cameras, telephoto and macro lenses, various filters, batteries, chargers and a tripod. A water-proof plastic crate filled with empty journals and pens for recording his observations completed his inventory. That was all. Everything else he would need should be waiting for him at his camp.

Arrangements had been made for Drew to live at a research station called South Camp, near the headquarters of Mazarie National Park. The camp was centrally located in the park, despite the name—the camp was named for its position south of the Equator, established and named fifty years before the park boundary had been drawn. It would provide a good base for studying hyenas throughout the sprawling park. His research grant had paid for a small cabin that would be his home and research office, sole access to a Toyota land-cruiser, diesel fuel as needed and meals in the mess tent run for the park staff.

He called the research grant "his," but, of course, the grant had been submitted and received in the name of his advisor at Virginia Western University. That was how such things were done at a university. And, yes, his advisor, Dr. Malcolm Burns, had the kind of reputation that opened doors and made granting agencies confident. But Drew was the person who had the idea to study hyenas in Africa, he was the person who read about and wrote about hyenas every chance he got. Drew had used charm and persistence—whatever it took—to convince most professors that he should do his assignments on hyenas, regardless of the specific topic. Consequently, when it came time to defend the research project before the grant foundation's review committee, he answered all questions with a knowledge that impressed the committee and landed the grant. So, regardless of what anyone else said or thought, it was "his" research grant. And, here, in Tanzania, far from any competitors for fame or success, far from the bureaucracy that set up rules about what he could do and how he could do it, here he would make sure everyone understood that Drew Robbins was about to become the world's expert on hyenas.

A group of men were lounging in the shade of the airport's pavilion. One broke from the group, walked up to Drew, and offered his hand. "I'm Geoffrey, director of South Camp," he said, a broad smile spreading across his face, "welcome to your new home!"

Drew returned the smile and shook his hand. "Glad to meet you, Geoffrey. I'm so excited to be here. Is it a long way to camp?"

"No, not far at all," said Geoffrey and smiled, "superhighway all the way!" HIs friends in the pavilion laughed. They loaded his gear into the back of the land-cruiser, and Geoffrey threw Drew the keys. "This is your truck, so you might as well get used to being behind the wheel."

Drew opened the left front door. Geoffrey erupted into laughter at Drew's confusion, and his friends under the pavilion all joined in. "We drive on the other side in Tanzania," he said, and opened the right–hand door. "The driver sits over here. You'll get used to it."

Drew bristled at the joke, but knew better than to challenge the group of men. I'll need them, he thought, so let it go—for now. Drew started the vehicle. At least the pedals were in the same location. But the gear-shift lever wasn't, and he ground the transmission repeatedly as Geoffrey chuckled next to him. They lurched slowly down the road as Drew got the feel of the truck, sweat running down his forehead as he dealt with the strange controls and the embarrassment. Geoffrey pointed the way as the road got narrower and less distinct. Within minutes, they were driving along two ruts that veered off into the grassland, dust clouding up behind the truck.

Embarrassed as he was, Drew was even more awestruck. Animals were everywhere. Wildebeest mostly, but also zebras, Thompson's gazelles and Cape buffaloes. The outlines of giraffes stood out above the horizon. Ostriches, the world's largest bird, scrambled out of the way, and little bee-eaters, one of the smallest, flitted across the truck's path. They were seldom out of sight of elephants. The animals were wild, but they seemed almost tame to Drew. They took little notice of the vehicle. "Why don't they run away?" he asked Geoffrey.

"The animals here don't fear us. They aren't hunted, and tourists can't approach them on foot. The boys joke that the animals must think the trucks are just big moving rocks, no threat to them. We're in their home, but they don't pay us much attention."

Drew braked to a stop when he saw the hyena. It was running slowly through the short grass, easy to identifiy by its lopping gait. The hyena's rear legs are shorter than the front, producing a sinuous path unmistakable for any other predator. Drew had seen hyenas before in zoos, of course, and watched them on videos, but he had never seen them run freely through their own habitat. They were magnificent, with their massive shoulders and powerful jaws.

This, he reminded himself, was his animal. He loved the dog his grandmother had given him, but the hyena was the animal Drew saw in his daydreams as a boy. He learned early that hyenas were not members of the cat family, like cheetahs and leopards, or of the dog family, like wolves and foxes. Hyenas had their own scientific family. They were different and mis-understood, just like he had always been. The more he learned about them, the more he knew that he was a hyena at heart. A wily predator, strong and fearless, using his talents to achieve what he wanted, regardless of needs or feelings of others.

"If we sit here much longer," Geoffrey said, interrupting Drew's reverie, "we'll miss lunch. The cook doesn't like if we miss lunch, and you don't want to get on the bad side of the cook!" Drew let out the clutch and drove on. Never, he thought, will I forget this moment.

Within a few minutes, South Camp emerged unexpectedly over a small hill. The contrast was startling. A moment earlier, it was all raw nature; now he was back in the habitat of humans. All the buildings were tents, but built on permanent foundations. "Sometimes we move the tents for specific seasons or projects," Geoffrey explained, "but we always come back here, so these tent sites are permanent."

The camp had several buildings, arranged in two wings around a central hub. The hub held a large tent that doubled as mess hall and meeting room. A series of smaller tents, the sleep-ing quarters, formed the wings. One of these was for Drew's use, serving as both his office and personal space.

The cooking tent and garage were about a hundred yards away, isolated to keep the sounds, smells and waste from the living area. Between those and the main tent was a small administration building for Geoffrey's use. The only other buildings were a latrine and shower halfway down each wing of sleeping tents.

Drew parked alongside the other vehicles and stepped out of the truck. He was living his dream. He felt like a true reincarnation of Henry Stanley, the reporter who had searched the Tanzanian wilderness in pursuit of David Livingstone. Like Stanley searching for Livingstone, Drew would search here for the secrets of the spotted hyena. Stanley had succeeded and become famous; Drew was sure he would do the same.

Drew spent the next several weeks learning his way around. At first he could barely detect what the Maasai drivers and guides called roads from the grassland and shrub growth. He would follow what he thought was a road only to see it become narrower and more overgrown and then totally disappear. He tried to make maps, but the tangle of dirt tracks followed animal paths rather than any sensible grid; maps were useless.

Over time, however, and with the help of Geoffrey and others, he learned to read the Mazarie landscape. A central lake and wetlands stretched from west to east across the park, flanked on both sides by slightly elevated savannas. Stands of acacia and other trees grew at intervals, some dense but others with just widely spaced individual trees. The Maasai guides had names for all the stands of trees—big baobab, yellow bark, buffalo camp—and they taught Drew to recognize their landmarks and navigate by them.

He saw plenty of hyenas, too. He sometimes followed them as they ran ahead of his truck, before losing them in the brush. He watched them lying along the sunny shore of the wetland, engorged from devouring the previous night's successful kill. Through binoculars, he could observe small clans of hyenas moving across the savanna, the dominant female always maintaining careful watch over the landscape.

But he was still a tourist when it came to hyenas, watching the animals from afar and frustrated as they trotted away and disappeared into the brush when he approached. He couldn't tell one individual from another or whether any particular group was a clan he had seen before or a new one. His task was to get close, though, to learn their behavior and explain its mysteries. But he was failing, and failure wasn't on Drew Robbins' agenda. The intended world expert on hyenas needed to get better, and fast.

He had resisted the advice of his supervising professor until now, but Drew knew the time had come to admit he needed help. That evening at dinner, he approached Geoffrey.

"Geoffrey, have you ever heard of Dr. Thomas Hyde-Martin?"

Geoffrey grinned and nodded. "You mean Old Tommy Tonic?"

"I don't know," Drew said. "My advisor gave me a letter of introduction for him. He's supposed to be some sort of hyena expert. My advisor says he went to Tanzania many years ago to work on hyenas, published some papers, but hadn't been heard from for a long time. I'm supposed to try to find him if I need help."

"That's Old Tommy, for sure. But I don't know if he'd be able to help you. He's pretty old, and he drinks a lot. That's why everyone calls him Tommy Tonic—he is always looking for more tonic water for his gin."

"Where can I find him?" Drew asked.

"The last I knew, he was staying in the little market town, Carmo, just outside the main entrance to the park."

The next day, Drew went in search of the old man. Geoffrey told him to see Markall, the Maasai warrior who owned The Hyena Bar in Carmo. When Drew asked for Thomas Hyde-Martin, Markall just nodded towards the corner.

At a small table in the corner sat the wreckage of a man. Obviously once large and strong, with hands that engulfed the tall glass in front of him, the old man appeared shrunken, as though he were a child dressing in his father's clothes.

"That's him?" Drew asked.

"Yes," said Markall, "that's him alright."

"Are you sure?" pressed Drew. "He looks like an old bum. What happened to him?"

"I don't know," said Markall. "When I took over this place from my father—he was called Markall, too—he told me that Tommy came with the bar. He told me to just keep him in gin and tonic and he'd never give me any trouble. He lives in a little hut out back."

"You know he used to be a scientist, right?" asked Drew.

"Yes, my father told me that, too," said Markall. "My father actually named the bar after him and his students, who were doing research on hyenas. It's been The Hyena Bar ever since."

"But how did he get this way?"

"I don't know," said Markall. "My father never said. He told me to just leave him alone in his grief and treat him with respect."

"How does he live?" asked Drew.

"I cook some food for him every day, but he doesn't eat much. He just sits there and sleeps and drinks. Every month he gets a small money order from England, a pension, I think, and he signs it over to me for his room and board."

My advisor obviously didn't know what had become of his friend, thought Drew. But the crumbled lump in the corner seemed to be his last option for rescuing his research, so he walked over to the table. "Dr. Hyde-Martin?"

The man looked up slowly. Behind the drooping eyelids stared a pair of searching eyes, eyes that still held a glimmer of intelligence and curiosity. "Who told you to call me that?" he demanded, "nobody should call me that anymore. I'm Tommy Tonic. Old Tommy Tonic."

"My name is Drew Robbins. I'm a student of Dr. Malcolm Burns. I've come to Tanzania to study hyenas. Dr. Burns told me to ask you for help. I have a letter from him."

"Milky Burns sent you? I figured that old stick-in-the-mud was surely dead by now." His gaze grew distant, his mind taking him back somewhere in his past. After a moment, he returned to the present. "I suppose Milky is some kind of distinguished professor somewhere, eh? He always was the responsible one."

"Yes, Dr. Burns is a highly regarded professor at Virginia Western University. He's my advisor there."

"And what did you say your name was?"

"Drew Robbins. That is, Andrew Robbins, sir."

Old Tommy stared at him for a long time. Finally he motioned and said, "Okay, Andy, you say you have a letter for me? Let me see it." Drew handed over the letter. Old Tommy read it slowly, several times it seemed. Once again, he was somewhere else, not sitting friendless in the dingy corner of a shabby bar.

"So, Milky wants me to teach you about hyenas, eh? Why should I do that?" Old Tommy growled. But the gruffness in his voice was having a hard time disguising his interest.

Drew was ready with his answer. "Hyenas have been my favorite animals since I was a boy. I've studied everything I could find about them all the way through school, right up to my doctoral work. I've read your papers, and they are wonderful. I want to make hyenas as well understood and popular as Jane Goodall has made chimpanzees and Dian Fossey made gorillas. I'm pretty sure I can't do that without your help."

The old man didn't look convinced, so Drew continued. "Dr. Burns also said that you owed him a favor. Something about a border crossing in the middle of the night."

Old Tommy broke into a grin, then a chuckle and finally a laugh that echoed through the bar. Markall looked over with raised eyebrows. "I owe him one, eh? Let me think it over. Come back tomorrow."

The next day Drew was back, but Old Tommy was asleep at his corner table. "I would just leave him alone," suggested Markall. "He's pretty grumpy if you wake him up and he's still drunk."

Drew was back again the next day, and found Old Tommy awake. "Hello, Dr. Hyde-Martin. It's me again, Andrew Robbins."

Old Tommy was writing in a journal. He looked up, and his eyes were sparkling. "I decided yesterday that I wouldn't help you," he said. Drew's face fell in disappointment. "But then I thought for a long time about the debt I owe to Milky Burns. If it wasn't for him, I never would have made it out of a Rwandan jail. So, I changed my mind." He called across the bar, "Markall, bring us two gin and tonics—one for me and one for my new friend, Andy Robbins!"

"Thank you, Dr. Hyde-Martin," said Drew. A surge of relief and excitement coursed through his body, along with the stinging taste of the gin and tonic.

"We'll see whether you need to thank me later. For now, Andy, let's just share a drink or two."

His happiness was tempered by being called Andy. He hated that name. He had lived through years of being called Andy and all the nicknames that went along with the name. He had blackened the eyes of boys who called him Raggedy Andy or Andy Pandy or any other rhymes an unwary rival might blurt out. But his grandmother was never persuaded to call him anything but Andy. He changed all that when he got to college— he became Drew. That, he thought, was a name that befitted a field biologist and adventurer. He wondered now if he should confront Old Tommy about his name, risking the good will of the old man. But the gin loosened his tongue.

"People stopped calling me Andy a long time ago, sir. I'd prefer if you called me Drew, short for Andrew. That's what everyone calls me now, even my professors."

The old man thought for a moment before answering. "Well, let's try to make this fair. I'll let you call me Old Tommy, and you'll let me call you Andy. How does that sound?"

Inside, Drew seethed, but his instinct for getting what he really wanted took over. He had to have the man's help. So he smiled. "Okay, sir—I mean Old Tommy. Andy it is."

For the rest of the field season, Drew and Old Tommy were inseparable. Every day, Drew drove to The Hyena Bar to pick up his mentor. He'd bring Tommy a sausage roll and coffee from South Camp, and they would set off into the bush. The work had breathed new life into the old man. He seemed to grow back into his skin. His complexion turned from the pallid grey of a habitual drunk to the deep brown tan of a field biologist.

He showed Drew where the five known clans of hyenas lived —one at each end of the wetland and three more distributed around the higher habitats. He gave Drew the ingenious template he had developed to diagram the location, size, shape and color of a hyena's spots, and together they learned to tell individual animals based on their distinctive spot patterns. Soon, they had documented twenty or more hyenas in each clan, each led by a dominant female, and several dozen males that roamed more broadly across the park.

Old Tommy taught Drew how to approach the animals on foot, avoiding movements and postures the hyenas found threatening. The largest clan, at the eastern end of the wetland, seemed particularly tolerant, so the men concentrated their efforts there. This had been the clan that Tommy had studied most extensively during his years of active work, and although the individual animals had long since died, the personality of the clan seemed largely unchanged. While Tommy waited in the truck, Drew approached the clan, a little closer and a little longer each day. Within two months, the animals were ignoring him, allowing Drew to get within a few yards and sit for hours, making notes of his observations and taking photos and videos.

Tommy generally watched from a distance, sometimes sitting

in the truck but other times sitting in the shade of an acacia. He would pour a little gin from his flask into a metal cup and add chilled tonic from a thermos. When Drew returned from his observations, he usually found Tommy dozing in the late afternoon sunshine, his face reminiscent of a napping child, content and worry-free.

When the end of the field season arrived, Tommy helped Drew pack up his notebooks and photographic equipment for the long flight home. Tommy watched the small plane take off from the South Camp landing strip, staring until it became a tiny speck and then disappeared into the sky.

When Tommy walked through the door of The Hyena Bar, Markall feared for the worst. The empty look that had filled Tommy's face for so many years was back. "Gonna miss the kid, aren't you?" Markall asked.

"Yeah, of course I will. But he'll be back next spring."

"So, want a bottle of gin, Tommy?" Markall asked.

"Just a short one for now," Tommy said. "I've got something to do." He sat down in the corner table and began to write. Markall watched with interest, and it seemed that as Tommy progressed on his writing, his emptiness began to refill.

5

Thursday

Desdemona White heard the report crackle through her police radio as she pulled into her parking space at the university's police department. "Suspicious death reported at 218 Monroe Ave."

She recognized the address immediately, shifted in reverse and headed to the scene. When she arrived, four police cruisers were at the curb, blue lights flashing. Two belonged to the town of Stone Valley, the other two to the university. A pair of town cops were standing by their car, one talking into the radio.

She met her chief assistant, Jimmy Nesbitt, coming around the corner of the house. "What's going on?" she asked.

"The resident called 911, in hysterics, saying that her boyfriend was dead, stabbed. The dispatcher called in the town guys; they were here first. But when they realized this was university property, they called us. We've been here about ten minutes. Jessie and one of the town cops are inside, and I've been checking around the outside of the house."

Des nodded her approval. "Thanks, Jimmy."

She slipped on gloves and shoe coverings and walked through the open front door. She found the town policewoman in the kitchen with Gina, who was sitting on a tall stool at the counter. "Hello, Gina. What happened?"

Gina looked up at the familiar voice. "Oh, Des," she cried and lunged from the stool into her arms. "I, I can't believe it. Drew is dead!"

"I can't believe it either. I'm so sorry, Gina. Can you tell me what happened?"

Gina brushed the tears away from her cheeks and tried to clear her throat. "I don't know. I came downstairs to go for a jog. Drew wasn't in bed, so I knew he'd be at his desk. I fixed some coffee to take to him. When I walked in the room, there he was, lying on his desk, dead."

"Ok, kiddo. You just try to settle down. I'll take care of things. Is there someone we can call to be with you?"

"No," said Gina, sighing heavily, "but if you're here, I'll be fine." Then a puzzled look crossed Gina's face. "But why..., why are you here?"

"Well, I'm police chief for the university, and this is university property. So, I'm in charge."

Gina looked even more puzzled. "No, no. This is Drew's house."

Des shook her head. "Actually, it isn't his. He leased it from the university some years ago. The university has several houses like this around town that they rent to special faculty members. This is one of them, so any crimes that occur here are in our jurisdiction."

Gina waved her hand in front of her face. "Whatever. I don't care. What am I going to do? We're going to be married." Gina caught her mistake. "We *were* going to be married."

Just then, Jimmy knocked on the front door frame. "Boss," he called, and Des came to the door. "This is the next door neighbor, Mrs. Heinz. She's wondering if she can help." Mrs. Heinz stood on the front steps, looking very concerned.

Des recognized Mrs. Heinz—Judith—immediately from the provost's office. "Judith, I didn't realize you lived here."

"All my life," said Judith. "Has something terrible happened?"

Des explained that Drew Robbins had died, but gave no details. "Judith, I wonder if you could take Gina back to your house for the time being. She needs something to eat and someone to sit with her for a bit."

Judith forced a smile across her worried face. "Of course, I'm glad to help."

Gina had followed Des to the door when she heard her neighbor's voice. Her tears began again, and Judith held out her arms. Gina fell into her motherly hug and sobbed. "Let's go sit on my back porch for a while, sweetie."

Almost robotically, Gina nodded her head and followed Judith across the lawn.

Des heaved a sigh and turned to her deputy. "Okay, Jimmy, let's get started. Where's Jessie?"

"I'm in the study, Des," came Jessie's reply from farther inside the house. Jessie Hunt was the third member of their investigating crew. Together Des and Jimmy walked into the study to join Jessie, careful not to touch or disturb anything. Drew Robbins' body lay on his desk, just as Gina had described, the Maasai spear still firmly lodged in his back. She looked across the room at the fireplace. Another spear was attached to the wall, resting on a pair of iron brackets. A pair of identical brackets above the spear was undoubtedly the home of the spear now in Robbins' back.

"You haven't touched anything, have you, Jessie?" asked Des.

"No, ma'am. I've just stood watch over the body and the scene. Except for the mess of the broken coffee mugs on the floor by the door, it doesn't look like anything else has been disturbed."

"Okay, let's get the experts here. We're going to need every-one's help on this. Jessie, please coordinate with the town to get their medical examiner and forensics team on the job." Jessie headed out the door to confer with the town cops. "And, Jimmy, go talk to the neighbors on the other side. Maybe they saw or heard something." Jimmy followed Jessie out the door.

Des walked back outside in the morning sun to get her thoughts together. She had been the university's police chief for the past five years, but nothing like this had ever happened. Murder, she was told when she accepted the job, was as rare as a professor with a small ego. Her previous stint with the Richmond, Virginia, police force and two deployments as a Marine MP in Afghanistan had given her plenty of experience with violent crime, but this job was supposed to get her away from all that. Student pranks, drinking in the dorms, and stolen bicycles were about as serious as it got. The violent murder of a faculty member was unheard of in the safety of a quiet place like Stone Valley, Virginia.

While Des and her team had been in the house, Stone Valley's police chief, Frank Marin, had arrived. He was talk-ing with his officers when he spotted Des on the porch. He walked to join her. They exchanged friendly greetings. The two police chiefs had worked side-by-side often over the years, as they sorted through town-gown issues that never seemed to go completely away.

"A homicide, eh?" Frank said.

"Yeah. One of the university's faculty members."

Frank nodded. "That's what the boys told me. Famous guy, too, they say. Got a big award last night."

"Yes," Des said. "This sort of thing isn't supposed to happen around here."

"How can we help?" Frank said.

"Thanks, Frank. What we need now is your crime scene folks to take over. We can do fingerprints and that sort of things, but we're not equipped for detailed forensics like you are. And we'll need a complete work-up on the body."

"Of course, Des," Frank said, "whatever you need." He walked back to his officers and gave them instructions. One officer moved to the front door of the house to take over security of the crime scene while the other began relaying Frank's instructions through his radio.

Des realized how fortunate she, and the university, were to have such a cooperative partner with the town officials, including the police. With them taking care of the in-depth forensics work, she could concentrate on the crime itself and all the people whose lives had changed with Drew Robbins death.

And the first of those was Gina Rahim, the victim's fiancée and the person who found the body. The situation was going to be complicated, because she and Gina were close friends. They had met almost as soon as Gina got to campus three years ago, at the new graduate student orientation where Des gave the usual safety warnings. They took to each other immediately, despite the difference in their ages. Gina was considerably older than most graduate students, having spent close to a decade working on wildlife conservation in Scotland before deciding to pursue a doctorate, but at 32 she was still several years younger than Des. They were like sisters, one older and more responsible, the other younger and more enthusiastic. But they got along well. They belonged to the same running club, and they competed in triathlons together. Perhaps "competed" wasn't the right term. They generally swam, biked and ran next to each other, talking and laughing on the course and finishing tied for whatever prize, if any, they earned. The companionship, not the medal, was the reward.

Des had been at the banquet the night before. She had been in charge of security, making sure the pampered celebrities, rowdy students and bored faculty all stayed in line. But she had been glad to be there for Gina, too. And when Drew proposed in front of the crowd, her heart raced for the joy of her friend and the romance of the moment.

Now romance had turned to tragedy, and it was her job to figure out what happened. Her thoughts were interrupted when Jimmy returned from the neighbors.

"Nothing to report from next door," he said. "One man lives there, a music professor, who has been home since yesterday about suppertime. He was working on a piano composition until early hours, but the room where he works is pretty well sound-proofed and doesn't have windows, so he didn't hear or see anything. And he just woke up this morning when he heard all of us arriving."

"Okay, kiddo," said Des. "let's get back inside."

Robbins lay across the desk, looking like he was taking a nap. Nothing was disturbed, except for the spear that had been moved from the wall and was now lodged in the victim's back. There was no sign of a struggle. It looked as though he had been taken completely by surprise and had been instantly immobilized by the stabbing. Blood had spread across his back and run down his right side, opposite the archway that separated the study from the base of the stairway and the foyer.

They checked all the doors and windows on the first floor for signs of forced entry. There were none. Either Robbins had let the killer in or the killer had a key. Obviously, Robbins knew the killer and wasn't surprised or afraid that the killer—he or she—had shown up at his house sometime in the night or early morning.

"Or the killer might have been here already," said Jimmy. "There was another person in the house. The girlfriend."

Des looked hard at Jimmy. "I know," she said, "we have to consider the possibility that Gina did this. But it's very unlikely. They just got engaged last night, at a banquet in front of a couple hundred people. I saw her there, so did you. She was so happy. We've got to be looking for someone with a motive to kill him, not to marry him."

Des tried to imagine the confrontation that had occurred. Robbins and the killer had been talking, perhaps as friends. But they could have been arguing, too. The killer took the spear down from the wall and brandished it at Robbins. Perhaps he thought it was a joke, or perhaps he didn't believe that his assailant had the courage to attack. So, Robbins kept sitting at his desk, perhaps ignoring the other person as a show of defiance.

The killer walked behind the desk and plunged the spear in Robbins' back, one swift, sure motion that set the blade firmly in his heart. He might have held the spear in place while Robbins squirmed a bit, the life running out of his body.

"Jimmy," she wondered out loud, "how does someone take a spear off the opposite wall, walk around behind the desk and stab the victim in the back without him putting up a fight, or even noticing?"

"Maybe he was already unconscious," Jimmy guessed. "Maybe he was drugged or poisoned first."

"Makes sense. We'll need to wait until the forensics report is finished to know one way or the other."

Des stepped closer to the desk. "Let's see what he was working on in the middle of the night." She carefully slipped the stack of papers from beneath the victim's stiffening arms. "It's a contract with a television network for a new science series." She read enough to get the idea. "Looks like Drew Robbins was about to hit the big time."

The police officers heard new voices outside the front door. The ambulance had arrived, along with one of the university's physicians who acted as medical examiner when there was a death on campus. The town's forensics crew also arrived. Des released the scene to them, and they began their examination of the body, the study and the rest of the house. She left Jessie to coordinate at the scene, and she and Jimmy went next door to talk to Gina and her neighbor. Judith Heinz let them in and she led them to the back patio where Gina was pacing.

She was clearly agitated and hadn't settled down since Judith took her away from the murder scene. When she saw Des, Gina ran to her and nearly collapsed into her arms. Jimmy looked on from the edge of the patio, almost embarrassed to be witnessing the emotions between the two women.

"Des," said Gina, "I can't believe this. I can't stop seeing him lying there. Des, who would do this to Drew? I love him. I, I don't know what I'm going to do."

"You'll be okay," Des reassured her as she hugged her friend. "You're in shock right now, so neither your mind nor your heart is reacting normally. But, listen, I have to ask you a few questions now, before things get any more confused in your mind. You okay with that?"

"If it'll help you, Des, yes, I'll try."

Des asked Judith to go back in the house so she and Jimmy could talk to Gina alone. "Okay. Let's sit down so we can concentrate." They sat next to each other on a small settee facing the back yard, while Jimmy continued to watch and listen from the periphery. "Now think hard. Did you hear anything before you came downstairs, anything at all?"

Gina sat silently for a moment, trying to focus. "No, I didn't. We had a very late night, you know, after the banquet and all. We'd had a couple of drinks. No, I don't remember anything until I woke up."

"And when was that, when you woke up?"

Gina thought again. "The sun was in my eyes—that's what usually wakes me up. It happens about seven this time of year. Then I get dressed and go for a jog, just like this morning."

Des moved on. "When you came downstairs, you didn't look into the study, you know, to say hi or make sure Drew was at his desk?"

"No," said Gina, "it's our routine. If I can't smell the coffee, that means Drew went straight to his desk to work, without stopping to make coffee. I just yell hi and go into the kitchen to make it. He really doesn't like—didn't like—to be disturbed in the morning. That's when he did his best thinking and writing."

"And you didn't touch anything when you went into the study? You didn't run over to him?"

It was only a few steps from the archway to the desk. "Yes, I did, of course. I ran behind him and grabbed his shoulders. But he didn't move. Then I saw the blood, and I knew he was dead."

"Did you touch anything else? The spear or the blood?"

Gina was losing her composure. "I don't know. I don't remember. I could have touched the spear, maybe, or put my hand on the desk or chair. Oh, god." She started crying again. "He was dead, Des. How could this happen?"

Des took both of Gina's hands in her own, in a futile attempt to settle her down. "I know, Gina, I know. It doesn't make any sense. But one last question. After you decided he was dead, what did you do?"

"Nothing. I couldn't move. I just stood there, shaking. I bent down because I thought I might faint. I took out my cellphone and called 911. Then I just sat on the floor and cried."

"Okay, kiddo, that's all we need for now. But, listen, you can't go back into the house until our folks have finished going over it for evidence and such. Okay?"

Gina stared vacantly at Des as if all this was too much to handle. Eventually she nodded her head.

Des smiled in return. "Good. We'll get this figured out, Gina, I promise." Des walked Gina back into the house, where Judith was waiting.

"Judith," Des asked, "will you please look after her for a while. I'll be back in a few hours, as soon as I can."

Judith smiled. "Of course. Don't worry, I'll take care of her, poor thing."

6

Tanzania, seventeen years earlier

Dr. Thomas Hyde-Martin was excited that Drew Robbins was arriving soon for a second field season. He had continued his new leaf after Drew had returned to VWU to analyze the year's results and show Milky Burns what they had accomplished together. He chuckled to himself often when he thought how Milky would react to the news that Old Tommy Tonic was on the job again. And he relived the moments that he and Milky had shared during their years together when they were both young, just as young and brash as Drew Robbins.

He sat at his corner table in The Hyena Bar, but now he worked through his old data for days on end. Markall marveled at the transformation in the man. Markall had expected Old Tommy to revert to his drunken ways as soon as Robbins departed in the fall, but that hadn't been the case. He occasionally got packages of papers from Robbins, and he would review them, make notes and send them back.

He also continued writing other letters, like the one he had worked on as soon as Drew had flown out. About once each week, he'd write several pages and then walk the letter to the post office to mail it. For a month or two, Tommy would return from the post office in a melancholy mood, obviously disappointed that he had received no return mail. But then, one day Tommy returned with a letter in his hand, the joy on his face bright enough to light the entire bar.

"Who's the letter from?" Markall asked.

"Never mind that," Tommy said. "Bring me a bottle of gin and lots of tonic." Markall brought the drinks and watched Tommy as he opened the letter. His hands were shaking as he pulled the pages from the envelope and saw they were covered front and back with beautiful script.

Tommy sat perfectly still and read the letter, beginning to end, forgetting about the drinks in front of him. He re-read the letter several times as Markall watched. Tommy's hands stopped shaking, and his face continued to beam.

He eventually laid the letter on the table and looked up at his friend across the bar. "Markall, perhaps it's not too late."

"Too late for what, Tommy?"

"For life to start again. Real life, I mean. Not just chasing hyenas with Andy Robbins, but maybe, just maybe, to have a real life again."

"Who wrote you a letter?" Markall asked.

But Tommy wasn't listening anymore. He had drifted off to somewhere in his mind, and Markall knew that whoever had written that letter and whatever memories it triggered were locked in Tommy's heart and mind, not to be shared.

The letters kept coming after that, not often but steadily. His ongoing work with Robbins and the exchange of personal letters kept Tommy occupied and away from his drink. If the interval between letters lasted too long, though, the demon of too many gin and tonics would take over again. But then the next letter would arrive, and Tommy would right himself.

The day Drew Robbins arrived for his second field season was like a holiday at The Hyena Bar. Tommy and Markall had cleaned the place from top to bottom. They had also installed a light above the corner table so Robbins and Tommy could work there together.

Both Markall and Tommy were waiting at the door when Robbins drove up in his field truck. They hugged the young man and dragged him into the bar, firing questions about the months while he had been away.

The mood was joyous until Tommy asked, "And how is old Milky?"

"I'm afraid I have bad news," Drew said. "Dr. Burns had a serious heart-attack last month."

"My god," Tommy said, "is he doing okay?"

"No. I'm sorry. He never recovered. He died two weeks ago."

The air went out of Tommy like a punctured balloon. He sagged into the corner table and stared into space. "Oh, my dear old friend. I thought that we might just see each other again, sharing Andy Robbins as we do."

Then he remembered that Drew was still with him. "What does this mean for your dissertation research?"

"The university has assigned another professor to be my advisor," Drew said. "He's a physiologist, though, and doesn't know anything about the kind of work that we do. So, he's told me to just keep following what Dr. Burns had told me and he wouldn't get in the way."

Andy pulled an envelope from his pocket and handed it to Tommy. "Dr. Burns gave me this for you."

Tommy opened the envelope and read the short note inside. The air was coming back into him. "Well, Drew, Milky told me to take care of you now that he wouldn't be able to anymore." Then he smiled. "And he told me to call you Drew."

And that's what Old Tommy did. He took a much more active role in the research that Drew was conducting. The first year, Tommy mostly taught Drew how to deal with the hyenas—approaching, observing and identifying them. He loved seeing the young student take his advice and succeed with the animals. Drew was a skilled observer and a clever interpreter of animal behavior. He had a way with the animals, for sure, a calmness and lack of fear that the animals seemed to recognize. Faster than anyone Tommy had ever seen, the animals accepted Drew's presence.

But that was only the first step in understanding animal behavior. The observations needed to be pieced together into a coherent story of the hyena's life history. And now, with the sad death of Milky Burns, it became Tommy's role to help Drew make sense of it all. He had been Drew's field guide; now he was his academic mentor. So he asked questions about Drew's research strategy and and the overall design of his project. They worked together to hone a hypothesis for hyena behavior and optimized their field observations to test their hypothesis.

With a firmer approach to their work, the second field season was even more successful than the first. Often splitting up to double their field time, the pair studied the hyena clans and the other animals of Mazarie. Tommy shared more of his earlier data, years of work that no one had ever seen before.

They built sets of observations and conclusions that were rock solid. Before Drew left for VWU at the end of the second field season, they drafted a paper on hyena behavior that contained more data and conclusions than had ever been published before. Their plan was for Drew to submit the paper once he returned home, with the pair as co-authors.

For Tommy, the work with Drew was a re-birth. Their first field season together had gotten Tommy back on his feet, but the second season saw the return of his love of science. His own research had been so promising, so fruitful. Like Jane Goodall, he had followed the famous anthropologist Louis Leakey to Tanzania. Leakey had steered Goodall to study primates, but he'd recommended that Hyde-Martin study a predator. Understanding the violent and cunning nature of predators, Leakey had said, would help explain the human penchant for competition, dominance and war. Among the predators, hyenas were especially interesting because their behavior was so plastic, adapting to the opportunities and conditions of any particular environment.

So, Hyde-Martin studied hyenas. His initial work was well received by the scientific world as he began to unravel the mysteries of hyena life history. Evolutionarily, hyenas fit between the big cats and the smaller dog-like species. Their bodies were more like dogs, but their behavior more like cats. Their behavior was exceptionally complex, from hunting strategies to clan dynamics. The same things that attracted Drew to hyenas—their defiance of conventional stereo-types—also fascinated Tommy.

He became friends with other researchers in the region, especially one Malcolm "Milky" Burns, who was studying zebras. We called him Milky, he once told Drew, because of the way he drank his coffee—equal parts milk and coffee. The young researchers worked hard and played hard. Drinking was about the only vice available, and they indulged aggressively.

When the other researchers headed home annually to work on their data and plan the next year's studies, Tommy stayed behind. The hyenas and the African savanna had captured him completely. He assured his friends that he could do the necessary analysis and report writing from Tanzania and that he had no reason to return to England. The animals stay here, he told his friends, and important things happen after the rest of you leave. He published several papers over the next few years, some in collaboration with his colleagues in England and the U.S. As the other researchers moved on to projects in new locations and with different species, Tommy stayed in Mazarie, working alone on his beloved hyenas.

Gradually, his colleagues lost touch with Tommy. He stopped publishing papers and also stopped answering their occasional letters. Malcom Burns persisted the longest, but when his letters came back from South Camp marked undeliverable, he too gave up. Unknown to him, his friend had become Old Tommy Tonic, the sad drunk living in a hut behind The Hyena Bar and spending his days alone at a corner table.

Not everything was perfect in Tommy's reincarnation, of course, not in the first season nor in the second. The old man slipped back into his old habits now and then, becoming Old Tommy Tonic again, drinking too much and turning sullen. When these bouts of despair occurred, Drew tried to help, but he could never penetrate the wall Old Tommy hid behind. He and Markall talked often about what might have happened in the past to destroy Old Tommy, but Markall was as mystified as Drew. Markall had heard vague stories from his father about a romance gone wrong, but he knew no details. So, they just waited for the malaise to pass. After a few days, Tommy would sober up and get back to work.

For his part, Tommy also saw some signs in Drew's behavior he didn't like. Drew was at home with the animals, but away from them he was a different man. There was an urgency about him, and Tommy couldn't tell if it was born of personal ambition or a true commitment to understanding as much of the natural world as possible so he could protect it. He was impatient, eager to draw conclusions after just a few observations. "I don't have time to keep sitting around watching the same thing day after day, week after week," Drew often said. "We need to draw our conclusions and move on to the next predator and the next habitat. We don't have the luxury of formal scientific protocols if we're going to save these animals."

"But animals are as complex as humans," Tommy told him. "They can fool you if you judge them too soon."

Drew scoffed. "Humans aren't complex. They're as easy to understand as those hyenas. Easier, really. Feed them what they need, and they'll do anything for you. Some want flattery, some want money, some want 'love.' All you have to do is figure out what they want—and then you can get people to do whatever you want. Just like trained seals."

That disdain for people bothered Tommy. "Drew, my boy, it isn't that simple. You'll learn, either the easy way or the hard way, that people aren't so easy to figure out. And sometimes they might turn out to be more formidable than you think. Making enemies isn't the best strategy for a happy life."

"I'll take that chance," Drew said, his temper flaring, "and I'm not your boy."

7

Thursday

Ted Graham leaned back in his chair, struggling to absorb the news. Drew Robbins was dead. More than that, he had been murdered.

The news had come first in a campus-wide email, the kind of alerts that federal law now required when a violent crime occurred on or near campus. A call from the dean of the College of Biological Sciences followed quickly. The provost had called the dean, letting him know that a member of his faculty had been killed. But it wasn't the dean's faculty, Ted thought, Drew Robbins is—was—one of my faculty members, in my Department of Renewable Resources.

Ted's thoughts bounced around like a pinball game. He was a practical man, and he moved almost immediately from the tragedy—someone he knew had been murdered—to the tasks he would have. People would be upset, especially Robbins' students, so some on-site counseling would be needed. He'd need to assign someone to take over Robbins' duties, his classes and research projects. He'd have to seal off his office, he guessed, in case the police wanted to search there. The police. Right. The police would want to talk to him.

Then there would be a line of people at his door all day. Gossipy faculty wanting to get ahead of the news, frightened staff needing reassurance that a maniacal killer was not on the loose, students concerned about their classes and grades. And the phone and email would be alive with colleagues from other schools, also wanting to know what happened.

He'd get to it all, that's what he was good at. Maybe he wasn't a visionary leader as a department head, but he could handle problems as they arose and get the necessary work done.

Right now, though, he just wanted to think. Drew Robbins was dead. The final scenes from *The Wizard of Oz* popped into his head. The wicked witch is dead. Someone had poured water on the evil villain's head, and he melted away. Cripes, Ted told himself, can't you show a little respect? Sure, Drew was a pain in the ass, but he was a human being after all, and he had been murdered.

More than that, he'd put their little department on the map. The famous Drew Robbins was a faculty member in DRR, the department formerly known as, well, as nothing. Basically unknown. When Ted arrived five years ago, he learned that the Department of Renewable Resources had never gotten much attention on campus "before Drew"; most people had never heard of it. But then Robbins hit the big time, and the DRR fell into the university's spotlight, featured in recruitment brochures, fund-raising promotions and even half-time spots on sports broadcasts. Robbins had sucked in resources from the university administration—new facilities, lower overhead rates, extra staff and graduate fellowships—and all that spilled over to benefit the whole department. Robbins' rising tide had raised the department's ship as well. By the time Ted had been recruited to become department head, DRR had long since hit the big time.

But being the boss of a prima donna had downsides. Major downsides. Robbins never wanted to follow the rules. Rules, he regularly told Ted, were fine in general, but most of them were made for people who couldn't think for themselves. I won't do anything evil, he had always promised Ted, but I can't be expected to jump through every piss-ant hoop if I'm going to save the endangered predators of the world. So, Ted was always in the middle. Robbins tugging on one sleeve, central administration offices tugging on the other. Glad that's over, he thought.

And then there were the department meetings. He remembered his first meeting as the new department head. He'd expected things to go smoothly, at least during his "honeymoon," but no such luck. Robbins and his primary nemesis, Aaron Schmidt, professor of wood anatomy, had gotten into it from the start. He could recall the exchange almost word for word.

Robbins: We're all very glad you've joined our department, Ted. We need your new leadership to break out of our worn-out traditions. We've got to redirect resources from last century's work to this century's.

Schmidt: Here we go again. In case you're confused, Ted, the esteemed Dr. Robbins is talking about me when he says "worn-out traditions." He wants my lab space.

Robbins: Well, you finally got something right, Aaron. I'm trying to save the world's biodiversity, and you've got half a floor of the building filled with old wood samples. Who cares?

Schmidt: The world's trees are a lot more diverse than the kitty-cats you study. DRR has the best collection of wood samples in the world. I get inquiries every day based on this resource.

Robbins: Right. "Can you tell me what kind of wood my desk is made of so we can repair it?" Call that important? Give me a break.

Schmidt: That call was about the Resolute Desk, you cretin. You know, the one in the Oval Office. Listen, sonny, I was helping identify the trees for ecosystem restoration before you were potty trained.

Robbins: And who's wearing the diapers now? Why don't you retire and let us hire someone relevant in your place? Give it up, old man.

The acrimony had just grown during the past five years. Almost any idea proposed by the younger faculty, voiced by Robbins, was immediately rejected by the more traditional faculty, voiced by Schmidt.

Ted avoided wading into issues like past versus future, faded and worn versus new and shiny. He was a problem solver, not an idea-man. Status quo with a bit of tinkering was fine with him. The dean and provost could make big decisions, that's why they made the proverbial big bucks. So, Ted just tried to keep the arguments to words rather than fists. Robbins' high-profile also meant that the university's pocket book was wide open, so meeting Robbins' needs didn't really require eating into Aaron Schmidt's.

But overnight everything had changed. Robbins was gone. Ted did not approve of murder, of course, but if it had to happen, it happened to the right guy. The big man on campus had just become the dead man on campus.

Ted was jolted out of his thoughts when Chief Desdemona White knocked on his open door. He flushed momentarily, hoping that she couldn't read his last thoughts. "Good to see you, Des. Oh, sorry, I didn't mean that the way it sounded. I guess you're here about Drew Robbins."

Des managed a smile for one of her favorites on campus. "Yes, Ted. Serious business today, I'm afraid, not just a critter at the campus pond that we need you to rescue."

The two weren't friends, exactly, but they met often. Usually the reason was injured wildlife or a snake napping on a sunny sidewalk, frightening students on their way to class. Ted had often wondered why all campus problems with wildlife landed in his lap. Did the police call in the mechanical engineering department when their patrol cars broke down or the accounting head when the budget needed balancing? Of course not, those departments were too important to be bothered. For today, though, he skipped the usual banter about not running a pest control business.

Des continued. "I need to know a lot more about Robbins, and in a hurry. Can we chat for a bit?"

"I was just heading out for lunch," Ted said.

Des looked at her watch. "At 11:15? That's a little early even for a full professor, isn't it?"

"I like to beat the crowds. But this is important. How about if we get some lunch and talk? Okay?"

That was fine with Des. She liked to have lunch out, where

she could be seen eating with students or faculty. It showed she was a partner rather than the big bad cop. "Great, but today I'd rather not be seen idling in a restaurant when a murderer is on the loose, so let's grab a sub and go to the arboretum. And let's take your car."

After getting their lunches through the drive-up window of a local deli, they walked to a less visited corner of the arboretum, designed for quiet meditation, and sat on a bench under a large Japanese myrtle.

Between bites, Des began her questions. "Tell me about Robbins. Was he a good faculty member? A good colleague?"

"Depends on what you mean," Ted said. "He was a good faculty member in the sense that he brought in lots of grant money, published a lot and had a bunch of graduate students. I wish they were all like that."

"So everyone liked him?" Des continued.

Ted winced at the question. "You know what they say about not talking bad about the dead." He paused, but Des' intense stare told him to continue. "But the truth is, no, hardly any of his colleagues liked him. And to be perfectly frank, neither did I. He was a royal pain."

"Details, Ted, details."

"First off," said Ted, "he thought he was better than anyone else—smarter, more productive, deserving of special treatment. He also thought his work was more important than anyone else's, and that doesn't sit well with the other faculty egos."

"Anyone's ego in particular?"

"Well, the guy who put up the biggest fight was Aaron Schmidt. He tended to speak out whenever Drew started preaching or complaining."

Des looked puzzled. "Isn't Schmidt that nice old guy who identifies wood? He's always seemed like the perfect 'gentleman and scholar' to me."

"And generally he is," Ted said. Aaron Schmidt was a fixture at the university, not just in his department or college, but everywhere. People liked him because he cared about the university as a whole, not just about his narrow specialty. "But Drew went after him every chance he got. To Drew, Aaron represented everything ridiculous about the university. Tradition, protocol, resistance to change. And when pressed, Aaron could be pretty nasty."

"Like impaling Robbins with a Maasai spear?" Des asked.

"Good lord," Ted said, "is that how Drew was killed? Stabbed in the back with a spear?"

Des nodded her head. "Yes, but I shouldn't have told you that, not yet at least. So let's keep that between us, okay?" She also made a mental note that Ted said Drew had been stabbed in the back. Was that just a lucky guess, or did he know?

"Sure, fine," said Ted, but it was hard for him to dismiss the image. It seemed like the perfect way to do away with Drew Robbins. Then he answered her question. "Well, I don't think Aaron would do anything violent. I don't think. But last month, when the university announced that Robbins was going to be awarded the Wallace Prize, things got heated at the department meeting. Drew was lording it over the rest of us, comparing himself to Jane Goodall and Dian Fossey."

Des interrupted, "You mean the Sigourney Weaver character in 'Gorillas in the Mist'?"

"Right, she's the one. Aaron had had enough, and he slammed his hand on the desk and shouted at Drew, 'Better watch out, sonny, or you might end up more like Dian Fossey than you wanted!' Then he stormed out of the room. You could feel the walls shake when he slammed the door."

"What did he mean? What happened to Dian Fossey?"

"She was murdered in her research camp in Africa."

8

Tanzania, sixteen years earlier

Drew returned for a third field season, ready to put the finishing touches on his dissertation research. With him was a new field assistant, Russell Bronoski, who had recently finished his own doctorate in animal behavior. Drew's productivity in his first two seasons had convinced the granting agency that more investment in his research would pay off, so they added funds for a second researcher. Drew had picked Russki, as everyone called him, from the large pool of candidates that was always available for field research on African predators.

Drew had talked often about the colorful figure of Old Tommy Tonic, and Russki was eager to meet him. But when they went to see Tommy at The Hyena Bar, they were shocked by the old man's appearance. He was drunk and shrunken again like he had been when Drew came to the bar for the first time two years earlier.

"This isn't the way I left him last fall," he told Russki, "but it is the way I found him two years ago."

Drew asked Markall what had happened, but Markall just

63

shook his head. "I don't know," he said, "he had a visitor about a month ago, and since then he's been like this. Before that, he had been happy, just like when you were here before. When I ask him what's wrong, he just growls and tells me to, well, to go away."

Drew walked over to the table and sat down. "Hey, old friend, what's going on?"

With an effort, Old Tommy looked up from his slumped position. In a voice filled with venom, he rasped, "You betrayed me, that's what's going on."

Drew straightened up, his own anger rising at the accusation. "What do you mean? How could I have betrayed you?"

Old Tommy's voice gained more strength as his hatred surfaced. "Last month, I saw an old colleague who had just given a seminar at the park headquarters. He had the latest issue of the Journal of Wildlife Ethology. He said that a promising young scientist was taking the wildlife behavior world by storm and that this article would surely be an instant classic. He asked me if I knew the author, Drew Robbins."

"That's true," Drew said. "That article about our work is getting lots of attention. It's great."

Old Tommy spit out his words. "But it's not 'our work,' is it? The author is you, not you and me. Just you. I read the article. It describes my methods, uses my data, draws conclusions that you and I formed together, based on what I taught you."

"I can explain," said Drew.

"I'll bet you can, you thieving bastard."

The rage in Drew's eyes spread to his face, blotching his skin in patches of deep red. "Well, what does it matter? You were never going to do anything with those data. You're just an old drunk. You should be glad that somebody finally found a way to benefit from your good years. We need those data to help save hyenas, and no one was ever going to see them if it was up to you. You've been happy working with me, it gave you back some self-respect, whether you deserved it or not. And it gave me what I needed—a jump-start in the profession. I don't need you anymore, so just sit here and drink yourself to sleep each night. And, here, I brought you a present, so be happy with what you're getting and leave me alone."

With that, Drew slammed a large bottle of gin on the table and walked away, dragging a confused Russell Bronoski in his wake.

When they got into the truck, Russki said, "What's going on? Is what the old man said true?"

Drew bit back fiercely, "That's none of your business, so just forget it."

"But he was accusing you of stealing his research."

"And you believed him?" said Drew. "Think about what you saw there—a credible scientist or an old drunk that no one would ever believe. So just drop it, okay?"

Russki sensed that he had pushed Drew as hard as he should, so, yes, he did drop it. But a nagging doubt lodged itself in his mind: Who is Drew Robbins, really?

Later that field season Drew heard from Markall that Old Tommy Tonic was getting ready to die. He went to see him one last time. Markall pointed to the hut behind the bar. "He's too sick to even come in here now."

Drew went out the back and entered Old Tommy's hut through the open door. The man looked like a decaying carcass lying on his cot, his glazed eyes staring vacantly at the ceiling. He barely turned when Drew walked into the room. Drew stood by the bed for a moment, but then scoffed and walked past him into the adjacent closet. He emerged carrying a wooden box. It held the original notebooks that Old Tommy had filled with data and notes over his years of research.

Drew grinned as he stopped by the bed. "You won't be needing these any more, Tommy. So I'll just take them with me. There might be something in here that is worth sharing with the world."

Old Tommy tried to form words in response, but while his lips moved, no sound came from him. "You don't have to tell me what you're thinking," said Drew. "I know what you want to tell me. Well, you can go to hell, too."

Drew never saw Old Tommy again. He died a few weeks later and was buried without ceremony in the only graveyard in Carmo, behind the only church in Carmo. Markall gathered the few personal items in Tommy's hut and mailed them, along with a final letter that Tommy had managed to write and begged him to send, to the address on the envelope. As far as the world was concerned, neither Old Tommy Tonic nor Dr. Thomas Hyde-Martin would ever be heard of again.

Drew returned to Virginia Western University with an amount of data that staggered his advisor and the other faculty on his supervisory committee. They knew Drew was a hard worker, totally focused on hyenas, but his results were almost manic in their scope and depth. On the basis of those data, Robbins wrote a doctoral dissertation that sailed through faculty review and approval. And the university's leaders, unwilling to let this new prodigy of wildlife behavior get stolen by Harvard or Cambridge, offered him a faculty position without even conducting an interview.

9

Thursday

When he finished his lunch with Des, Ted knocked on another door in the department, the office of Elena Bertoni. "Got a minute, Elena?" he asked.

Dr. Elena Bertoni was an associate professor of animal behavior in DRR. She had been Ted Graham's first hire as the new department head five years ago. It was a good hire. Elena was both a fine teacher and a solid researcher, growing in status and confidence every year. She had come from the University of Bologna, where she spent several years studying the European lynx in the Alps. Born of American and Italian parents, she had lived in both countries while growing up. She was fluent in both languages, but her English was tinged with a European accent that made her voice sound slightly exotic, especially to undergraduates. She joked that her accent was worth two tenths of a point on teaching evaluations.

Elena looked up from her computer screen and smiled. "Always for you, Mr. Department Head."

"Good," said Ted, and sat down in the stiff wooden chair

beside her desk. "When are you going to get a more comfortable chair for your visitors?"

"You want me to spend money on furniture? Don't you read your own memos? We barely have enough money for pencils, let alone for new chairs."

Ted grinned. "Tell you what, I'll make you a deal. I'll buy you a new chair if you do a little favor for me."

Elena smiled back. "I don't want a new chair. And I don't have time to do anyone any favors. My department head told me not to."

Ted winced slightly at the dig, but he knew Elena didn't mean it. In fact that was her biggest problem, doing favors for anyone and everyone. She liked the university too much, so she got herself involved in activities well outside her primary area of responsibility. Ted kept trying to keep her focused, but it was like winning at whack-a-mole. No sooner would she finish chairing the art and environment taskforce than she'd sign up to be a host for international graduate students during holidays. Ted regularly told her that if she wanted to be the next Drew Robbins, she needed to concentrate on just three things—grant money, graduate students and publications. Those conversations never went well.

"Don't be like that, Elena," said Ted. "This is an opportunity more than a task."

"I can't wait to hear it."

Ted got serious. "You've heard about Drew Robbins."

Elena nodded and frowned. Events like this had consequences for everyone, and she had already fielded several emails from students who were jittery. "Terrible news," she said, "and a lot of work for you, I'll bet."

"Oh, yeah," said Ted, "there's lots to do. That brings me to the favor. I need you to take over Drew's course and his research."

Elena jumped to her feet. "Are you kidding? I wouldn't cross the street to spit on that guy. Sorry, I know he's dead, but still, no way. I detested everything about that man. You know he tried it on with me when I started here."

"Sit down, Elena," Ted said, "and he 'tried it on,' as you say, with everyone. You're not special in that way."

That comment did nothing to cool Elena down. It wasn't because she was sensitive about her looks or her attractiveness to men. The same Italian-American heritage that had given her a melodious voice also blessed her with good looks and an eye-catching physique.

"That's just the point, Ted," Elena said. "He is—was—the epitome of a vulgar bully. How could you ask me to do this? It's insulting. You should know better."

"Relax, Elena. You know I have the utmost respect for you. That's why I'm asking. You are the most reasonable, competent person we have in the department, level-headed and practical. Besides, you're an animal behaviorist, just like Robbins. It wouldn't make sense for anyone else to do this."

Elena just glared back at him, but at least she sat down again.

"It won't be that bad," Ted continued. "He didn't have much of a teaching load—he was a prima donna, remember? He was just teaching a senior-level seminar course this semester, in wildlife behavioral ecology. You know just as much about that as Drew did, probably more. And his teaching assistant, Melissa Campbell, was helping with the course and she'll continue. All you need to do is supervise her and show up for the discussions. All we really need is a new teacher-of-record."

Elena found her voice again. "Yeah, well, that doesn't sound so bad. I'm sure that Mel was doing all the real work anyhow. Maybe I could even teach the students a little something, rather than just having a look-at-me session with the big shot."

Ted tried to keep from smiling, but he knew he was winning. "And the research shouldn't be a problem, either. Russell Bronoski, his research associate, knows the projects in and out. Just like for teaching, though, we need a faculty member to be the replacement principal investigator. The grants don't allow a research associate to be the PI."

That made sense to Elena, too. "Russki is a good scientist—better than Drew ever was—and he's a good organizer, too. But I don't think it will be as easy as you say. For one thing, if my name is going to be on the grants, that means my reputation is on the line. I won't do it unless I can dive into the projects, figure out what's going on, and be confident that what we say we're doing is what we're really doing."

Now Ted did smile. "Conditions accepted."

"Hold on, I'm not done yet." Elena knew Ted was counting on her to say yes, so she pressed the advantage. "I want the department to take over funding of my post-doc, so she can take my place on our research. I'm a lot more confident that our work will be done right with her in charge than I am about Drew's work. I'll need to put all my efforts on his stuff, not mine. But I'm not willing to lose momentum on what we've been doing. You always tell me to concentrate on my research, remember? So, without funding for my post-doc, you can find yourself another soft-touch. You could always try Aaron Schmidt."

Ted thought about sparring longer to see if he could negotiate her down a bit, but he decided against it. Elena was as close to a perfect faculty member as he'd ever known, and Ted often thought of her more as a daughter than an employee. No need to risk her good will by being cheap. He was already planning how he could shift some of the funds that had been earmarked for Drew over to covering Elena's needs.

He stood and extended his hand. "Okay, it's a deal." They shook hands, and Ted headed out the door. This will all work out just fine, he thought. He stopped in the doorway and looked back. "But you can forget about that new chair."

10

It was mid-afternoon before Des White could get back to Judith Heinz's house, next door to the crime scene.

As she rang the bell, Judith came quickly to the door and held a finger up to her lips. "Gina is sleeping, finally. Come in."

Des stepped into the front foyer. The house wasn't as she expected. Judith was old enough to be Des's mother, and she expected the house to look like her mother's, with too much furniture, all the surfaces covered with knick-knacks and crocheted lap blankets on the back of every chair and sofa. But Judith's house was the opposite, what Des supposed designers called minimalist. A few pieces of sleek Scandinavian-style furniture created an open and airy feeling, and big, bright canvases graced the walls. And Gina lay peacefully on the couch, covered with a silk throw that looked like an impressionist painting.

Judith motioned for Des to follow her through the kitchen and directed her onto the back patio. This yard looked nothing like Drew Robbins' next door. Rather than covered in flower beds, the yard was a manicured flat green lawn, edged with precisely trimmed miniature boxwoods. Edward Hopper might have painted this yard.

Judith followed a few moments later with two glasses of iced tea. Des complimented her on her design taste. "You have a beautiful home and yard. I love the simple look, too."

Judith smiled. "Not what you expected, huh? Not Nana's fussy little house? I like open space and lots of color, big color."

"The paintings in your living room are breathtaking. Did a local artist paint them?" Des asked.

Judith smiled again. "You might say so. A very local artist— me. I taught art history at VWU for 30 years before I retired. I'd be up in my studio painting right now, if it weren't for what happened. How horrible."

Des agreed. "Yes, horrible is the only way to describe it. But I'm sorry that I didn't know you were an artist. I only know you from the provost's office."

"No need to apologize," said Judith. "I retired from teaching art before you started at the university."

"You should know that Gina and I are friends," said Des, "so, in addition to my police duties, I care for her a lot. Thanks for taking care of her since this morning. How has she been doing?"

"Not very well," Judith said. "She paced around the room for a long time after you left. She broke out sobbing several times. I finally got a little food into her and gave her some hot cocoa. I suppose I shouldn't admit this, but I slipped half a sleeping pill into the cocoa—I take them sometime when I can't sleep—and she's been asleep now for a couple of hours."

Des' police instincts came out. "No, you shouldn't have done that. I understand, though, and I'm glad she's resting." Then she smiled. "I'll let you off with just a warning, but lay off sharing your drugs. Now forgive me, but I need to ask you some questions."

"Of course. I know you have to ask all the neighbors questions."

Des first asked Judith to tell her a little about herself. She had lived in the house her whole life, except for her college years and a few years studying art in New York City. The house had belonged to her parents, and she moved back in with them when she got her job at the university. She never married—married to her art, she said—but loved kids. She was active in the children's art programs at local schools. She had retired about a decade ago. After that, she substituted in the provost's office, filling in for staff when they went on vacation or were ill. Just about everyone at the university knew Judith, and vice versa.

After her parents passed away, Judith inherited the house. She remodeled it completely, converting her old upstairs bedroom into her studio. The bedroom faced Robbins' house and had windows on three sides, perfect for a studio. She enlarged the windows and added a big skylight. She spent many hours every day in that room. So, yes, she told Des, she saw a lot of what went on next door.

"Were you and Drew Robbins friends?" Des asked.

Judith shook her head. "No, not really. We said hello when we saw each other, but that's about it. He wasn't very friendly. Of course, this neighborhood is filled with professors, most of whom aren't the kind to sit on the front porch and strike up conversations with passers-by. But, even though he wasn't all that neighborly, there was lots of action at the house."

"What kind of action?" Des asked.

"Well, he had lots of visitors," Judith said. "He always had a student working in his yard. They changed every term, but they all had one thing in common—they were all girls, cute little things. I'm pretty sure they did more for Drew than just tend his garden, if you know what I mean."

Des was a police officer, so she liked clarity. "You mean sex?"

"Yes," said Judith, "that's what I mean. I never saw anything, of course, but the girls would finish the gardening and then go into the house for a long time before leaving. That all stopped, though, when Gina moved in."

"What other kind of company did Robbins have?" continued Des.

"His assistant, Russell Bronoski, came by a lot. He had a key, I know, because he would let himself in when Drew was gone for a few days."

"Anyone else?"

"Another young woman came by often, but I don't think she had a key. She looked older than the students that tended his garden, maybe a graduate student or technician. She didn't look like the others, either. You know with long blond hair tied in a ponytail. She had short dark hair, curly. She didn't stay long, maybe just half an hour or so, and she was always carrying lots of papers and books and things." This was a new person, and, Des thought, probably a person-of-interest.

"And he had one other regular visitor," continued Judith. "The person who keeps track of money for the provost, she's been coming ever since Drew moved in. Sheila Cummings is her name. She's a sweetheart. I've gotten to know her since I've been subbing in the provost's office. She told me that she and Drew were good friends. They met many years ago, when she was a new bookkeeper in the Department of Renewable Resources and Drew was a starting Ph.D. student. She's got a key, too. She used to check on the house, too, especially when Drew was away for long field trips."

"What about Gina?" Des asked.

"Oh, Gina's a sweetheart, too. She's about the opposite of Drew. Very friendly. She came over often for a chat. And she's so beautiful. Not just pretty, you know. There's a radiance about her, a glow. It made the artist in me excited. We talked about me painting her portrait, but we never got around to it. I think she was hoping to surprise him with it as a wedding present. That is, she said, if he ever got around to asking her."

"Do you know that he proposed last night, in front of everyone at the award banquet?"

Judith frowned. "Yes. Gina told me about it when we came back to the house, and she showed me her beautiful ring. Sort of doubles up the tragedy, doesn't it? A little bit like Romeo and Juliet, except that Juliet is still alive to live with the pain."

Des changed the subject. "I know you don't sit around looking out the windows all day and night to spy on your neighbors…"

"Some people think that, though," laughed Judith, "because they see me up in my studio at all hours with the shades open and the lights on. And, like I said, I do see a lot."

"What about last night and this morning?" asked Des.

"I wasn't invited to the award banquet, but I did see Drew and Gina leave. She was wearing an elegant long white dress, so beautiful. It inspired me to work on a painting, and I stayed in my studio all evening. I saw Sheila Cummings drive up and park a bit down the street. Then Drew and Gina came home,"

"What time did this happen?" asked Des.

"Sheila arrived maybe half an hour before Drew and Gina. And then they got home about eleven, I think. Then I went to bed."

"What about this morning?"

"I do get up early," Judith said, "partly because the light is so good, but also because I don't sleep all that soundly. Remember, I've got some sleeping pills? I didn't take one last night, though, because I felt really tired. But I was wrong, I guess, because I woke up early. I heard a car start up and drive away, and I looked at the clock. It was about 5:30."

"Did you see the car?" Des asked.

"No, but I could tell it was a diesel, the way it clanked as he drove away."

"Why do you say it was a 'he' if you didn't see the car?" Des asked.

Judith shrugged. "Oh, I'm just guessing. But Russell Bronoski has a car that sounds just like that."

"You'll need to stop by the police station and make a formal statement, I'm afraid," said Des. Judith nodded. I wish all witnesses were that competent and cooperative, Des thought, and maybe as nosy.

The back door opened, and Gina walked out on the patio. She looked groggy, probably still feeling the effects of the sleeping pill. But the sadness in her face and the slump of her shoulders told the unmistakable message of sorrow.

"Hi, Des," Gina said. She looked at Judith and started to cry again. "Thank you so much for taking care of me today. You're an angel."

"How are you feeling now, kiddo?" Des asked.

Gina managed a small smile. "Better. I feel a little rested, and maybe the shock is starting to wear off. I just don't know what to do now. I don't know how to take care of a person's death, let alone a murder."

"Don't worry," Des said, "I'll help you out on the funeral—as your friend. It's going to be hard, Gina, with me being both your friend and a police officer, but we'll work it out."

"I knew I could count on you. Can I go home now?"

"I'm afraid not. You can't stay in the house until the town police department's forensics team finishes, and I'm not going to rush them. They're doing us a favor, and this is too important."

Gina looked confused again. "Where am I supposed to stay?"

Judith came to the rescue once more. "You can stay here, Gina. I've got plenty of room, and I don't mind the company."

"Okay, I guess," stammered Gina, "at least I'll be close to home."

Des took over. "But I can go into the house for a few minutes to get you some clothes and personal items. We'll be right back, Judith, and thanks for being such a good friend to Gina."

Des and Gina walked back to the front door of the Robbins' house. Yellow crime tape blocked their entry, and a town police officer stood nearby. Gina hesitated at the doorstep, frozen by a combination of fright and uncertainty.

"Let's go around back and sit in the garden," said Des.

She led Gina around the house. The bushes along the side of the house were overgrown and crowded the sidewalk. "The shrubs need some trimming," Des said.

"Yes," Gina said, "I kept telling Drew to get his horticulture tart to trim them, but she hasn't gotten it done."

The backyard, however, was beautifully cared for. Not manicured, but a bit wild, packed with beds of colorful flowers and blooming shrubs. It reminded Des of how a Hollywood stylist might spend hours making her celebrity client look like she had just stepped out of the shower, her tousled hair just naturally beautiful.

Gina told Des what she needed from the house and where to find it. Gina also showed Des where they kept a back-door key hidden under a flower pot.

"Who knows about this key, Gina?" asked Des.

"As far as I know, just Drew and me," Gina answered, "but maybe Russki knows about it. And maybe Sheila Cummings. Drew might have told them both."

"Judith mentioned that another young woman often was here," Des continued, "but she didn't know her name. She said she had dark curly hair. Do you know who she meant?"

Gina nodded. "Yes, that would be Melissa Campbell. She's Drew's teaching assistant. She's around every once in a while."

"Would she have known about the key?" Des asked.

"Maybe," said Gina, her voice starting to crack, "I don't know." Des sensed that she had pushed Gina as far as she should right now.

Rather than using the key to enter the door, Des slipped on latex gloves before picking up the key and putting it in an evidence bag. Telling Gina to wait, Des went around to the front door and spoke for a moment to the police officer. She put on shoe coverings and entered the house. A few minutes later, she came back with a small bag and walked back to Gina. "I think this will do you for a day or so while we finish working up the house."

Gina thanked her and then pointed out into the garden. "The flowers are still here," Gina said, "blooming their hearts out. It's as though nothing has changed. But everything has changed." Then she sat straight up and cried out, "Oh, my god, that's what he said!"

"What do you mean, Gina?"

"Last night, as Drew was getting dressed for the banquet, he said 'it all ends tonight.' Something like that. When I asked him what he meant, he just shrugged it off, saying that the stress of trying to succeed would end. But I wasn't convinced. Do you suppose he knew he was in danger, that something bad might happen?"

"We'll never know that, I'm afraid." Des waited a moment to let Gina recover. "And since you brought it up, can we talk about last night? Are you ready to do that?"

Gina swallowed hard. "I guess. We have to do it sometime, don't we? Better to get it over with, I guess."

"Okay, let's start before the banquet. How did Drew seem? Was he acting normal or not?"

"He was acting fine," Gina said, "a little nervous maybe, but it was a big night, and a lot was happening. Not just the award. He was also signing a contract for his own series with the television company. That's why Jamie Nelson was here, to finish up the deal."

Des added, "And don't forget that he was going to ask someone to marry him. That would make me nervous enough all by itself." Gina gave Des a mournful and hurt look. "Sorry, Gina, that wasn't very thoughtful. Sorry."

Des waited a minute to let the emotions die down, but she knew she had to continue. "Now, at the banquet, did anything happen that seemed out of place?"

Gina tried to focus on the previous night. It seemed a year

ago, not just yesterday. "Jamie Nelson was in a terrible mood, especially for a celebration. He hardly spoke to me, or to that girl he had with him. Once, though, he leaned over to me and said, 'Your lover boy is quite an ass, you know.' I couldn't believe he was talking that way, sitting up there with us. 'I gave him his big break,' Jamie said then, 'and now he thinks he's the alpha dog. We'll see about that.' I was so angry. I just ignored him after that."

"I'll find out what that was all about," said Des. "Anything else out of the ordinary?"

"You mentioned Mel a minute ago," Gina said, but Des looked confused. "Melissa Campbell, I mean. We call her Mel. She wasn't at the banquet. I'm sure she was invited and would have had a seat at the tables for Drew's staff up front. I hope Drew didn't notice; he'd take that as a slight, and I don't think things were going well between them anyway."

"What do you mean?" Des asked.

"I don't really know," Gina answered, "but she seemed unhappy whenever she was over here lately."

Yes, Des thought, Melissa Campbell was certainly a person-of-interest. "Anything else happen at the banquet?"

"Yes, one other thing," Gina said. "While we were having dessert, just before the speeches started, Russki walked up to the head table and handed Drew a note. I'd seen him writing it on the back of the program a few minutes before. Anyway, Drew read it, frowned, and put the note in his jacket pocket. He flashed his biggest smile—the one he uses when he's not happy about something—at Russki and said, 'Not on your life, Russell, old buddy, not in a million years.' I asked Drew what that was about, but he said it was just a joke among old friends and to forget it."

"Any idea what the note said?"

"No," said Gina. "But I'll bet it's still in his jacket pocket, upstairs in the bedroom."

Des told Gina to wait, got outfitted again to enter the house and went up to the bedroom. The bedroom hadn't been touched yet, forensics would get to that tomorrow. Drew's suit jacket was on the floor in the tangle of his and Gina's clothes. Des picked up the jacket and took it outside to Gina.

"Is this his jacket?" Des asked.

Gina nodded. "Yes. And he stuck the note in the inside pocket on the left side."

Still wearing gloves, Des reached in and lifted out the note. As Gina had said, it was written on the backside of the one-page program.

"What does it say, Des?"

Des read the note silently first before looking up at Gina with a question in her eyes. "Maybe we shouldn't talk about this right now."

Gina looked confused. "Why not? What does it say? You have to tell me, Des."

Des sighed and read the note. "It says, 'I want half of the prize money, or your life won't be worth living.'"

Gina cried out in agony. "Oh, my god. Oh, my god. Russell killed him."

11

Sheila Cummings sent a message to the provost's assistant at six in the morning, long before anyone would be at work. She was ill and wouldn't be in today.

The thought of seeing anyone today is what made her ill. How could he have done this to her? After all the years they'd been together, after all that she'd done for him, all that she had sacrificed. How could he?

She thought back to last night's award banquet. She had chosen a seat at a table near the back, so her overwhelming happiness wouldn't be too obvious. There he was, her Drew Robbins, about to get the most important award in the entire conservation world. She wished that she could be up there, sitting next to him, where she belonged. But she understood that their love would always need to be private, shared just between them, kept secret from the jealous campus community. She couldn't let anything, not even her gnawing desire to be his wife, interfere with his success.

She glowed inside as the speakers said the nicest things about Drew. She tried not to clap too enthusiastically, cautious so that others at her table wouldn't gossip later, wondering why she was so excited.

And then he had crushed her. Rather than her heart beating fast because of joy, it had pounded with horror. He had done the unthinkable. He asked that girl to marry him, there in front of hundreds of people. She had almost fainted at her table. When everyone rose to their feet to cheer the proposal and Gina's whispered yes, she slunk out of the room as quietly as possible, bitter tears streaming down her face. She felt light-headed, but managed to make it to her car before totally losing control. She sat in the car crying for a long time. The voices of other people leaving the building roused her from her trance. Somehow she made it home, but she could not remember the drive.

Sheila now thought even farther back, back to the beginning. It was her first week as a junior bookkeeper in the Department of Renewable Resources, in January, 2003, and it hadn't gone well. The job was more complex than she had expected from her community college courses. There were dozens of accounts, many with dozens of sub-accounts. Most were for research projects, each with differing rules set up by the funding agencies. Others were accounts of state money that had what seemed like arbitrary and illogical restrictions on how funds could be spent. Whatever you do, don't try to buy pizzas for graduate students on a state account, her boss had told her the first day, as the rest of the office staff looked on and laughed.

She had been young then, shy and inexperienced. The faculty talked down to her, as though she were a hick from the mountains. She was a local girl who had been raised on a farm outside of town, but she was also smart and hard-working. But she shriveled like a raisin in the sun every time professor so-and-so questioned her about what invoice she had charged to what account.

Then, on the last day of her first week, Drew Robbins had walked in the door. He looked as lost as she was. He caught her eye and smiled. She looked down, turning red. When he walked up to her, she could hardly breathe.

"I'm Drew," he said, "Drew Robbins. I'm a new graduate student."

" Sheila," she managed to squeak out.

"Sheila, hi. I have a cousin named Sheila. It's a nice name." The other staff didn't even look up from their work. "My advisor told me to turn in these forms here, so I can get paid. Can you help me?"

Sheila took his forms, and Drew left, smiling at her again and saying thanks. It was the first time all week that someone had thanked her for her work. She sat with the forms in her hands for several minutes, unable to shake Drew's image. She had never met someone so handsome but also so nice. Earth to Sheila, someone said, and she snapped back to the moment. She hadn't processed forms like this in her first week, and she needed to ask for help. Her colleague frowned over the forms, saying what a bother it was when a student started at an odd time rather than in the fall. But Sheila kept both of them at it until Drew Robbins was fully and properly on the payroll.

And Drew Robbins was fully and properly lodged in Sheila's heart. The whole weekend she fantasized that they might become friends, that maybe he would ask her on a date. Then reality would take hold, and she would chastise herself for being so ridiculous. Someone like him would never go out with someone like her. But no sooner had she dismissed one fantasy when a new one would pop up.

He returned to her office the next Monday with more papers to be submitted—key request forms, his rabies vaccination record, new employee safety checklist—and Sheila made sure she was the one to help him. He asked her if she would have lunch with him, because he had a lot of questions about how to do things and could really use her advice.

Her heart leaped into her throat at his offer, but then reality took over again. "I bring my lunch from home. Sorry," she murmured.

"Me, too," said Drew. "I can't afford to eat in a restaurant. I was thinking we could just sit on one of the picnic tables I saw in the little woods outside the building."

And that's how their relationship began. Drew treated her differently than all the other faculty and students. He didn't make fun of her, and he encouraged her to speak up around the office. He encouraged her in other ways, too. While Drew worked on his doctorate, she took classes in the business school, first getting her Bachelor's degree and then a Masters of Accounting.

Sheila became Drew's watchdog in the department. After every departmental event, when she put out the leftover food for students, she kept some in her desk just for Drew and her to eat at a secret lunch or dinner. If there was an opportunity to meet a visiting scholar or be on a committee with influential people, she made sure Drew got included. If he lacked a few receipts for his travel vouchers, she wrote the kind of explanation that she had learned higher levels would accept. She kept track of his personnel file, assuring that he got raises the minute he was eligible and any extra benefits she could stir up.

The truth was, Sheila loved Drew. And she knew Drew loved her. She gave herself to him, body and soul, the first time she had given either to anyone.

But she never demanded anything from him. She understood his ambition and his need to get ahead. He was brilliant, she knew, and the passion that he put into their love-making was the same passion he had for saving the endangered animals he studied.

They always kept their relationship secret, though, partly because of the university's rules and partly to avoid the jealousy that might develop with other staff. All the women in the department, from the oldest secretary to the youngest undergraduate, had a crush on Drew, and he told Sheila that he didn't want any office gossip to get in the way of her success, or his.

Sheila wished their love could be public, but she accepted the need for secrecy. She even grew to enjoy the idea that Drew was hers and that no one knew it. She felt superior to all of them because Drew loved her, shy Sheila from the farm. She had also learned from Drew that knowledge was power—he always tried to know more about what was going on than anyone else. By keeping their love to themselves, she could use that knowledge for their benefit.

And they both did succeed. He became a full professor in record time, and she steadily moved up the university's administrative ladder. She became the head accountant in DRR, then moved to the Dean's office and finally to the provost's office. As she advanced, her secret knowledge allowed her ever more and bigger chances to promote and protect Drew.

She knew that he slept with other women. But she didn't care. Those graduate students and young office workers served him well as a way to satisfy his sexual energy, but she knew he never loved any of them. Sheila told herself that a man of Drew's passion needed to express that passion in all kinds of ways. He used those casual flings to satisfy his lust, but he loved only her. She knew he'd come back to her when he tired of this one or that one. And he always had.

Until now. Sheila had begun to worry about Gina Rahim as soon as she saw her and Drew together. Drew had kept her around longer than the others. He even let her move in with him. Sheila thought that wouldn't last long, but they had been living together now for close to six months. Sheila kept close tabs on that girl.

And then last night. Last night he had proposed. Sheila was shattered.

Sheila's email pinged just after 8 o'clock. The provost's assistant had sent the tragic news that Drew was dead. The message sent Sheila into a new shock wave, the second woman that morning to be overcome with grief. She moaned and sobbed, alone in her kitchen. No one could know of their love, and now no one could know of her heartbreak.

She looked down at the table. Fear replaced grief as she stared at the handgun lying there. She had always kept a gun at home. Growing up on a farm, guns were part of life. She had liked to shoot targets as a girl and had won ribbons for her skill through 4-H. When she moved to the university, her father had given her this handgun for protection.

She shook from fear as she thought about what she had almost done last night. Enraged at the proposal Drew had made to Gina, Sheila had driven home. She hadn't been thinking clearly. She got the gun, loaded it and drove to Drew's house on Monroe Avenue. A calmness came over her as she waited for them to return, knowing they would be delayed as they greeted all the well-wishers.

She crept out of her car and hid behind the shrubs at the corner of the house. In her deranged state, she had determined to shoot the evil whore who had put a spell on the man she loved.

When Drew and Gina pulled into the driveway, Sheila watched as they kissed in the car before getting out. The bile rose in her throat, nearly gagging her. Drew got out and came around the passenger side of the car and helped Gina out. Gina looked in Sheila's direction for just a second and paused. Sheila held perfectly still, hoping that she hadn't been spotted. Then Gina looked away, hugged Drew and they kissed again. They were so close together Sheila couldn't get clear aim at Gina. The pair staggered to the door, laughing and caressing, never giving Sheila the chance she so wanted.

Sheila crept back to her car, and drove home.

She was heartbroken, first because she had been betrayed and second because she had failed to destroy the woman who caused the betrayal.

Now, however, as she sat at her table and contemplated the gun in front of her, she shook with a different kind of fright. Suppose someone had seen her? That nosy neighbor next door was always looking out her window.

Dear lord, she thought, I've lost Drew, and the police might think I did it.

12

Friday

When Des arrived at the police station the next morning, Jimmy was already there, looking eager. Sometimes she wished he wasn't such a lap-dog, constantly seeking her attention and approval. But he had good instincts and was growing as an investigator a little every day. She poured herself a cup of coffee and headed to her desk. Jimmy tracked her through the door.

"Okay, kiddo, what are you dying to tell me?" she asked.

Jimmy put the forensic report in front of her. "You won't believe this. The murder weapon, the spear..."

"Yes, I know the murder weapon was a spear," she snapped, and was immediately sorry. Jimmy looked like a scolded child. "Sorry about that, Jimmy, I didn't mean to jump on you like that. So, what about the spear?"

"Forensics found two sets of fingerprints on the spear," Jimmy said, "and we got matches for both of them in the university database." The university had instituted taking fingerprints of all employees and students a few years earlier, including taking prints of all existing employees. Faculty objected at the time, as expected, but the need for enhanced safety and security trumped their concerns.

"Let me guess," Des said, "Drew Robbins and Gina Rahim."

Jimmy shook his head. "Nope. You're half right. Gina Rahim's were on the spear, but the others belonged to Russell Bronoski."

"Things are starting to look bad for Bronoski," said Des. "What about the note that we found in Robbins' coat pocket?"

"Two sets of prints on the note. Robbins', of course." Jimmy paused for effect, irritating Des again.

"And the other?" asked Des.

"Bronoski."

Des and Jimmy reviewed the evidence stacking up against Bronoski. Gina said he had passed Robbins a note that made Robbins mad. Judith Heinz thought she heard his car outside the house early in the morning, and she said he had a key to the house. And now this—his fingerprints on both the incriminating note and the murder weapon.

"What's that they always say on the cop shows, Jimmy? Means, opportunity, and motive. I think we better have a talk with one Russell Bronoski."

They found Bronoski in the Carnivore Research Center a little after ten that morning. Des had sent officers the day before to secure Robbins' office, but had decided not to make the laboratory off limits because there was no suspected connection between Robbins' death and the university research he oversaw. The lab was busy, despite the fact that the boss had been murdered. Two staff members were working at lab benches, and Russell was talking to a small group of young men and women, obviously students and obviously in distress. Des and Jimmy overheard him as they walked in.

"Yes, it was a terrible thing that happened yesterday," Russell was saying. "Drew was special is so many ways. He was a great scientist and an inspiring leader. But you know what he was like—the work always mattered most. And today, like every day, he'd want you to take a few deep breaths and then get back to saving the animals he loved so much. So, that's what we're going to do. But Ted Graham, our department head, wants you to know that if you need to talk with someone, you know, a counselor, we can arrange that. The university has people on standby to help us out. Okay?"

The students nodded their heads and drifted back to work, but clearly neither their heads nor their hearts were focused on their tasks. Des caught Russell's attention, and he walked over to them.

"Russell, I'm Desdemona White, the university's police chief. And this is Jimmy Nesbitt, my chief assistant."

Russell frowned. "Yes, I know who you are. I expected that you'd be wanting to talk with me. Should we go into my office?"

They followed him out of the lab and down the hall to a faculty-style office. All faculty offices were small, but his was truly claustrophobic because of the mess inside. The desk and shelves were stacked with the miscellaneous dregs of years of research and travel—books, papers, notebooks, and computer outputs, of course, but also cameras, animal traps and specimens of bones, plants, insects and other formerly living things neither Des nor Jimmy could identify. It was the figurative rat's nest, but Des was pretty sure some real rats were probably in residence.

"Sorry about the mess," said Russell, moving some stacks

off two camp stools so the police officers could sit down. "I keep a very neat laboratory—that's where accuracy and precision matter. But my office, well, who cares?"

Des offered something between a smile and a grimace. "Yours isn't the first messy faculty office I've seen. But let me offer some friendly advice. If the fire marshal comes through here, he's going to go nuts that your window ledge is so covered with stacks of paper and other, uh, specimens that you couldn't use it in an emergency. That's why the window is made to open, you know, for use if the building needs to be evacuated." Or exterminated, Des thought.

"Okay, advice taken," Russell said. Des was sure it wouldn't be.

Jimmy interrupted. "Excuse me, but is that a spear in the corner?"

"Yeah," said Russell, "it's a Maasai spear, from Tanzania. I got it when I was working there with Drew. It's pretty cool. Would you like to look at it?"

As Jimmy was about to reach for it, Des held up her hand to stop him. "Not now. Maybe some other time. We're on much more serious business this morning. With Drew Robbins' murder, we have to talk with everyone who was close to him, personally or professionally."

"I understand. Ask away."

"Had you and Drew worked together for a long time?"

Russell nodded. "Yes, ever since I finished my Ph.D. I did my dissertation research on the tundra wolf in Russia—that's why they call me Russki around here. Well, that and because it is easier to say Russki than Russell Bronoski. When I finished, I came to work with him, just as he was finishing up his dissertation at Virginia Western. I went with him on his third year studying hyenas in Tanzania. And I've worked for him ever since."

"How did you get along?"

"Just great," Russell said. "Drew treated me like his research partner rather than as someone who worked for him. You know, worked 'with' him rather than 'for' him. We ran everything together in the beginning, which was great. When things started getting really intense for him, though, after the book and TV show, then I started doing more of the management of the projects. That's the part that I love, being in the field, observing animals, helping the students learn the ropes. And then analyzing the data. Drew did really well getting the grants, setting up the research projects at the start and then with the lights and cameras at the end. But I'm not that way. I don't like being in the spotlight."

"With all of Drew's success, and yours, too, why didn't you start your own lab, like at another university? You're not tenured here, are you?"

"No," said Russell, "I'm a research associate, but I'm not classified as a faculty member. So, no, I don't have tenure. The truth is that I'm not very good at publishing, either. Just like I freeze up in the spotlight, I freeze up starring at a blank screen and keyboard if I have to write. That was also Drew's thing. He could tell a story that kept people entranced, and he could get it down on paper, too. I probably never would have gotten tenure anywhere. We're a great team, I mean, we were a great team. Me running the field operations and churning out the data, Drew taking it to the world."

Given what she had been learning about Robbins, Des wasn't

buying the brotherly love bit. But she let it go for the moment. "So, tell me about last night. I saw you at the awards banquet, sitting right up front."

"Yeah, I was there. It was a great night, wasn't it? And him asking Gina to marry him? That was great, and it was just like Drew. No sense wasting a moment like that." Russell stopped for a moment, his words now coming haltingly. "I'm sorry, I didn't mean to…you know, make light of what happened. It's horrible."

"We heard that you passed Drew a note at the banquet, and that it seemed to make Drew angry."

Russell's face flushed, and his composure slipped even more. "That was nothing. Just a little issue about the research."

"Why did you bring it up during the banquet?" Des asked. "It doesn't seem like the right moment, does it?"

"No, of course not," Russell said. "It was my fault, you're right. I shouldn't have disrupted the evening."

"So, what did the note say?" Des asked.

"Well, uh, I asked him if he was going to get the latest proposal done by Friday, today. It's due early next week, and we needed time to review it over the weekend."

"Try again, Russell," said Des. "We've seen the note."

Russell's hands started to shake and sweat began to bead up on his forehead. "I'm sorry. That was stupid of me to lie. I'm sorry."

"You're right about that," agreed Des. "What did the note say, Russell?"

"I told him it would be nice if he gave me equal credit for our joint work when he accepted the award. He just laughed at me. He said not in a million years." His voice quivered as he talked. "I know I just said I don't like the spotlight, but I would appreciate being given some credit sometimes. And the award presentation would have been the perfect time."

"Okay, Russell," Des said, "I'll give you one more chance. This time it better be the truth. What did the note say?"

Russell looked straight at her, his eyes never waivering. "That is the truth. Honest."

Des reached into her notebook and pulled out a piece of paper. "Here's a copy of the note. Why don't you read it to us."

Russell looked at the note and read it aloud. "I want half of the prize money, or your life won't be worth living." He stammered as he said the words, barely able to reach the end. He looked up, bewildered. "I never.... This isn't the note I wrote, not what I gave to Drew. Where did you get this?"

"It was in his suit jacket pocket, where he put it after you gave it to him and he read it."

"No, no, no, I didn't give this to him. Someone else must have done this."

"Sorry, Russell," said Des. "Your fingerprints are all over it. And the only others are Drew's."

"What?" Russell looked like he might faint. "I didn't write this note, I swear. Give me half the prize money?" He looked back at the note. "And then to say his life wouldn't be worth living? That's a threat. God, I could never do that. I didn't write this note. No, no, no."

Des and Jimmy stood up. "You're going to have to come with us, Russell," Des said. "You are in serious trouble."

13

Elena Bertoni was not a procrastinator. As soon as she finished teaching her Friday morning class, she set out on her new task as the successor to Drew Robbins.

Fortunately Ted Graham wasn't a procrastinator, either. He had already done his part. He informed the registrar that Elena was the new teacher of record for Drew's seminar class. He also contacted the research office and made Elena the principal investigator on all his research grants. Ted also sent an email to the department's listserv, telling them that Elena had been so gracious as to take over Robbins' workload.

That morning the comments from her colleagues ran the gamut. You're a great departmental citizen, Elena. You're really a soft touch, aren't you, Elena? Good on you, Elena. Gonna ride Robbins' reputation to full professor?

Teasing aside, her colleagues all knew this was the right move. Elena had the reputation of being a straight arrow, sometimes annoyingly so. Other faculty members cringed when she reviewed one of their draft reports or papers, knowing that she would do a thorough job, not just rubber-stamping, even if it was a routine committee report no one really cared about or would ever read. Her students knew her as a stickler, too. Don't get caught using the wrong format on your literature citations, they all said, because she'll kick your butt right back to the Harvard style guide. But when you wanted something done right, well, give it to Elena.

When Aaron Schmidt met her in the hallway on her way to get coffee, he had a twinkle in his eye. "Great day for the department. Robbins is gone, and you're taking over his kingdom. The king is dead, long live the queen. It's a good day, that is, as long as you don't turn into a hedonistic jerk like Robbins. No plans for that, eh, Elena?"

"I don't know, Aaron," Elena winked. "Wait until our next department meeting. Maybe I'll give you a bunch of trouble, just so you don't get too complacent."

Elena and Aaron had gotten along well right from the beginning. He noticed something special in her, an interest in the work of the whole department, not just her specific research. She wanted to learn about his wood identification program and visited his lab frequently, just out of curiosity and collegiality. Her intellectual curiosity went much farther than that, as he had learned as he got to know her better. She loved every corner of the university, from art to nuclear engineering, from English literature to veterinary medicine. Aaron had found a kindred spirit.

Aaron laughed, but then got serious. "I know I should feel bad about what happened, but I don't. I really don't. Deep down, Drew Robbins hated the university, what we do and how we do it. We're all a bit self-centered and egotistical, but he was manic. Many was the time I'd day-dream about bumping him off myself."

"Better not say that to the wrong person, Aaron. You might find yourself as the prime suspect."

After class, Elena set about getting acquainted with Robbins' various projects and his seminar course. She emailed Mel Campbell, his teaching assistant, asking for a time when they could get together to discuss the course before Elena took over the next week. In the afternoon, she met individually with each of Robbins' graduate students. They were all rattled, given that they had seen Russell Bronoski leaving with the police and it hadn't looked like they were going out for a friendly cup of coffee. Rumors were flying, but Elena tried to keep the students focused on explaining their work to her.

The range of projects interested her greatly. Each student was working on one of Robbins' grants, but each also had a project of their own that would become a thesis or dissertation. Most of the six students she met with were working on animal behavior projects, some in Tanzania, where Robbins had maintained research ever since his dissertation, and a few on scattered projects both nearby and around the world.

The students were smart and conscientious; Robbins' high profile meant that he had a line of high-quality students waiting for a chance to work with him. And the troubles they shared with Elena were the standard variety. Animals were hard to find and capture, there wasn't enough time or money, the field telemetry equipment often broke down, remote links with satellites sometimes failed, and other typical trials of field research. She talked each of them through their specific problems, set up a plan to address them and worked out a schedule for regular meetings over the coming weeks and months. Each student left feeling that he or she had found a new sympathetic and capable mentor.

In late afternoon, she met with the final student, Timor Madras.

Elena smiled and started the conversation. "So, Timor, tell me a bit about yourself before we get into your research."

Timor was visibly nervous. "Thank you, Dr. Bertoni. This is my first year. I am from India, and I am—was—very fortunate to have the chance to work with Dr. Robbins."

"Do you like it here, Timor?"

"Oh, yes," he answered, "I love the university. Everyone has been very welcoming to me."

"And you got along well with Dr. Robbins?"

"Oh, yes, of course." Timor hesitated then, and he seemed undecided about what to say next.

Elena tried to ease his discomfort. "It's okay, Timor. You can say anything you need to say."

"Thank you again, Dr. Bertoni. Well, I hadn't really gotten to spend a lot of time with Dr. Robbins. He was gone quite a lot, and when we did have time to talk, he was so busy that our meetings were brief. And I haven't really started on my thesis research project yet, so he told me I should keep talking to the other students and do library research to get my ideas narrowed down."

"That seems reasonable," said Elena. "I'm sure that we can find a project that both of us are interested in. What do you like about studying wildlife?"

"Well, I like the animals themselves, of course, and protecting their habitat and all. But I'm really good at computer modeling and mapping, so I'd like to work more on that—making better predictive models of how animals behave in their natural habitats."

Elena was impressed. "Most graduate students want to be in the field, becoming the next Steve Irwin."

"I'm sorry, Dr. Bertoni," said Timor, slightly embarrassed, "I don't know who that is."

Elena chuckled to herself. Time, and fame, pass by fast, she thought. "Never mind, Timor. He was a famous wildlife expert who loved to get close to the animals, too close in one case. But doing the statistics and building good models is just as important. Good for you for wanting to do this work."

Timor nodded his head and smiled, happy for the positive reinforcement. But once again, he seemed hesitant. Elena jotted down a note to help him with his self-confidence. "Is something bothering you, Timor?"

"Yes. I mean, no, not really. It's just that I've been working on something that has me puzzled, and I was hoping to talk with Dr. Robbins about it."

"Well," said Elena, "I'm afraid you're stuck with me. What is it?"

Timor opened up like a dam bursting. "Because I'm new here, Dr. Robbins' wanted me to take his undergraduate seminar class, even though I'm a graduate student."

"Faculty often recommend that, Timor," said Elena. "Are you having trouble with the level of the material?"

"Oh, no," Timor said, "I love the class. Although most of the time we work with Ms. Campbell, not with Dr. Robbins." Elena made another note, remembering that she still hadn't heard from Mel. "We have to do a research project on some aspect of animal behavior. Ms. Campbell gave us access to the data files for Dr. Robbins' published studies so that we'd have some real data to work with. So, I started to study the behavior of the India plains wolf. Dr. Robbins did a project about them several years ago. That's how I learned about him, reading his papers for my undergraduate class in ecology in India."

"I'm familiar with the project," Elena said. "He published several major papers about their behavior and habitat use."

"Right, it is very interesting information," Timor said, his nervousness giving way to excitement. "Dr. Robbins reported on various traits of the wolves, like their home range size, average daily distance traveled, things like that. What I wanted to study was how these traits changed across the seasons. So, I divided his observation season—about six months—into one-month intervals. Then I calculated the data for each month and compared them."

"Sounds interesting," Elena said. "What did you find?"

"Well, first off, it wasn't very interesting at all. I found no significant differences among any of the months. The means of the home range area, daily distance traveled, hours of activity, and several other measures changed a little from month to month, but they were all statistically the same."

Elena nodded. "So, I guess the India plains wolf is a creature of habit, isn't it?"

Timor laughed. "Yes, ma'am. For sure. But then I looked a little deeper, and I found something I can't explain."

"You've got my attention, Timor. Keep going."

"Take home range, for example. When I looked at the standard deviations around the average home range area for a particular animal, the value was almost identical for every set of monthly samples. All six of them. And not just close, but almost identical. To two decimal places."

"That is strange," agreed Elena. "Was your computer model doing something you hadn't asked it to do? Was it rounding the numbers, or truncating them, covering up the differences and making them all look so similar?"

Timor shook his head. "No, nothing like that. I checked. And, if I might be allowed to say so, I'm very good at these models. No, the model was working fine. So, I went back and chose different monthly intervals. I started the first monthly sample two weeks later and calculated the traits again. Same result. Every time I calculated a standard deviation with any of the data, arranged in any way, I got the same result. Every standard deviation was almost exactly the same. It's really weird."

Elena agreed. "It is unusual. Well, more than unusual. It's basically impossible for two reasons. First, because animals aren't ever that consistent; that's why we have to study their behavior. Second, groups of data don't turn out that similar in biological situations; physics maybe, but not biology. Did you talk to Dr. Robbins about this?"

"No," said Timor, "I didn't know how to approach him about it. I didn't want him to think I was questioning his research. So, I just kept checking, re-running the data like I said. I was going to try to talk to him about it at our next meeting. But, well, now I can't do that."

"I'm glad you told me, Timor," Elena said. "Send me the data files and let me see how it turns out when I run the data. Then we can get back together. I'm sure we can figure this out."

Timor stood to leave. "Thanks, Dr. Bertoni. I feel a lot better."

Unfortunately, Elena did not.

14

A university police station is normally a pretty quiet place. Most of the activity involves police officers going on and off duty, or getting keys to open the office door for some absent-minded professor. Occasionally a student stealing from dorm rooms or peddling drugs gets dragged in, but not often.

The station was buzzing today, though, as Des and Jimmy brought Russell Bronoski through the front door. The desk officers and other support staff stopped what they were doing to watch the murder suspect be led to the back of the station where a pair of interview rooms were located. It wasn't as dramatic as the cop shows on TV—reporters stacked outside the door shouting questions, the suspect's hands cuffed behind his back—but the tension was real. Faculty members didn't get murdered on university campuses every day.

Russell walked between Des and Jimmy to one of the interview rooms. Boxes of files and supplies were lined against the walls; space was always short on university campuses, even for the police, and the interview rooms doubled as storage space. A staff member brought bottles of water for all three, and they settled into the plastic chairs.

They had read Russell his rights on the way from his office, and now they let him know that he could have a lawyer present if he wished.

He declined. On the short drive from his office, Russell had regained some of his composure. "I haven't done anything wrong," he said, "so I don't need a lawyer. Let's just get this over with so I can go back to work."

"I wish it were that simple, Russell," said Des. "So, tell us again about what happened last night."

Russell frowned. "Nothing happened. I passed Drew that stupid note at the banquet, not the note you showed me, but the one asking him to share some credit, and he pulled his usual prima donna attitude. It was foolish of me to try that stunt. I knew he wouldn't recognize me." He looked in turn at each of the officers. "He was a self-centered, selfish bastard."

"I thought you were best buddies," Jimmy said.

"Yeah, that's what everyone thought. And don't get me wrong, working for Drew had been good for my career. But that doesn't mean I liked him, or that it wasn't all about him all the time. You want to know the truth? Drew had some good ideas, and he was good with animals. In the field, though, he was basically a distraction. He expected it all to be easy. But it isn't. You've got to get up early, even if it is cold or hot or rainy, go out and sit there for hours, days, maybe weeks, in order to learn anything. You've got to be patient, and recognize that the animals are the stars of the show. That wasn't for Drew. He was good with the ideas and he was good at the end, like I said—writing the papers, making the speeches, smiling into the cameras. But he was crap in the middle, when the real work gets done. If it weren't for me and his students—who I taught how to really be scientists—he'd have ended up teaching biology in some podunk school somewhere."

Des heard the bitterness in his voice and words, and it just added to the strikes against him. "Okay, so you're the hero and he's the pretty boy. What did you do after the banquet?"

"I went home and went to bed. That's all."

Jimmy asked, "Were you alone? Can anyone vouch for your story?"

"I live with my older sister," said Russell, "but she won't be able to help. She goes to bed early, and she sleeps soundly. I checked on her when I got home, but she didn't wake up."

Jimmy continued, " So, you were there all night? You didn't leave for a while?"

"No," said Russell, "I mean yes. Yes, I was there all night. No, I didn't leave."

"What would you say," asked Jimmy, "if we told you a witness claimed to have seen you at Robbins' house early before dawn on the next morning?"

Russell jumped up from his chair. "That's a lie. I'm telling you, I was home all night. Your witness, whoever that is, is lying. Or mistaken. I was nowhere near his house." He sat down again.

"I'm afraid there's more than the note, Russell," said Des. "Drew was stabbed in the back while he sat at his desk. He was stabbed with a Maasai spear."

"A spear, my god," Russell said. Then his face blanched with fear. "You don't think I did it with my spear, do you?"

"No," said Jimmy. "Your spear is in your office. The one that killed Robbins was left in his back."

"One of his spears?" asked Russell. "The ones hanging on his wall?"

Des took over. "Yes, one of those. Now here's the bad news for you, Russell. Your fingerprints are all over the spear handle."

"What? Wait. What? My fingerprints? How could that happen?"

Des said, "We were hoping you could tell us. We think you grabbed the spear from the wall and drove it into Robbins' back."

If possible, Russell turned even whiter. "No, no, no. I didn't do that."

"Well, then, how did your fingerprints get on the spear, Russell? Can you explain that?"

"I don't know. I'm over at the house a lot, so maybe I touched it some time. Maybe I took it down once to look at it. I don't know. I can't remember." Russell was panicking, grasping at straws. "Those prints could be years old. The spears have been there for a long time."

"Possible," said Des, "but we don't think so. Those spears were Robbins' prized mementos of his work in Tanzania. They looked nice and clean to the forensics team."

Russell sunk deep in his chair. "I don't know. I just don't know. Maybe it is time for a lawyer."

Russell did get a lawyer. Des instructed the lawyer that they weren't charging his client with anything yet, but that he should stay in town and be available for further questioning.

In Des' office, she and Jimmy discussed the murder.

"Something about the fingerprints bothers me," said Jimmy. "We found Gina's prints on the spear, and Russell's. Why weren't Robbins' prints on it as well? You'd think that he would have picked it up at some time."

"I agree that it seems strange," said Des. "Have we checked the fingerprints on the other spear?"

"No, we haven't," Jimmy admitted. "I'll get our guys back over there to dust it down. And maybe Bronoski is telling the truth. The killer could have worn gloves, so that his or her fingerprints wouldn't be on the spear."

"Yeah, I know," said Des. "That's why we haven't charged him with anything yet. I'm sure that his fingerprints are all over that study. He said he went over there a lot. Right now, we don't have a lot of concrete evidence. His fingerprints are just circumstantial. And Judith Heinz's statement that she heard a car that sounded like his doesn't mean much. The biggest piece of evidence is that threatening note, but the note is just that, a threat. It's not a smoking gun. We need one of those."

"No," said Jimmy, "we need a smoking spear."

Des looked at her watch and stood up. "We need to go, Jimmy. It's spring rush for the fraternities and sororities this weekend, and everything starts in a couple of hours. We need to put the murder investigation aside and get our officers set up for whatever ruckus breaks out tonight."

They stopped by Jessie's desk to pick her up for the evening's patrol work. "Look at this," she said, holding up a set of papers. "This is the contract that was lying on the desk under Robbins' body. Forensics just got it back to us. It's between him and the Canadian production company. It's an interesting read."

"I'll read it later," Des said. "Just give us the bottom line, because we all need to be somewhere else pronto."

"Well, the contract is for a television series that Drew

Robbins was going to do with the company. He was going to make a lot of money. But that's not the interesting thing. The contract includes an addendum that says Robbins gets to pick his own producer for the series, and that Jamie Nelson—you know, the Canadian guy who was seated up on the stage for the award banquet—will not be employed in any way on the series."

Jimmy's ears perked up. "You mean Robbins was having him fired?"

"Looks that way," said Jessie, "and the company had already signed off on the paperwork, so it was a done deal."

"Forget about a lazy Saturday morning, both of you," said Des. "First thing tomorrow, Jessie, you need to be back here organizing all the information we've gotten so far. And Jimmy, we need to have a chat with Jamie Nelson."

15

Saturday

Elena loved Saturdays. The contrast with weekdays was like, as Aaron Schmidt might say, the difference between a redbud and a redwood.

Weekdays were a blur for her. She taught a large general education class about biodiversity conservation on Monday, Wednesday and Friday mornings. Just keeping up with class preparation was a major task. Conservation changed continuously, and she needed to keep up to date. If not, one of her students who had watched Nat Geo the previous night or gotten the latest newsletter from the World Wildlife Fund might know more about the morning's topic than she did. Then there was the continuing stream of emails from the nearly 300 students in the class. She loved students, and helping them along on their academic journeys was a joy, and she made herself answer all her emails every night before going to sleep. Being constantly available to a hoard of figurative nieces and nephews was rewarding, but it was also a grind.

And then there were her graduate students, not as needy as

undergraduates but still requiring oversight, and research grants and committees and papers to be written. Promotion to full professor required a much longer resume than she currently possessed, and Elena was constantly aware that her progress wasn't as quick as she wanted. Ted Graham, her department head, had told her many times to not be such a perfectionist. Sometimes, he told her, "good" is good enough. Associate professors needed to be practical, he always said, full professors could be idealistic.

She had a hard time with that. She was a just a few clicks away from being obsessive-compulsive. The fact that good never sounded good enough to her was the major point of contention between her and her department head. It also got her sideways with her faculty colleagues at times, when they had declared a job done and she still wasn't satisfied. She winced every time she heard "give it a rest, Elena."

And she also loved all aspects of university life and wanted to participate in them fully, whether or not they filled an important category for promotion. So, she walked a tightrope, balancing the bar with have-to-do on one end and want-to-do on the other. The old adage—that if you wanted something done well and quickly, give it to a busy person—rang true with Elena Bertoni. She didn't procrastinate. She couldn't, or else the wave of responsibilities would wash over her like a tsunami.

But Saturdays were for her. Not the whole weekend, because Sundays were spent first at the campus ecumenical center and then getting ready for Monday and the rest of the week. She loved her small vintage home on the edge of town, far enough away to avoid the hustle-bustle of a university town but close enough to still be convenient. And she guarded her Saturdays there ruthlessly. She slept late, waking gradually rather than being jarred into action by an alarm. Rather than running her weekday morning three-mile circuit, she'd tackle the unforgiving list of household chores or putter in the yard.

In the afternoon, she'd head to a late lunch at the Scandia Café in the small downtown section of Stone Valley. Her friends would often be there as well—no need to plan to meet, because the café was their hang-out on Saturday afternoons. The pricey menu kept students at bay, so her friends—young faculty members and professionals without family responsibilities—were free to enjoy themselves without worrying about undergraduates watching their behavior. The outrageously decadent open-faced sandwiches, paired with a tall glass of Carlsburg and a couple hours of free-flowing conversation, were good for Elena's soul.

The one problem with the café was its owner, Hans Kjer. Hans had immigrated to Virginia from Denmark several years earlier. He started the café with money borrowed from his parents, who ran a similar business back in Denmark. The café had been successful since day one and had expanded twice into adjacent spaces. Hans had been able to repay his parents much quicker than they expected, and now he was riding high, his café on all the local "best of" lists and often featured in regional newspapers and magazines.

Elena and Hans had been dating for a few months. He was a good guy, they got along well, and Elena enjoyed being part of Hans' circle. His friends weren't all university people, a refreshing change from the usual men that Elena socialized with at receptions and occasionally dated. She enjoyed her colleagues, of course, but who wanted to discuss existential literature over a candlelit dinner? Much better to laugh with Hans as he described his ancestors as the role models for Game of Thrones.

The trouble with Hans, however, was that he wanted to get serious, much more serious than Elena could handle. Elena would probably never be ready to become "partners" with Hans —whatever that meant to a Danish man—but certainly not now, at the point in her career that demanded her full attention. Besides, Elena was enjoying her life just as it was, without someone who called himself her partner.

Whenever Elena came to the café, there was always the chance that Hans would make a pest of himself. He wasn't obnoxiously intrusive, but just pushy enough to put her off sometimes. So she usually came during the busiest times, when the flow of customers kept Hans busy in the kitchen or behind the bakery counter. For Elena, time at the Scandia Café was for all her friends, not just one.

Today, however, was going to be a different Saturday. No yard work or smoked salmon and tilsiter on pumpernickel. Today was devoted to getting inside the research brain of Drew Robbins.

Elena sat down at her home computer with mixed emotions. On one hand, she didn't need the work, and she was personally repulsed by Drew Robbins and his world of "smile for the camera." On the other hand, the research was interesting, complimentary to hers and was sure to yield some outcomes that would satisfy Ted's advice to be practical. Some "good," practical results.

And then there was the problem that Timor Madras had presented. Something wasn't right, and, as usual, Elena couldn't make herself walk away from a challenging problem. She loved puzzles of all kinds. That was another reason she loved Saturdays—the New York Times crossword puzzle on Saturday was the hardest of the week. So, teasing an answer to Timor's problem out of Robbins' data was compelling enough to capture the day. Besides, her need to correct errors made her want to dig deeper to see if Robbins was really the superstar everyone said he was.

She logged in with her new access to Robbins' computer files, took a deep breath and dived in. To her delight and surprise, the data files were surprisingly easy to navigate. Each project had its own three-letter designation, which she quickly recognized as an acronym based on the subject animal's common name. SHY, for example, was the spotted hyena. Within each of those, the data were simply organized by animal, year and season. She suspected that Russell Bronoski was responsible for the order. All the graduate students had told her that he was the go-to person on any of the details of the research, from what to expect in the field to taking field notes to running the statistics. That jived with Elena's opinion of him. Whenever they had served on committees and other tasks together, she always found him to be pleasant, reliable, and focused.

Elena realized that she needed to get a sense for how the data were organized and analyzed. The best way to do that, she thought, was to work through one set of data from beginning to end. And Timor's issue with the India plains wolf data would be the perfect data-set to explore. She checked her email and found Timor's message with the data set he had used for his analysis.

The file was labeled IPW, for India plains wolf. The data file contained a long string of individual excel sheets, one for each wolf in each year and each season. She copied the files onto a blank flash drive so she could run her own statistics without risking corruption of Timor's files. Now the fun could begin.

She began with the data for the first wolf, IPW-1. First she coded the data so that they would run in the standard analysis software used by wildlife behaviorists. She allowed herself a smile, thinking about how confusing this task was to students in her classes, who sometimes spent all-nighters getting the program to run. Score one for old and experienced over young and sleep-deprived.

Then she ran all the normal statistics on movement data, first for the season as a whole and then for the monthly periods that Timor had used. And just as he said, although the means for the data bounced around a bit, the variability around the means was astonishingly close from month to month. Elena stared at the screen, totally puzzled. The odds of something like that happening randomly were vanishingly small.

She repeated the process for each of the wolves in the study, thirty-two in all. The means and standard deviations for each wolf were different; at least that made sense. But for every individual animal studied, the standard deviations around any calculation were nearly identical. Now it made no sense at all. Maybe, just maybe, this could happen for one of the thirty-two wolves studied, but never, absolutely never, could it happen for each of them.

The ring of her cellphone jolted Elena out of her intense concentration. She recognized the number. "Hello, Hans," she said.

"I missed you today at the café, my dear," Hans said. "What have you been doing?"

"Oh, just some extra work that the boss gave me," she answered. "Today is a very unusual Saturday."

"Have you eaten?" Hans asked.

Elena realized that she hadn't, not since a quick PB and J sometime during the day. "Yes. Well, not really." She looked at the clock. It was already late afternoon.

"How about I bring some dinner from the café," Hans offered, "and we can spend some time together this evening."

Elena hesitated for a moment, considering her options. Now that her focus had been broken, she was aware of how tired she felt, how stiff her neck was. She needed to work on the data more, but that could take many hours, even days. The decision was obvious as she felt the emptiness in her stomach. "It's a deal, Hans. Come by after you close."

"Ciao, my dear. See you about nine."

16

"When can we get out of this place?" Misty Stanhope was not happy to still be on the campus of Virginia Western University.

Jamie Nelson cringed. His current girlfriend was turning out to be a mixed blessing. She was stunning to look at, of course, and she had no problem showing it to the world. Everything she wore was tight, cut low on top and high on bottom. He enjoyed the lust and envy he saw in other men's eyes as he walked with Misty on his arm. She was the definition of eye candy, the kind of treat you looked at in duty-free stores and knew you couldn't afford.

But she also irritated him to no end. She expected to be treated as the beauty she was, and she constantly complained about, well, everything. She was too cold or too hot, the champagne was too sweet or too dry, the sex was too rough or not rough enough. And the campus hotel was deficient in about every way a hotel could be. Even the reach of Nelson's credit card couldn't keep her satisfied.

Nelson had planned to spend several days in Stone Valley and had scheduled their departure for Saturday morning, just

119

before lunch. He figured that after the Wednesday banquet, he'd need a couple of days to work on production details with Drew Robbins. Instead, he was on and off the phone with his bosses in Toronto, filling them in on the murder and trying to talk them into letting him take charge of the proposed television series, including finding a star to replace the murder victim. He placed calls to other wildlife experts who had been on his earlier series, but he was getting mostly voicemails and a few outright rejections. His inability to get anything done left Nelson worrying about his future and grumpy.

The idleness put Misty Stanhope in a permanent huff. "I need to get back to Toronto," she said. "I've had enough of this camping trip! Look at my nails. I need my nails done, Jamie. Get me out of here!"

"We're leaving today," said Jamie. "Just be a little patient, will you? And quit complaining for a minute or two." Biting back at her was risking a day of the silent treatment. He was looking forward to it.

Jamie Nelson wasn't exactly Mr. Wonderful himself. In the television industry he was considered a whinny little brat, more confident of his reputation than most thought he deserved. His *Africa Wild* series had been successful, to be sure, reaching a global audience and stacking up awards and profits. But the animals made the show a hit, not Nelson's skill directing the cameras or in the editing studio. People loved wild animals, and they especially loved the famous species of Africa—lions, cheetahs, giraffes, elephants, gorillas and more. "Charismatic megafauna" is what the experts called them.

Nelson's success came from another source, his aunt Clara,

a wildlife professor at the Namibia Polytechnic University in Windhoek, Namibia's capital. When Nelson graduated from film school, he convinced Clara to let him film her field work. She introduced him to other field naturalists, who also let him film their work. His amateurish filming style lent an innocence and authenticity to his work that the U-Tube generation found watchable. As cable networks kept expanding their animal-based programming, his style caught traction. Soon he was on his way to producing a hit wildlife series.

But *Africa Wild* had run its course, and Nelson needed a new property. His recent luck with show ideas had been on par with his choice of girlfriends—glossy on the surface, but lacking depth. He tried several pilots, but they all flopped. A show about an aquatic veterinarian wasn't "charismatic" or "mega" enough. One that showed wildlife professionals catching and killing nuisance animals was exciting enough, but no network would risk alienating the animal welfare community. People loved animals, and they didn't want to see them being harassed or killed, even if they were nuisances. One night, drinking in a bar, he told a colleague about his idea to do a series featuring the world's most extreme national parks; the next week, a rival network announced that his friend would produce a new show based on exactly that idea.

So, when the network suggested he go back to Drew Robbins, Nelson grabbed the lifeline. "Robbins in the Wild" promised to be a great hit. Viewers loved Dr. Drew, so an instant audience was assured. Expanding the show past Africa, including the studies that Robbins had led around the world, and focusing on predatory animals, that was the ticket. He negotiated with

Robbins, and they were ready to sign the new contract. That's why he had come to the award ceremony, to get the contract signed and make a big splash announcing the new show.

And now this. Robbins was dead, and so was Jamie Nelson's career. All he had to show for it was the company of Misty Stanhope. He was beginning to think he might be allergic to eye candy.

When he heard the knock on the door, Nelson was even more irritated. "We don't need the room cleaned," he yelled through the door, "we're leaving in a minute."

"It's the police, Mr. Nelson."

He opened the door and apologized. He'd learned to be polite and careful around police. "I'm sorry. I thought you were one of the maids. They've been bothering us since we got here." He gave them his biggest PR smile. "I guess they don't get many celebrities at, what's it called, West Virginia College?"

Des wasn't impressed. "What it's called is Virginia Western University." She introduced herself and Jimmy. "May we come in?"

Jamie opened the door wider. "Of course. The room's a mess, though, because we're packing up to leave. Hope you don't mind. Misty, clear off the chairs." Misty looked up from her packing, her face showing a faint spark of interest. That young policeman is kind of cute, she thought.

Des and Jimmy walked into the room and sat down in the chairs offered. Jamie and Misty sat on the unmade bed.

"Have you found Drew's murderer yet?" asked Jamie. "What a terrible thing."

Des shook her head. "No, we haven't. And that's why we've come to talk to you."

"I don't know how we can help, but we're happy to try, right Misty?"

"Of course," purred Misty, a note of excitement in her voice. She looked right at Jimmy, and he blushed like a teenager. "This is just like one of those police shows on television. I had a part in one once. I was the killer's girlfriend."

Des thought she might have underestimated Misty. "Could you tell us what you did, where you went, on the day of the banquet?"

"We arrived on Wednesday morning, before the banquet. We drove down from Toronto."

Des was surprised. "That's quite a drive. I wouldn't figure you had that kind of time on your hands."

"I like to drive," Jamie said, not admitting he really wasn't very busy at the moment. "And as a television producer, I like to get a feel for the countryside. I do outdoor shows, and you never know when you might need a setting for a show. We also stopped for a couple of days in New York City, to see some business contacts and enjoy the big city."

"I love New York," added Misty. "It's so exciting. Do you like the city, Jimmy?"

Jimmy stammered, "Uh, I don't know. I've never been there. Or Toronto, either."

"I'd love to show you all around Toronto, Jimmy," Misty purred, "you should come up and see me sometime." Jimmy's mouth hung open. Des rolled her eyes and made a mental note to ask him if he knew who Mae West was.

Des got them back on track. "So, you arrived on Wednesday morning."

"Right," said Jamie. "Our room wasn't ready—of course—so

we found a restaurant for lunch and then came back to check in. We stayed here for the afternoon and then got ready to go to the banquet."

Misty cut in, eager to be involved. "Wait, Jamie, you forgot to tell them we went over to Drew's house right after lunch."

Jamie looked daggers at her, but he recovered quickly. "Oh, yeah, right. We stopped by to say hello to Drew and his girl-friend. Gina, right? Sorry, that slipped my mind."

Jimmy picked up the questioning while Des focused on Misty's face. Misty was looking at Jamie like she knew he was lying. "What happened when you visited them?"

Jamie shrugged. "Nothing much. We just wanted to con-gratulate him. We knew he'd be covered up with people later at the banquet."

Des saw the cloud pass over Misty's eyes. "Misty, anything you'd like to add?"

"Well, yeah," said Misty. "Jamie said he and Drew needed to talk business, so Gina took me into the backyard to look at the flowers. The flowers were beautiful, and so was Gina. She could be an actress, she's so pretty and poised."

Jimmy resumed the questions. "Mr. Nelson, what was the business you had to discuss?"

"Call me Jamie, Please. We just needed to go over some details about our upcoming show. You know he was going to start a new series with our network, don't you?"

Jimmy nodded. "Yes, we do. In fact, we have a copy of the contract. We found it under Robbins' body on his desk."

Jamie lost a bit of his bravado, but before he could speak again, Misty piped up. "It must have been pretty serious, be-cause Gina and I could hear them arguing through the back door." She was enjoying herself, playing a role in this real-life drama and irritating her boyfriend at the same time.

Jimmy looked back at Jamie. "Mr. Nelson?"

"Alright," he said. "Listen, we were having some issues about how the series would get produced. Drew and I didn't see eye-to-eye on everything."

"We've read the contract," Jimmy said. "He was cutting you out of the deal completely."

Misty was into the scene big-time. "That's right, Jamie. You were really mad at him, muttering the rest of the afternoon that Drew was a double-crosser." She turned to the officers. "And at the banquet, Jamie was in a terrible mood. He kept grumbling that Drew wouldn't be so happy when he got done with him. He ignored me the whole evening. I was never so humiliated in my life."

Jamie had to admit the truth. "Okay, okay, she's right. We argued. Robbins told me I was out. That was news to me, but he showed me the new contract he got from the company, the signed contract." Now the words started flowing out of him in a torrent. "He was two-faced. He acted like we were pals when we first met, all smiles and yes, sir, no, sir, whatever you say, sir. When his episode of *Africa Wild* aired and he got great reviews, then he changed. All of a sudden, he had his own ideas and didn't like mine. I created him and then he couldn't be bothered to even take my calls. When I approached him about this new series, he was all smiles again, all buddy-buddy. And then he went behind my back and aced me out of the deal. He was a snake. I won't cry any tears over him, that's for sure. But I didn't kill him."

Des and Jimmy stood up to leave. "Thank you for speaking with us. We'll be back to talk again later. And you better let the hotel know that you'll need the room for a couple more days because we need you to stick around, what's it called, Virginia Western University."

17

After the interview with Jamie Nelson and Misty Stanhope, Des dropped Jimmy back at the office so she could swing by the Robbins' house to check on Gina. Forensics had finished going over the house on Friday, and Gina had been able to move back in.

When Des arrived, the front door was ajar, so she opened the screen door and stepped in. "Gina, are you here?"

Gina popped around the corner from the dining room, almost running to the door to meet her friend. "Oh, Des, am I happy to see you!"

Des hugged her. "How are you doing?" It seemed to Des that Gina wasn't doing very well at all. She was dressed in baggy sweat clothes and her hair was bunched up under a baseball cap. Her eyes had dark bags, and her cheeks looked hollow. She obviously hadn't been sleeping well or eating much.

"Okay, I guess. I mean, I don't know how someone is supposed to feel when their fiancée is murdered—in their own house. I can't get motivated to do anything much. Just sitting around. It's so quiet. The house feels more like a tomb than our home."

"I know, Gina," Des said, "it'll take some time before you start feeling normal again."

Then Gina's eyes lit up, making her look more like her beautiful self. "Hey, Des, want to do something? Go for a run or to a movie? Anything to get me out of the house."

Des frowned, knowing she had to disappoint Gina. "I'd love to, kiddo, but I can't. I'm running this investigation, and I can't get my police business and my personal life mixed up. So, for at least a while, we can't be doing friend-things."

Gina's spirit immediately dropped, gloom again taking over her face and posture. "I understand. I guess. You don't think I had anything to do with this, do you?"

"No, of course not. But that doesn't matter. Perception is reality, they say, and neither you nor I need to be causing anyone to think the investigation isn't objective."

"Well, how about a glass of wine then? Nobody is in here to 'perceive' that!"

Des smiled but shook her head. "I'd love a glass of iced tea. But no wine. And the reason I'm here—well, first it is to check on you—but I do have a few more questions to ask."

Gina retreated to the kitchen. "Okay, Ms. Police Chief. Give me a few minutes to get the iced tea, and I'll meet you in the backyard."

Des walked through the back kitchen door and out to the backyard. A young woman was doing gardening chores. Des walked over and introduced herself.

"I'm Maryanne," the girl said, "Maryanne Creamer. Drew, I mean Dr. Robbins, hired me to look after his yard and flowers and things." She welled up a bit as she spoke his name. "What a terrible thing this is. I can't really believe it."

"It is hard to believe," said Des. "Tell me about your arrangement with Dr. Robbins."

Maryanne looked surprised. "Arrangement?" she asked.

"Yes," Des said, "the arrangement for your work here."

"Oh, okay. Now I understand. Well, every term he hires, I mean, hired, a horticulture student to tend to his yard. He wanted students to get a chance to do something in their profession—other than watering the plants at a big-box store—you know, for resume value. So, I came twice a week in the early evening or, like today, on Saturdays, in the morning, for a couple of hours. Mow the lawn, weed the flower beds, deadhead the blooms, trim the hedges, that sort of thing. It's a great job. I was really happy to get it."

"When were you here last?" Des asked.

"My usual day was Wednesday," Maryanne said, "but last week Dr. Robbins asked me to come on Tuesday because of the award banquet. He wanted everything to look nice for Wednesday, in case someone wanted an interview or something during the day."

"Do you know if that happened?"

Maryanne shrugged. "No, I don't. I didn't have a chance to talk with him on Wednesday."

"Were you at the banquet?" Des asked.

Now Maryanne smiled. "Oh, yes, I wouldn't have missed it. It was great to see him get the award and all."

"And how about the proposal to Gina?"

Maryanne's smile turned into a frown. "Yeah, I guess that was good, too."

"What's the matter?" Des asked. "Don't you like Gina?"

"Not really, to be honest. Everyone said she was really sweet, but she treated me like crap. If I asked for some water, she'd just point to the hose and tell me that was for the workers. But if Drew was around, she was all polite and friendly. Being nice was just a big act."

Des redirected the conversation. "So, Dr. Robbins was a good boss?"

Maryanne smiled and shook her head enthusiastically. "Oh, yes, he was. He paid us a lot more than necessary, and he said he'd give me a good recommendation at the end of the term."

"Did anything personal develop between you and Dr. Robbins?"

Now Maryanne's face turned redder than the roses she was tending. "Uh, well, if he was here, he'd invite me in for a snack and a beer or glass of wine. I'm twenty-one, so it's okay." It wasn't okay for a faculty member to do that with a student, regardless of age, but Des let it go.

"And that was it, just a beer before you took off?"

"Sort of, yeah, that's all."

Des gave her a hard steady stare. "What does 'sort of' mean?"

Maryanne's coloring hadn't faded. "Well, Dr. Robbins was quite popular. All the girls have, I mean, had, a crush on him."

"Having a crush is one thing," Des said, "acting on it is another."

"Yeah, well, some of the girls had a fling with him."

"By a fling," Des said, "do you mean that they had sex with him?"

"Yeah," said Maryanne. She realized that the police chief wasn't going to stop asking questions, so she decided to keep talking. "Everyone knew that if you took the job, Dr. Robbins would flirt with you. And if you showed interest, you'd end up in his bed. Most of the girls took the job because they wanted to hook up with him. He was handsome and exciting, and they all said he was a great, uh, …well you know."

Des knew. "So this was common knowledge, was it?"

"More than that," Maryanne admitted. "It was sort of like a little sorority. The girls who had worked here and hooked up with him called themselves Sigma Delta. It stands for Screwed Drew."

"Had you made it into Sigma Delta?"

Maryanne looked disappointed. "No, I didn't. Not that I didn't try. And, you know, I'm not gross or anything."

Des certainly understood why Robbins would have been tempted. The tight denim shorts and deep-cut t-shirt did little to hide Maryanne's figure. A long blond ponytail and pretty smile completed a package most men would appreciate.

"He didn't make a play for you?" Des asked.

"Nope," said Maryanne. "He liked to look, that's for sure, but nothing more. The other girls said it must be because of Gina."

"So, that was another reason for you not to like her, right?"

Maryanne pouted. "It was my chance to join Sigma Delta, and he had to pick now to fall in love. And now I'm sure Gina will get rid of me. No job, no reference and no tumble with Drew. My timing really sucks."

Des didn't think Maryanne was a praying mantis, ruthless enough to kill her man after mating—or before mating in this case. Nonetheless, the list of possible suspects was growing. First Jamie Nelson and now the unrequited Sigma Delta wannabe.

18

Gina came out to the yard with the iced teas, and Des returned to the patio. They sat at a table looking out at the flower gardens. "Maryanne seems nice," she said to Gina.

Gina looked at the girl and scowled. "Yeah, I guess so. She likes showing off her body, that's for sure. Drew couldn't keep his eyes off her when she was working in the yard. But bedtime was always worthwhile on the nights after she had been here." Gina smiled at the memory, but then started crying quietly.

Des concentrated on the iced tea and gave Gina a chance to regroup. When she seemed somewhat back in control, Des said, "Okay, now let me put my police officer hat on and ask you some questions."

Gina nodded. "Okay, I'll do my best."

"First off, why did you say that Russell Bronoski killed Drew when we talked earlier?

"Well, the note, the one Russki gave him at the banquet," said Gina. "The note threatened Drew."

"Yes, but that was just a threat, and also somewhat vague," said Des. "Was there anything else going on? Were Russell and Drew on good terms, or not?"

Now Gina hesitated. "That's a tough question. They worked well together, but we never did anything socially with him. But, then, Drew wasn't much into socializing with anyone in the lab or the department. Well, or with anyone, to be honest. He didn't like to be around people all that much. I loved him, but the truth is that Drew was no boy scout. If he thought you could help him, then he was your friend. But if not, he had no time for you."

This was the first negative thing Gina had ever said about Drew, and Des tucked it away for when she and Jimmy reviewed the case later. "Russell's demand for half the prize money is a pretty serious demand. Where did that come from?"

"I do think he was jealous of Drew's fame," said Gina. "Drew was the one with the ideas. He had the good research brain, you know, a way of looking at questions and designing a way to collect data that would answer the questions. But Russki is terrific in the field. He worked with me my first season studying wildcats in Scotland. He was strict about the work getting done and getting done right. We were in place to observe animals before dawn, or well into the night, depending on the need. Rain, cold, heat, whatever, it didn't matter. " Gina stopped to chuckle. "Not a lot of heat in Scotland, but there was plenty of rain and cold! The animals are 'behaving,' he always said, no matter the weather, and our job was to watch them."

"No short cuts in the field, then, right?" said Des.

Gina shook her head in agreement. "No way, Des. He was like a drill sergeant." Des thought back to her experience with drill sergeants when she was in Marine boot camp. It wasn't a pleasant memory.

"We had a strict routine for what we did," Gina continued. "Standard data sheets, codes for every type of behavior we might observe. Everything was by the book. He even made us all print our data in block letters so there would be no mistakes in transferring it from data sheet to computer and so on."

Des broke in. "Wait just a minute, Gina. So, the printing on that note we found in Drew's coat, that could have been made by anyone who had worked in the field with Russell? It wasn't distinctive to him?"

"I guess so," said Gina. "Our printing was all pretty similar, so, yes, it could be anyone's. But, of course, it was Russki's. We saw him hand the note to Drew, and Drew put it in his pocket. That's where we found it."

"Right," said Des, but she wasn't so sure. She only had Gina's word that Bronoski had written the note and given it to Robbins. Bronoski had admitted to writing a note, but not the threatening one they had found in Robbins' coat. If handwriting analysis couldn't confirm that the writing was Bronoski's, then the note didn't mean much. Then she remembered that the only fingerprints on the note were his. And there was no sign of the note he claimed to have written. So, for now at least, she'd keep operating on the premise that the note was legitimate.

"Okay, back to my basic question. With Russell wanting half the windfall that Drew was about to receive, there must have been some issues between them, huh?"

Gina frowned. "Yes, I guess so. The truth is that Drew didn't like to share the credit. And he deserved the credit, of course, because he was the scientist. Russki was more of a technician, like the rest of us. But it did seem to me that Russki had been acting kind of nasty the last few weeks. Like when we learned that Drew was going to get this television series. He was here, at this table, actually, to discuss some research matters, when the mail came. I brought it out, and Drew opened the letter from the television network and read it to us. I was thrilled, so happy for Drew, and me."

"What about Russell?" Des asked.

"He got all huffy. He said to Drew, 'So, it happens again. You get the money and glory, and I do all the work.' Then he banged down his coffee mug and stormed around the side of the house. We could hear him peel away in that noisy truck he drives."

It was looking worse and worse for Russell Bronoski, but Des had other questions. "Let's leave Russell for the moment. Is there anyone else that you can think of who might have wanted to hurt Drew? Another colleague in the department, maybe? Anyone?"

Gina actually laughed. "Well, that Aaron Schmidt was Drew's sworn enemy in the department. But that old guy couldn't hurt a flea. He's a big talker, but that's all. No, no colleagues, I'm sure."

Des pressed a bit more. "What about Melissa Campbell, his teaching assistant? Would she have the same issues as Russell? Did all the work and got none of the credit?"

"Maybe," Gina said. "Mel came here the same semester I did, working on her doctorate. Drew wasn't her advisor at first, but he agreed to take her on later. She wasn't working on one of his research grants, so she didn't have funding. Then the department gave her a teaching assistantship, to help Drew with his classes. She did a good job for him, so I guess he decided to take pity on her."

"Pity?" Des asked.

"I didn't mean it like that," Gina said, but Des heard the negative vibe. "Drew liked how she handled his classes. You know, he didn't like teaching much. Got in the way of his research. And students like Mel a lot, so it meant he got good teaching evaluations because of her. But she didn't have much to do with me. She wasn't around the lab much, and I never worked in the field with her."

Des saw a questioning look on Gina's face. "What's wrong, Gina?"

"I was just thinking," Gina said, "Mel wasn't at the banquet."

"Should she have been?" Des asked.

"She certainly would have been invited. And I'm just remembering that there was an empty seat at the table with Russki."

"You can actually remember that?" Des asked.

"Yes," said Gina, "I remember thinking that Drew wouldn't like an empty seat at a table right up front."

Des made a mental note to check up on Melissa Campbell. She kept coming up, around the edges of the investigation. For now, though, she went on. "What about Jamie Nelson, the television producer?"

Gina looked serious now. "Oh, well, yeah, he was a jerk. Drew never liked him. He tolerated him at first, because that's how Drew got his big break, with the *Africa Wild* episode that Jamie produced about Drew. But he hated the way that show tried to present animal behavior in human terms. Nothing made Drew angrier than when someone described wildlife, especially predators, in human terms. You know, like, 'the mother lion lovingly watches over her babies, imagining that one might become king of the jungle.' If anything, Drew believed that humans acted like animals, not the other way round."

"Gina, we've read the contract that Drew signed with the television network about the new series. Do you know what it said about Jamie Nelson?"

"No," said Gina. "Drew had just gotten the final contract the day of the banquet, and we hadn't had a chance to talk about it."

"The contract cut Jamie Nelson out of the deal," Des said. "It gave Drew the right to name his own producer and it said that Nelson was to have nothing to do with any aspect of the show."

Gina's mouth dropped open. "Oh, my god. No wonder he was so nasty at the banquet." Gina looked directly at Des. "Do you think that he might have killed Drew?"

"I don't know. But we'll be checking him out, at least. Okay, now I have two questions that are bothering me about the murder itself. I need to ask you these things, Gina, but I know answering will be tough."

"I'll try, Des, I'll try."

Des said, "Okay, the first thing is that we found two sets of fingerprints on the spear that killed Drew. Yours and Russell's."

Gina hadn't heard this before. "Russell's fingerprints were on the spear? Oh, god. It must have been him who killed Drew then."

"Not necessarily. He claims he was over to the house a lot, probably touched the spear at some time or other. So, his fingerprints aren't proof that he had held the spear that night. And we can't figure out why Drew's prints weren't on the spear and yours are. Why do you think that is?"

"That's easy," said Gina. "Drew was very particular about the spears. He used to clean them and oil them about once per month, he told me. But when I moved in, I said I'd do that for him. So, I started wiping them down and putting a thin coat of oil on them at the first of every month."

The murder had occurred on April 3. Des asked, "So, you would have cleaned and oiled both spears just a couple of days before Drew was killed?"

"Yes," said Gina. "I did. And Russell hadn't been over since then."

The forensics team had been back to the house to dust for fingerprints on the spear still hanging on the wall. Des had gotten the results late on Friday. "And that explains something else," said Des, "because yours were the only fingerprints on the other spear, the one still hanging above the fireplace."

"Right, of course. We don't take the spears off the wall for just any reason. Drew occasionally took one down and held it for a while, if he was tense or in a thoughtful mood. Not often, though. And Drew never let guests touch them. Except Russki. He would take one down sometimes, again, when he and Drew were trying to work out some problem or other. Those spears were like talismen for both of them." Gina looked deeply concerned. "All this is really bad for Russki, isn't it?"

"Yes," said Des, "it is. But we're not ready to make any conclusions yet. And here's one more thing we're wondering about. We can't figure how anyone could come into the house, get the spear off the wall, walk behind Drew and stab him, without Drew realizing what was going to happen and trying to stop it. Do you have any explanation for that?"

Gina looked distraught. "I've wondered that, too. It doesn't make sense. Unless Drew thought his attacker wouldn't really do anything. It would be like Drew to ignore someone threatening him—just like he did at the banquet when Russell passed him that note. I could imagine Russell, or someone else, Jamie Nelson maybe, arguing with Drew, getting the spear and threatening him with it. Drew would just laugh and ignore the threat, challenging the person. Drew wasn't afraid of anyone or anything."

Des sighed. "This time, he should have been afraid."

19

Elena needed to talk to the graduate student who had done the original research on the India plains wolf. She located the published papers about the work on the university library's website. The first author on all the papers was Drew Robbins; of course, thought Elena, don't give up the top billing to a graduate student. The next author was Sanjay Smythe. Smythe had been a graduate student at the university, but the most recent paper listed his current position as a staff scientist at the International Wolf Heritage Institute, headquartered in Sun Valley, Idaho. Nice gig, she thought.

Elena calculated the time difference. It was about seven in the evening in Virginia, so would be about four in Idaho. She called the institute on the chance that Saturday might be as busy there as at VWU. The recorded message gave the extensions for all the principal scientists. She punched the code for Smythe, and someone picked up immediately.

"This is Sanjay Smythe. May I help you?"

Jackpot, thought Elena. She identified herself and explained her reason for calling, including the death of Drew Robbins.

"I'm so sorry to hear this," said Sanjay. "Dr. Robbins was a wonderful mentor for me and so committed to saving predator species."

"We are still pretty much in shock," said Elena, "but I've been tasked with keeping his research and teaching moving. And a current student who is using your wolf data for a research paper has come up with some results that we can't explain."

"How can I help?" Sanjay asked.

"Thanks for being willing to help us," Elena said, "and thanks for answering the phone on a Saturday afternoon."

"You're welcome. I was back in India visiting my parents for two weeks and just returned last night. My body has no idea what time it is, so I'm in the office trying to catch up on things. What results are you confused about?"

"Several things," Elena said. "Usually data files contain the name of the person who collected the data in the field. But these files don't have that information."

"Right," said Sanjay. "Russki, that is, Dr. Bronoski, told us that wasn't necessary. In fact, he said Dr. Robbins didn't want the names on the files because we shouldn't be able to associate the data with specific observers. This was science, they said, and science wasn't about the people who took the data, but just about the data itself. "

"But what if you found out a person hadn't been taking the data properly?" Elena asked. "With the names attached, you could eliminate those observations. Without the names, you'd have to throw out all the data, maybe wasting a whole field season."

Sanjay agreed. "Yes, I feel you are correct. We always need to know who took the data. I understand that now. But Russki insisted that everyone who worked on their projects was carefully trained and that he reviewed each set of data personally. He was really tough in the field."

"Okay, thanks," said Elena. She knew that wasn't the right way to collect and register data, but she had other questions. "Can you go over specifically how the data were collected in the field."

"Sure. After we caught a wolf, tranquilized it and put a GPS collar on it, we waited until the wolf recovered and then we watched it until it ran away, just so we'd know it was okay. Then I'd test the GPS device and the satellite link to be sure they were working. I would track the animal for two days, but not record any data, letting the wolf get accustomed to the collar. Then, on the third day, I would collect data for the day and record it. Then I'd collect data for three more days, just to make sure that everything was working and making sense. After that, we turned the data collection over to a company that recorded the data for the rest of the season. I went through that process for each of the wolves we captured, all thirty-two of them over the three-year study."

"So," asked Elena, "did you supervise the people hired to collect the data?"

"No. Russki did that. I never met the people. They were working remotely from the United States. Atlanta, I think. All the data were retrieved via satellites, so they didn't need to be on site."

"Do you know if just one person worked on the data from your project, or were there several?"

"I'm sorry, Elena," Sanjay said, "I don't know. Like I said, Russki handled all that. I just kept catching new wolves and making sure the wolves were healthy and the equipment was working well. That was a big enough job, as you know, so I was happy that I didn't have to keep track of all the data. Russki and Dr. Robbins both said that we needed to tag as many wolves as possible to get reliable data. And I was the one who knew the habitat because I'd lived there and studied the wolf when I was doing my other degrees. That's why they recruited me for the study."

"Do you know the name of the company that Russki hired to collect the data?"

"No," he answered, "not off the top of my head. But they are listed in the acknowledgements sections of each of the papers we published. Do you have those?"

Elena replied that she did, thanked Dr. Smythe, and hung up. She looked up the papers again and found the acknowledgement. The company was International Bio-telemetry Services. Elena opened the website for the university's research office. She located the grant given to Drew Robbins by the International Wolf Heritage Institute. The organization had given Robbins a $500,000 grant to study the India plains wolf.

She checked the expenditures and found the payments to International Bio-telemetry Services. Over a three-year period, the grant had paid the company nearly $190,000 in monthly payments of $10,500 each that covered the eighteen months of the three field seasons.

She leaned back in her chair and sighed. She didn't like where this was going. The research hadn't been done correctly. It wasn't Sanjay Smythe's fault—he had been following his advisor's lead. But there just wasn't enough transparency in the process to make her comfortable.

Elena jumped when the doorbell roused her from her thoughts. She opened the door to find a beaming Hans, holding a wicker basket covered with a blue and white cloth.

He came through the door and kissed Elena. "Hello, my dear. Ready for a picnic?"

Elena laughed. This was vintage Hans, always twisting the situation just a bit. "It's a little late for a picnic, isn't it?"

"Not in Alaska!" He pushed the furniture around the living room to make a space large enough to spread out the blue and white tablecloth. Then he began removing treasures from the basket. First an appetizer of pickled herring in cream sauce with Danish hard rye wafers. Then a salad of cold grilled salmon over mixed greens. And finally mini crab cakes on a bed of palenta.

Elena laughed at the riches before her. "What," she teased, "no dessert?"

"Ah," said Hans, "I saved the best for last. Wild Alaskan berries sautéed in brandy. Hungry?"

"Famished," said Elena. She ate as if she had run ten miles. The food was heavenly. "My god, Hans, you do make it hard for a girl to maintain her independence."

Hans grinned. "That was my intention. Just wait to see what I've brought for breakfast."

20

Sunday

Russell Bronoski decided it was time to clean his office.

He had spent Saturday with his sister. She didn't like to change their usual routine, so although his mind was occupied, he tried to make the day as similar as always for Amy. They ate breakfast at their usual restaurant, went for a walk through Stone Valley's small downtown to window-shop, and then had a picnic lunch at the campus pond so Amy could feed the ducks. By evening, she was tired and went to bed right on time.

But Russell's mind roiled. The murder of Drew Robbins was upsetting enough, but that the police thought he had done it was almost more than he could handle. Even worse, he worried that the murder was not the end, but probably just the beginning, of his troubles. He needed to clean his office.

Sunday morning was the perfect time to do it, because even in the university, almost no one worked on Sunday morning. Faculty members had families to look after, undergraduates were sleeping off the previous night's revelry, and because it was a beautiful spring morning, graduate students would be doing anything—bird watching, biking, fishing—other than cranking on their theses.

Looking at the mess in his office, Russell admitted to himself that he didn't really know what was there. Being in the field was his first priority. Transferring the data to the computer and then analyzing the results was second. Helping the students when Robbins wasn't paying attention to them came next. Keeping up with the paperwork didn't even make the top ten. When he was finished with a stack of data sheets, he just put a rubber band around them, if he could find a rubber band, and dropped them on the closest pile.

But he also knew that there were things in all that mess that could get him in trouble. Old data sheets held information that could be checked to make sure their research was on the level. Original receipts and invoices, if they were in there, might not add up right if they were balanced against official university records.

And then there were the things that no one knew except Drew and him. No doubt, somewhere in those piles of paper, were notes they had made and that no one else needed to see. Drew had always been careful to get rid of compromising pieces of paper, and they never used email to discuss their under-the-table schemes. So, Russell wasn't worried that the police or any-one else would learn certain uncomfortable truths by searching Drew's office.

But they had needed to keep track of their tactics so they didn't make simple mistakes that a bookkeeper might catch—the same address for two different bills they submitted, or overlap-ping dates on travel reimbursements, that sort of thing. Drew had always said that keeping track of such details was Russell's job. So no doubt there were records in his office that implicated them in wrong-doing. Now that Drew was dead, the authorities might come looking at the next most obvious source—him. And Elena Bertoni was a bulldog when it came to getting to the bottom of things.

His strategy was simple. He carted the shredder from the departmental business office down to his office. He started at the top of the pile, shredding everything. It didn't matter what the contents were, he was going to get rid of it all. Everything of research value was already in the lab's computer, everything else was just a potential question that he would never want to answer.

After two hours of continuous shredding, he had filled eight huge trash bags with shredded paper. In the process, he had discovered a missing pair of binoculars, his framed graduation diplomas, and several pairs of woolen socks, no doubt set out to dry after a wet day in the field. The floor was clear, so was his desk and the offending window sills that the police chief had warned him about. He chuckled to himself, she told me to clean the place up and I followed her orders, so now I've gotten rid of all the evidence.

He was startled when he heard loud footsteps heading down the hall, approaching his door. He looked out and saw Aaron Schmidt advancing.

"Hello, my boy," said Aaron. "Having a little clean-out?"

"Hey, Aaron," said Russell. He tried to keep his voice and manner casual. "How you doing? Yeah, I decided that it was time."

"Good boy. Tidy office, tidy mind. Or maybe you subscribe to the theory that an empty desk is the symptom of an empty mind?"

Russell laughed. "Neither. I'm less of a theorist than an empiricist, Aaron. I was just afraid someone might find me dead in here someday, crushed under a pile of rubble."

That caused Aaron to laugh as well. "We don't need another death around here, but I get the joke. How are you holding up after what happened to your buddy?"

"Fine," said Russell, "just fine. I'll miss him, of course, but we'll all survive. We've got a good crew."

"My sense was that you were a good team," said Aaron. "You did most of the work, and that arrogant prick took all the credit."

"Easy, Aaron. Drew was my colleague and friend. No reason to call him names."

"Forgive me, Russell. But you know what I thought of that man. How did you manage to work with him all these years?"

"You were right," said Russell, "we were a good team. Truth is that my strength, like I said, isn't so much thinking as it is doing. Drew was good with ideas, you know, he thought like a scientist. Me, I just get on with the doing."

Aaron looked at one of the newly excavated chairs. "Do you mind if I sit down and rest my kness for a minute?"

"Of course not," said Russell. "I'm basically done anyhow. It took a lot less time to clean out this clutter than I thought."

Aaron sat down and stretched his legs. He noticed the Maasai spear in the corner. "That's a beautiful spear, Russell," he said. "The wooden handle is exquisite."

"Whatever you say," Russell said, "you're the wood expert.

But thanks for noticing. I love that spear. It's from my first year working with Drew in Tanzania."

"I had my differences with Robbins, as you know," Aaron said, "but one thing that always impressed me was how much work you two turned out. Even with a crew of eager graduate students and research assistants, it seems that your team was amazingly productive. And you are studying wild animals, predators no less. They aren't that abundant and they don't like to be seen. My trees tend to stay in one place. How you managed it all is quite admirable."

Russell sat down at his desk chair. He was warming to the idea that someone was talking to him about the research. Everyone usually looked past him to get to Robbins. "We had an efficient system in place. We always recruited a lead graduate student who was from the area where the research was going to happen. That saved a lot of time learning the lay of the land. Then I trained the lead student to locate and observe the animals —that's what I'm good at. We used the student to capture the animals, tag them and do the initial data collection. Then we turned it all over to a company that collected the routine data for the rest of the project. It works, pretty slick."

Aaron nodded. "And then you are off on the next project—next animal, next continent, next set of papers. Right?"

"Yes, that's the way we do it," said Russell. "Did it, I mean."

"And another feather in the headdress of Chief Robbins."

"Oh, give it a rest, Aaron."

But he wouldn't. "If I had been you, Russell, I'm not sure I could have stood being treated that way. And now, here goes Robbins and gets three million bucks for all the work you did. I'd go nuts. I might even kill the guy."

Russell stood up. "Who have you been talking to?" he yelled. "What right do you have to come in here and accuse me of murder?"

"I didn't accuse you of anything, young man," said Aaron, rising to his feet as well. "I said I might consider killing him. You don't have the backbone for it. Otherwise you'd have done something about being walked all over a long time ago."

Aaron turned and ambled off, the same measured steps now retreating from Russell's office.

Russell sat back down in the chair. His thoughts were running wild. Was he a coward, like Aaron had said? Maybe he should have demanded more from Drew than just a steady job and a decent paycheck. If he had, perhaps that three million dollars would have been split in two by the Wallace Foundation, half for Drew and half for him. He'd be set for life if it had. As it was now, he presumed that the award would go right back to the Foundation, none of it landing anywhere near him or Virginia Western University.

The more perplexing thought, though, was what Russell was going to do in the future. He had been content with the job, and it suited his lifestyle—living with his sister and supporting her. He knew the truth, that Drew was the rainmaker, bringing in the grants and getting the research products out to the world. What was going to become of the research program now that Drew was dead? He doubted the university would just put him in charge, and the thought of having to lead, rather than follow, scared him. Perhaps Elena Bertoni would take over, and maybe she'd want him to continue doing just what he had always done. But maybe not. She seemed like someone who did things right, not the way he and Drew had done them.

Russell looked at the spear in the corner. And why had Aaron brought that up? Does he know that Drew was killed with a spear, a Maasai spear? Has Aaron been talking to the police about him?

Finally, he looked around his clean office. At least, he thought, all the evidence in gone.

21

Monday

Ted Graham was happy. That wasn't typical for a Monday morning, but today he was happy.

He and Aaron Schmidt were looking over copies of the new departmental brochure that profiled faculty members and their work. Lots of color and trendy graphics. Not a lot of words, just the little snippets of text that young folks liked today.

In what he considered a stroke of creativity (for him, anyway), he had the idea to photograph each faculty member and sometimes one of their assistants holding something that related to their work. It would be a great recruiting piece. Elena Bertoni was there, holding a baby coyote. Cute animals always worked. Aaron Schmidt and his longtime wood technician were holding a tree cookie—a cross sectional cut through a tree trunk. It was astonishingly large, like those in museums. In fact, they weren't holding it but sort of draped over it as it sat on a wheeled cart in front of them. Drew Robbins and Russell Bronoski were pictured together, each holding an upright Maasai spear. Ted frowned. They'd have to edit that one out before the brochures started being used for publicity. But otherwise, it was a real beauty.

Elena knocked on the partially open door and looked in. "Got a minute, Ted?" Then she saw that he wasn't alone. "Oh, I'm sorry, I didn't know that Aaron was with you."

"No problem," said Aaron, "I need to get going anyhow. We were just admiring Ted's triumph—the new departmental brochure."

"Have you seen it yet, Elena?" Ted asked. He had put copies of the new brochure in all the faculty and staff mailboxes first thing in the morning, and he was looking forward to hearing praise from his people. "I put a copy in your mailbox. It looks great, if I say so myself."

Elena shook her head. "No, I haven't been to my mailbox yet today. I need to talk about something more important."

Ted grinned. "We've always got time for our favorite faculty member, don't we, Aaron?"

Aaron nodded, but Elena frowned. "I might not be your favorite after I tell you this."

Ted winced. "Come on, Elena, you agreed to handle Drew Robbins' stuff. You can't back out now."

"I don't want to back out," said Elena, "but I've found something that I'm worried about."

"I'm in a really good mood, Elena, and you're ruining it. What's up?"

Elena looked at Aaron and hesitated. She wasn't sure that anyone else but Ted should hear about this. Aaron sensed her discomfort and got up to leave.

"Wait, Aaron," said Ted. He had learned a few things

about procedure during his years as an administrator. "If this is something really serious, then I want a witness here to be able to verify what she told me and how I responded. You are my designated witness, Aaron." Aaron sat down again. "Okay, Elena, spill."

"I've been reviewing some of Robbins' data. Specifically from the India plains wolf study he did a few years ago."

"That was before my time," Ted said, "but I remember Drew talking about it. They had a big grant for that, and it got lots of attention. And several high-citation papers in journals with great impact factors, as I recall. Drew made sure I knew that."

"Yeah, that's the study. But there seems to be a problem with the data." Elena explained what she had found.

"So," Ted said, "you think the data may have been made up by the sub-contractor, this International Bio-whatever? How could they do that and get away with it?"

"I think I know how. The first few days of observations for each animal were legitimate. I talked with Sanjay on Saturday, and I'm sure he collected those. But then I think the company took those data, calculated the statistics about home range, daily movements and all, and then used those results in reverse to make up the rest of the data points about each animal."

Ted and Aaron looked confused. They were both botanists, Ted for wetland plants and Aaron for trees and their wood. They both knew that computer modeling was a big part of wildlife research, but neither really understood how it all worked. "You can do that?" Ted asked.

"Sure," said Elena. "It's done in population modeling. If you want to know the probability that a population will survive through time, you use mean values and standard deviations for reproduction and mortality and the like and create sets of artificial data points. You run it for a long time, maybe fifty years, and see how the population grows and shrinks. Because there is variability in the data, each time you run the model again, you get a somewhat different result. Sometimes the population dies out, sometimes it grows very large, but most times you get more intermediate results. Do that one hundred different times, and count up the number of times the hypothetical populations die out—that gives you a probability of extinction."

Ted hadn't followed exactly, but he wasn't about to make her go through it again. "And you think that's what happened here?"

"It's the only possible explanation," Elena said. "The company took the data from the first tracking days and used them to simulate tracking data for other days. They changed the mean values a bit from day to day, just so they weren't identical, but they didn't bother to change the standard deviations. I guess they figured no one would look that closely. But that's the only way it could have happened that all the standard deviations are virtually identical for every set of data for each animal."

Ted dropped his beautiful brochure on the desk. So much for being happy. "Okay, you two, beat it. I've got to make some calls."

They left, and Ted reached for the telephone. Then he put it down because he didn't know who to call first. He needed to inform the dean and the research office that there may have been research irregularities. He had to get the financial people on the track of International Bio-telemetry Services. But he chose to call Des White first. The police, he decided, needed to know what Elena had brought him. It might not have anything to do with Robbins' murder, but it might, and that decision was for the police to make, not him.

Des, Jessie and Jimmy were reviewing what they had learned over the weekend and planning the strategy for the day when Des got Ted's call. He briefly told her that they'd found some serious issues with Robbins' work that might be relevant to his murder.

"We'll be there in ten minutes" she told Ted. She stood up, and so did Jessie and Jimmy. "Let's go, Jimmy. There's trouble in research land."

When they arrived at the Department of Renewable Resources, they found Ted waiting for them in the hall. He was obviously agitated.

"Good morning, Ted," Des said.

"Not a good morning, Des, not at all. This place seems to be falling apart. You need to meet someone. Follow me."

Ted took them down to Elena's office. He introduced everyone and then grabbed a couple extra chairs from the hallway. Oh good, thought Ted, now all of us can be uncomfortable in those ancient chairs Elena liked so much.

Elena went through the story, quickly and clearly. Drew Robbins had a project that studied wolf behavior in India, before any of them—Ted, Elena, or Des—had come to the university. Now a new graduate student had done some independent research on the old data that came up with an impossible result: astonishingly equal statistics case after case after case. That could only mean the data had been fudged. The student who had done the original project, now working in Idaho, had only collected the initial sets of data, all of which were legitimate. After that, all the data had been collected by the same subcontractor, International Bio-telemetry Services. Russell Bronoski had supervised the subcontract

Des listened carefully. "So, does that mean the subcontractor was the culprit, or Bronoski?"

Elena shrugged. "I don't know. Could be either, could be both. And it might have involved Robbins as well; he was ultimately responsible, as the grant holder and principal investigator. Ted just thought you should know right away."

"Good thinking," Des said. "I wish everyone would call us right away instead of hesitating. Thanks, Ted."

Ted accepted the kudos and headed back to his office. He needed to start informing people up the chain of command that the university might have another problem, as if having a dead superstar wasn't enough.

"Elena," Des asked, "can we work on this together for a bit, in case I have questions that need your expertise?"

Elena nodded. "Of course. I'm the person assigned to take over Robbins' research, so, yes I need to know what's going on. What do we do next?"

"Let's see what we can find out about the, what's it called, International Bio-telemetry Services."

Elena got on the internet and entered the company's name into the search bar. The first entry that came up showed that the company was "permanently closed." When she scrolled down a couple of pages, though, she found a website address that still worked. The website was very plain, the kind you'd expect from a freshman web-design class rather than for an established business It showed a few photos of projects going on in various field locations around the world. The address listed was in Atlanta.

Jimmy entered the address into the GPS program on his cellphone. "Here it is," he said. He enlarged the map. "What do you know? The address is a vacant field." He switched to satellite view and zoomed in on the area. It looked like the entire block was deserted. "There's nothing there," he said. "Maybe the land is undergoing redevelopment."

Elena looked at Jimmy, then at Des. "How can that be?"

Des had a pretty good idea how it could be. "I think the whole thing is s sham. My guess is that no data were ever collected, given what you told me about the results and how they could have been made up. And my other guess is that Russell Bronoski knows all about it."

Elena nodded in agreement. She switched back to the research budget pages and found the invoices for the payments to International Bio-telemetry Services. The payments were electronic, of course, all routed through an Atlanta bank.

She scanned through each financial transaction form and found the name of the accountant who approved it. Every invoice was approved by the same person: Sheila Cummings.

"I wonder who Sheila Cummings is," said Elena.

Des knew the answer. "Sheila Cummings is the provost's budget officer. But this was several years ago. She's only moved to the provost's office recently. I wonder what her position was when this project was going on. Do you mind if I take over the computer?"

They shifted chairs, and Des entered her log-in codes. As the police chief, she had clearance to look at anything in the university, including all personnel records. After clicking through the string of pop-up menus, she accessed Sheila's personnel file.

"Here it is," Des said. "She started at the university as an accounting clerk in DRR, your department. But at the time of this project, Sheila was the head financial officer for the College of Biological Sciences. That would mean she had the final approval on all expenditures."

"It seems odd that every payment to this company would get approved by the same person, especially the head financial person," said Elena. "On my projects, the approving business person changes all the time. I always figured the accountants just took the next invoice in line and worked on it, at random."

"Well, kiddo, that might be how it usually works," said Des, "but I'm afraid there was nothing random about this. Our next stop needs to be Sheila Cummings' office. Do you have time to go with me? I'd like someone who understands the ins and outs of research funding to be there, if I have questions."

"All this stuff is my responsibility now, so, sure, I'm happy to help. But I have a class to teach from 11 to 12:15. Can we wait until after class?"

"Sure," Des said, and looked at her watch, "but you better hurry. It's 10:45 already. Is your class nearby or can we give you a lift?"

"No, my classroom isn't nearby, it's across campus."

"Then it looks like a police escort is in order." Elena gathered her class materials and they left.

Elena hesitated when they got to the police car. "I've never been in one of these before," she admitted.

Des chuckled. "It's just a car, Elena, but it does have some special features." Jimmy climbed into the front passenger seat, squeezing around the dash-mounted radio and computer terminal and moving several notebooks from the seat. "The back seat is for guests."

Des gave Jimmy a new task as she drove slowly through campus, stopping frequently for groups of students crossing the road. "While we're talking to Sheila Cummings, Jimmy, I want you to go find out what you can about Melissa Campbell."

"Who?" he asked.

"Melissa Campbell. She's a graduate student in the DRR and was Robbins' teaching assistant. Gina and her neighbor both told me she was occasionally at the house. And she was supposed to be at the awards banquet, but she didn't show up. All might not have been well between her and Robbins."

"You don't think Mel is involved, do you?" Elena asked. "I know her. She's great. And she's an excellent teacher. I'll be working with her now that I've taken over Robbins' class."

Des shrugged. "I don't have any reason to believe she's involved, but we need to check in with her anyhow."

Elena frowned, and Des noticed through the rearview mirror. "What's wrong, Elena?"

"I've been trying to get in touch with Mel, because we'll be teaching Robbins' course together now. She hasn't responded to my emails. And I just realized something else. The day after Robbins' murder, I met with each of his students and research assistants. I emailed them all and each one came by for a chat. But Mel didn't respond to that email, either. I should have noticed, but, forgive me, things have been a bit chaotic since the murder."

"You're forgiven," Des said and smiled at her new friend.

"But this just makes Jimmy's work a little more important—and urgent."

They reached the classroom building, and Elena jumped out. "I'll be waiting here when you get finished," Des said. "Have a good class."

Elena's heart was beating like she had just run a 5k as she walked from Des White's police cruiser up the steps to the lecture hall. Students who were arriving at the building and saw her get out of the car were looking at her with surprise in their eyes. One was bold enough to ask, "Everything alright, Dr. Bertoni?"

She was startled by the question, but quickly reassured her student. "Yes, everything's fine. My friend just gave me a lift to class."

"Nice wheels," he said and held the door for her.

She walked to the front of the auditorium and worked her way through the pre-class routine. Teaching a class of 300 was a production. Crank up the computer and projector, load the power point, fuss with the lighting, clip on the microphone and test the volume. She could do it pretty well without thinking, which was a good thing. Her mind was far away from the lecture she was about to give. I'm a professor, she was thinking, not a detective. How did I get here, trying to help the police track down financial crimes and research fraud? Even worse trying to catch a murderer. Ted Graham always told me to keep my nose down and just pay attention to my own work. Maybe he was right.

22

Des was waiting outside the classroom building as promised. Elena made her way out of the door along with the usual crush of students eager to get their cellphones out and get on to their next class. The student who had questioned her earlier saw her again as she got into the back seat of the police car. "Yeah, right," he said to his friend, "just getting a ride. Something's up, I'm telling you."

Des drove to the main administration building and parked in the service-vehicle-only spot. She and Elena walked up the imposing flight of marble steps. The steps ended at a portico with marble columns in a semi-circle and the university's crest—a soaring bird holding a quill pen in its talons—above the door. The inside foyer was just as grand, with the floors polished to a blinding sheen and the walls dressed in portraits of former university presidents. All men, thought Elena, of course. They walked up another marble staircase to the academic administration offices on the second floor. Less grand up there, but still exuding an air of power and the utmost respectability. They found Sheila Cummings in her office inside the provost's suite.

Sheila looked like death warmed over. Her eyes were puffy

and red, her face was blotchy. Her hair was fastened up in a bun, the kind of trick college girls used if they hadn't had time for a shampoo before class. Her clothes were neat and professional, but they couldn't hide the reality that Sheila wasn't herself.

Her office, however, was spotlessly tidy. Des had visited with university business staff members many times over her time at the school, and their offices were generally chaotic, with notebooks for different accounts and projects spilling off shelves, desks and credenzas. Any remaining spaces would be stacked with computer printouts, sticky-notes punctuating the entire mess in a rainbow of randomness. But not so in Sheila's office. She had a reputation for living the motto "everything in its place and a place for everything." A kind person would call her highly efficient; an unkind one would call her obsessive.

"Hello, Desdemona," said Sheila. She never used nicknames. She was polite, but Des saw a bit of caution in her eyes and manner.

"Hello, Sheila." Des had once called her kiddo and had received back a stare that could have frozen hell. She wouldn't make that mistake again. "We've got some questions about Drew Robbins and his research accounts." Des introduced Elena, explaining that she had taken over responsibility for Robbins' research.

Tears welled up in Sheila's eyes. "It's so horrible what happened to him. I just can't believe something like this could happen here."

Remembering what Robbins' neighbor had told Des about Sheila's numerous visits to his house, Des decided to probe deeper. "Yes, we're all puzzled about what could have prompted his death. You seem awfully upset. Were you and Drew friends?"

"Oh, yes," said Sheila as she magically retrieved a handkerchief from her sleeve and dabbed at her eyes. "We have been friends since we both started at the university. He was my first friend here, actually. We met just after I started working as an accounts clerk in the Department of Renewable Resources. He was just beginning his doctoral program."

Thinking through the timeline, Des asked, "So, you and Drew have been friends for, what, maybe eighteen years?"

"Exactly," said Sheila. "Eighteen years almost exactly. Our anniversary was just a few weeks ago."

"Anniversary?" asked Des. "What do you mean? What kind of anniversary?"

Sheila's face flushed. "Well, nothing really. Just the anniversary of when we first met."

"You keep track of that?"

"Yes," said Sheila, tears now starting to flow in earnest. "Drew was very important to me. I don't make friends easily. People think I'm unfriendly, just because I'm very business-like. But Drew and I had a special, you know, a special kind of bond."

Des kept up the questioning. "Yes, Drew's neighbor, Judith Heinz, told me that you often came to the house, and that you took care of it when Drew was out of town."

Sheila's face turned rigid. "That old busybody. Just like her to be spying on us from her window. She was always looking out of that window. I hate her."

That sort of outburst wasn't like Sheila, and Des made a mental note to look into the different perceptions of those two women. Judith had described Sheila as a sweetheart, quite the opposite of Sheila's reaction at the moment. Des chalked it up to emotional stress and moved on. "I'm sorry that you lost such a good friend. But we need to ask you some questions about one of Drew's research grant accounts."

"Okay," Sheila said, "but I'm not sure how I can really help."

Des let Elena take over at this point. Elena explained that they were looking into the sub-contract that Robbins had with International Bio-telemetry Services for his project on India plain wolves. "We've found some issues with the data, and we're wondering if that company might have been responsible for the problems."

Sheila looked shocked. "You mean they might have done something wrong? Wouldn't that mean Drew's results might be, you know, compromised?"

"That's exactly why we're worried," continued Elena. "This project was done while you were the head business officer in the dean's office, and we noticed that all the invoices had been approved personally by you."

Sheila reached for the only pencil on the desk and nervously picked at its point. "Well, I used to do some of the basic accounting work when we were busy, just to keep my hand in it. The exact procedures change a bit all the time, so it's good for the supervisor to stay connected with the basic accounting work."

Des took over again. "But it seemed really odd to us that over the course of three years, with close to twenty invoices, you had approved every one of them. If you were just reviewing invoices occasionally, some of the ones on this account surely would have been handled by someone else. Wouldn't they?"

"I don't know," said Sheila. "Maybe, but maybe not."

Des could see the increased tension in Sheila's face, and her fingers were making a mess of the pencil. "Let me put it this way, Sheila. Drew was your good friend, and this was Drew's project. Maybe, and there's nothing wrong with this, Drew brought his paperwork to you personally, because you were friends. And maybe you processed them yourself, you know, just to make sure they were done right and went through easily and quickly. We all know how sensitive faculty are about their research getting hung up in the bureaucracy. I know that my financial person has certain accountants that she prefers to work with up the line."

Sheila seemed to relax a bit. "Well, you're right. I did try to help Drew out in that way. He or Russell Bronoski would walk invoices over to the dean's office themselves and give them to me. Then I'd sign them and send them on to central administration right away. But, like you said, there was nothing wrong with that."

"Nothing wrong," said Des, "as long as you put them through the same sort of review that any invoice would get."

"Oh, and I did," said Sheila, her voice rising just a little. "I would never do anything that wasn't according to the accounting rules. I have a reputation for doing things correctly, you can ask anyone."

"I'm not questioning your integrity, Sheila," said Des. "I know you wouldn't do anything wrong. It's admirable you were looking out for your friend. So let's go on to another topic. How does a company like International Bio-telemetry Services get approved as a sub-contractor on a grant? You know, how does the university decide it is a legitimate outfit they want to do business with?"

Sheila's nervousness returned. "That's pretty much up to the principal investigators on their grants. They're the ones who choose the companies they're going to work with. Not for something like buying a truck or computer or something standard like that. But for technical things, we trust their judgment."

Elena jumped in. She knew it wasn't that easy for faculty members to choose a private company to work with. VWU was a public university, and it had lots of rules. "Don't you even check out the basic facts about the company? Like getting their company's official data."

"Oh, yes, of course we do that," said Sheila, "but once that's on file, then we don't have to worry about it anymore."

"Was the arrangement with this company a sole-source contract, or had it gone out for bids?" Elena asked.

Sheila was getting more stressed. "I don't remember those details," she said. "It was a long time ago."

Elena wanted to press farther, but she sensed that Des had heard enough. "So," Des asked, "could you get us the file on this International Bio-telemetry Services outfit?"

Sheila nodded and turned to her computer. With a few strokes she was at the vendor database. She used the search function to find International Bio-telemetry Services. "Here it is," she said, and turned the screen so Des and Elena could see it.

"How about making us each a copy of the file?" said Des.

Sheila pressed the print button, and a machine on her credenza started churning out the pages. When the printer stopped, Sheila carefully stacked the pages, stapled them precisely in the upper left-hand corner and put each copy in a separate green-and-gold folder. Elena was wondering if ribbons and a bow might follow. Des and Elena said their thanks and left.

As they walked down the hallway, Elena took a deep breath. "Is this what you have to do all day? That was exhausting."

Des took her own cleansing breath. "Yes, it is exhausting. What did you think of Ms. Cummings?"

Elena thought about Sheila as they walked to the car. After they were seated, she said, "I think she is a frustrated woman, and she takes out her frustration by being obsessive about her work. I'm sure that everyone she supervises is scared to death of her and that no one would cross her if she wanted something done her way."

"Yes," said Des as she pulled out of the parking spot, "I think you've got her figured out pretty well. Just one thing I'd add. She was lying."

23

Des stopped in front of the Biological Sciences Building. Elena started to get out, but Des motioned for her to wait.

"Elena, I appreciate your help today. But we need to talk about a couple of things."

"Sure, Des. What?"

"First, you can't share any of the things that we did or heard today with anyone else.'

"Of course," Elena said, "that goes without saying."

"Second, I'm afraid that I'm going to need your help a lot more on this case. I know you didn't sign up for this when you took over Drew Robbins' work, but if we're going to get to the bottom of his murder and all the rest of this, I'm going to need you to be, well, 'on the team' you might say."

"Again, of course. I'll do whatever you need me to do, but you know I don't have any experience with this sort of thing."

"I know that," Des said, "but I also know that you're a well-regarded faculty member who knows about this stuff—research, teaching, grants, all of it--how all of it works. And I don't have experience in that. So, we need to be a team, okay?"

"Okay," Elena said and got out of the car.

Elena walked up the stairs to her office, her head swimming with the day's happenings. Here she was, an ordinary associate professor, now she was becoming the sidekick for a detective. They all had one. Holmes had Watson, Poirot had Captain Hastings, Monk had Sharona. Now it seemed that White had Bertoni. It would be funny if it weren't so serious.

She had accepted an assignment to oversee a deceased faculty member's research, and now she was knee deep in a murder investigation. A few days into the assignment she had discovered what appeared to be gross research fraud by one of the university's star faculty members. And, after the interview with Sheila Cummings, she was pretty certain that he had been stealing money, too.

The field work on the India wolf project just didn't make sense. A researcher wouldn't take a few samples and then let a private contractor take over. If Elena were in that situation, she'd want to get a better feel for the data. Maybe take the first month's data herself, not just the first few day's. Besides that, you'd spot-check the data regularly to make sure they were being taken correctly. One set of observations doesn't mean anything; in science, accuracy and repeatability are what's important, and you need more than a few day's data to get a handle on both.

No, it didn't make sense at all. So, Robbins and Bronoski must have been cheating. They had the perfect opportunity. Most of their research was done in far-off places where the chance of being found out was low. And with Sheila Cummings running cover for them in the accounting office, nobody was going to question the paperwork they submitted. It was an ideal set-up for fake invoices, fake data, fake everything.

As Elena thought about the situation, a new worry gripped her. She'd presumed that the problem that Timor had found was an isolated case, but what if they had cheated on other projects? How much of their research might have been fraudulent? Such a level of cheating would be devastating to the university—and to the field of conservation. And now she was the person assigned to figure it out.

She needed to look at more of their projects. She decided to look first at Gina Rahim's doctoral work. Gina had just finished, and although her dissertation had been filed, her results hadn't been published yet in peer-reviewed journals. If there were problems with the data, Elena could limit the damage before the work got into print and had to be retracted.

She walked down to the departmental reading room, where copies of the theses and dissertations of all the graduates were lined up in bookcases along the walls. The most recent were displayed on a special shelf, to highlight the department's latest work. Gina's was there, on the very end.

Elena violated departmental policy by taking the dissertation out of the reading room. She was sure Watson would have done the same for Holmes.

Back in her office, she opened Gina's dissertation, "The ecology and distribution of the wildcat (*Felis silvestris*) in Scotland." It was a study similar to those of Robbins' other students. Gina studied an animal native to her home; although she wasn't from Scotland, she had lived in England for most of her life and understood the people and places where she did her field work. She had studied a relatively poorly known species, at least in wild settings, because the Scottish wildcat was nocturnal and stayed away from people. The species was protected because populations had been declining. So, it was important to understand more about them so conservation strategies could be planned and implemented.

After reading the abstract, Elena turned to the methods section. As she feared, Gina described the same data-collection strategy as on the India plains wolf project. Gina caught each of the animals, put on the GPS collars and tracked them through the first few days. Then the routine data collection was turned over to a private company.

She turned back to the front of Gina's dissertation and read the acknowledgments. Gina had thanked all the usual folks, of course. But then she gave special thanks to Russell Bronoski—she called him Russki in the acknowledgments, a familiarity Elena thought highly out of place—who trained her in the field, as well as the technicians who collected most of the data. She thanked those technicians as a group, along with the company they worked for, International Bio-telemetry Services.

Elena went back to her computer and opened the website for the Carnivore Research Center. She found the list of recently completed projects and chose one that occurred between the dates of the India wolf project and Gina's. The project studied hyenas in Namibia. The same data collection strategy had been used. Russell Bronoski trained the student and the contractor's technicians, the graduate student caught the animals, tagged them, and collected the first set of data, then the contractor took over.

Elena leaned back in her chair and rubbed her eyes. This was going to be a long process. She'd need to analyze these two data sets and, if they had the same problem that Timor had found with the India wolf data, then all the research done by Robbins and Bronoski would have to be reviewed. Ted Graham had told her that taking over Robbins' duties would be no big deal. She should have known better—never trust an administrator. And she had other work to do. She had not been able to get to her students' emails, and she wasn't prepared at all for her class on Wednesday, not to mention covering Robbins' class as well. She wished that Mel Campbell would get in touch with her.

A preliminary analysis of these two sets of data would take most of a day, at least. If the worst happened, there would be months of work ahead.

She needed some help, obviously. She emailed Timor Madras, asking him to come to her office. He had found the first problem, so she knew he had the skills and the interest to work with the data. She hoped he could get to it quickly.

Her hopes were fulfilled when Timor knocked on her door within a matter of minutes. "I was in the computer lab when I saw your email," he said, "so I came right away."

"Excellent, Timor," Elena said. "I have a job for you, if you're willing."

"Of course. I would love to help you if I can."

"Thanks," Elena said, "but I want to make something clear. What I'm asking you to do has important consequences for the university. So it needs to stay between just you and me. Okay?"

Timor looked unsure. "Will I get in trouble? I can't risk losing my visa."

"No, Timor, nothing like that," Elena assured him. "I would like you to run the same analysis that you did for the India plains wolf data on a couple of other projects. I need to see if the same thing happens with those data sets. Then we'll know if the pattern you found—which I confirmed, by the way, you were absolutely right—happened just once or more times. If we keep finding the same sort of thing, it'll mean we need to ask a lot more questions about how the research was done. "

That explanation seemed to satisfy Timor. Elena directed him to analyze Gina Rahim's dissertation work and the Namibian hyena data.

"Thank you for giving me the chance to help you, Dr. Bertoni. Perhaps this will lead to work that I can do for my degree."

"Yes," said Elena, "perhaps it will."

After Timor left, Elena tried to get Drew Robbins out of her mind. Investigating what other people might or might not have done wrong was high pressure work. She marveled that Des White could do this sort of thing full-time. How do you relax, she thought, when you are chasing a murderer?

She shook her head to dislodge such thoughts and opened the first email in her inbox. "Hey, Dr. Bertoni," it started, "I wonder if I can get an extension on my term paper. My grandmother died…" This, she thought, is a problem I know how to handle.

Elena logged off her computer just after six. Her shoulders hurt and her eyes were tired. She had managed to read and answer all the emails from her students. Deaths of relatives, car accidents, cases of mono, and many more were to be expected, especially if you taught several hundred undergraduates every term. So were the more serious issues that students often brought to her—sexual assault, alcohol abuse, depression. Life for a faculty member these days wasn't the ivory-tower existence the public imagined.

She filled her bag with books and notes she'd need to prepare for Wednesday's classes, and headed out of the building.

Aaron Schmidt waved at her in the parking lot and walked over. "My dear," he said, "you look like you could use a pick-me-up. How about I treat you to a cold one at your favorite watering hole?"

Elena knew Aaron wasn't actually trying to "pick her up." He'd been a mentor for her since she started, and she enjoyed his somewhat old-fashioned company. This evening she could really use a little frivolous conversation. "You got it, old man," she said. "Hawk's Den in ten minutes."

They found a quiet table on the patio. Less noisy would be a better description, as the bar was in full swing on a beautiful spring evening. The Hawk's Den was a favorite hangout near campus, named for the university's mascot. Elena cringed at the name—hawks didn't occupy dens—but she enjoyed the outdoor space, covered by an old grape arbor, with its picnic tables and plentiful ceiling fans. The first long swig of cold beer was like a gentle slap on the face. It jolted Elena to the present moment.

Aaron sensed her relaxing. "Ah, nothing like a tankard of mead to enliven the wearisome wench."

Elena laughed. "Stop it, you old reprobate. You aren't Shakespeare, you know?"

"Okay," he said, "let's try Doyle. How's the case going, Sherlock?"

"Maybe we should go back to old Will. I really don't want to talk about Drew Robbins."

If nothing else, Aaron Schmidt was a gentleman. He let it go, and they spent a pleasant time bantering over a wide range of topics. Conversation never lagged between the two friends, partially because both their interests ranged widely.

Eventually and inevitably, the topic returned to Drew Robbins. Aaron brought it up again. "Listen, Elena, I need to talk something over with you. I know you'd rather not be dealing with any of this, but you are the assigned point-person."

"That's okay, Aaron," she said. "I reckon this is going to be my burden for some time. The problems that we were discussing with Ted look like they might go a lot farther."

Aaron leaned toward her. "So let me add to the picture. Yesterday I was at the office in the morning."

"Not a church-goer, eh?" teased Elena.

"Well, yes," said Aaron, "but on the Sabbath, Elena. That's Saturday, not Sunday."

He was Jewish, Elena remembered, reddening. "Sorry, I wasn't thinking..."

"No problem," said Aaron. "But here's the thing. When I was at the office, I passed by Russell Bronoski's office. He was there, too. And he was cleaning his office."

Elena was surprised. "That rat's nest of his? He was actually cleaning it?"

"Yes, he was. He had the shredder there, and he had disposed of all that paper, bins and bins of it, all shredded to bits."

"Why do you suppose he was doing that?" asked Elena, her mind starting to add two plus two to make four.

"I don't think it was because he had just discovered that cleanliness was next to godliness. I think he was getting rid of anything that might be valuable if you, or anyone else, wanted to investigate."

"A murder investigation, do you mean?"

That stopped Aaron for a moment. "Well, no, I wasn't thinking about that. I was thinking about the data issues that we discussed. If he had been fudging the data, he'd want to get rid of any evidence of it. You know, things like data sheets that could be compared and ways to reconstruct all the steps in the research process. Why, do you think Russell is the murderer?"

Elena tried not to reveal more than she was supposed to know. "No, I have no idea about any of that. I was just wondering what you thought."

"Okay, forget murder," Aaron said. "There was something else, though. We started talking about how he and Robbins got all that work done. You know, they managed to turn out a lot of results in a relatively short time."

"Yes, I've always thought it was remarkable."

"Well," Aaron continued, "Russell described for me the same thing you told Ted and me this morning. They used sub-contractors to collect most of the data."

"Right, that's what I've learned. Why didn't you mention this when we were with Ted this morning?"

Aaron shrugged. "Ted hustled us out of his office, and I had a class starting in a few minutes. I stopped by your office and Ted's a couple times during the day, but I didn't catch either of you. And I sure wasn't going to send it in an email!"

"Good thinking about that, Aaron. I'm glad you're telling me now. I'll fill Ted in as soon as I can. It's incredible that they have gotten away with this for years."

"Well, it seems highly unorthodox to me," Aaron said. "And his only answer to how they assured quality control was that he, Russell, always checked the data carefully. That doesn't seem right to me. In my work, when we're trying to identify an unknown wood sample, we always go through a double-blind process to verify that our conclusions are accurate. You know, an explicit quality-control process. We record the results and keep them in case we have to justify our results later. Science depends on it."

Elena agreed. "I'm beginning to think that Robbins wasn't doing science at all."

24

After her meeting with Elena and Sheila, Des had driven back to the police station. Her desk was covered with messages to return calls, papers that she needed to sign and other dregs of routine police work. Can't the rest of the demanding world take a few days off, she thought, while we solve this murder? But both Jimmy and Jessie were out of the office on tasks Des had given them, so she spent the remainder of the afternoon dealing with the rest of the demanding world.

Jessie returned to the office just as the shift changed for the patrol officers. Jessie knocked on Des' door and stuck her head in. "I've got quite a bit of news to share."

"We need some news, kiddo. Come in and sit down." Before she asked Jessie to report, Des supplied some facts of her own. "I can clear up one of our mysteries. I know why Robbins' fingerprints weren't on the spears."

"Let me guess," she said. "He always handled them with museum gloves because they were such valuable artifacts."

Des smiled. "Close. Robbins cleaned them at the beginning of every month—because they were so valuable to him. He swept off the dust and then put a thin coat of oil on the whole thing, the metal ends and the wooden handle."

"Well, then, his fingerprints should have been on both of the spears, the one that killed him and the one still on the wall."

"Nope," said Des. "Gina told me that since she'd moved in, about six months ago, she had taken over the care of the spears. She had cleaned them just a few days before the murder, right at the beginning of April. That squares with our fingerprint analysis, showing only Gina's fingerprints on the spear still on the wall, and hers and Bronoski's on the murder weapon. And it still puts Bronoski in the cross-hairs for murder."

It was Jessie's turn to smile now. "Not exactly. So, I can clear up another of our questions. How the killer could have taken down the spear, walked around the room behind Robbins, and stabbed him without Robbins so much as raising his head."

"Okay, my turn to guess. The doctor found a sedative in Robbins' blood. He'd been drugged before he was killed."

"Not even close," said Jessie. "The doctor didn't find anything out of the ordinary in his blood stream. Some residual alcohol, no doubt from the previous night's big event, but no drugs, poison, nothing like that."

"Okay, so what gives?"

"Well," Jessie said, "what the doctor did determine is that the spear wasn't the murder weapon."

She had Des' attention now. "What? We found it stuck in his back!"

"Right," said Jessie, "but the doctor found that the wound caused by the spear wasn't deep enough to kill him. It hadn't reached into his heart or lungs. It was just in the back muscle between two ribs. Because the blade of the spear was broad, the ribs held it in place so it was there when Gina discovered the body."

"So how did he die?"

"There was a deeper wound that did puncture his heart. It was caused by a much narrower blade, from a knife of some kind."

Des needed a second to process this information. "So, someone stabbed him with a knife, then took the knife away, and stuck the spear in?"

Exactly," said Jessie. "The spear was inserted in the same wound as the deeper knife wound. And the doctor said the way the edges of the wound looked meant that the knife had been used first and the spear added afterward."

Des frowned. "Well, that solves another mystery, for sure. A killer certainly could have walked behind Robbins with the knife concealed, then pulled it without him seeing and stabbed him in the back. But that leads to more questions."

Jessie nodded. "Right. Now we don't have a murder weapon. The list of possible suspects also gets longer. Anyone who had a key to the house could have snuck in with a knife and done it. Or anyone that Robbins saw outside and let in. All we can conclude is that the murderer was known to Robbins and that Robbins wasn't worried about being harmed by him—or her."

"And the other question," continued Des, "is why would the killer bother to put the Maasai spear into Robbins' back? It's almost ceremonial, like the killer was setting a scene."

"Either that," said Jessie, "or the killer didn't think our forensics would be good enough to discover the real cause of death. Maybe he, or she, thought the spear had gone as far as the knife, obscuring the narrower wound."

"In either case," said Des, "there's some reason for involving a giant spear in the murder."

There's more," added Jessie. "We've also got the fingerprint analysis from the door that leads from Robbins' office out onto the patio. There are lots of fingerprints, of course. Robbins' and Gina's are all over the door, both inside and outside. So are the student's, you know, the girl who takes care of his yard."

"I guess we'd expect all of those, including Maryanne's, based on what she told me."

Jessie continued. "Several others are there also, more interesting ones. Russell Bronoski's are there, both inside and outside the door. So are Sheila Cummings' and Melissa Campbell's."

"All of that makes sense, Jessie. We know all those people came to the house regularly."

"Here's the really interesting one," Jessie continued. "Jamie Nelson's fingerprints are there, too."

Des let out a big sigh. "Well, so much for a simple case. We've got all sorts of people moving in and out of the murder scene. We've got a staged murder that we don't know the meaning of. And we've now got a different murder weapon. Did the doctor have any idea what kind of knife it might have been?"

"He says that it wasn't anything like a kitchen knife, nothing domestic, or even a big hunting knife or something like that. The wound was two-sided, so the blade was sharp on both edges. The blade was narrow. It made him think of military issue, the kind of daggers that soldiers use in wartime. Sharp, thin and long. It would readily penetrate clothing, even tough uniform material, and skin and muscle tissue. It was thin, so it would easily go between ribs, making inserting it easy, even for an inexperienced user; and it would go deep enough to cause lethal damage. Exactly what soldiers need, he said." Jessie consulted her notes. "I looked on the web, and there was a British weapon called a Fairbain-Sykes fighting knife that soldiers used all the way through World War II."

"Good work, Jessie," Des said, "really good work."

"We've also been through Robbins' cellphone records."

"Anything interesting there?"

"Not really," Jessie said. "He hadn't made or received any calls since the afternoon before the banquet. We looked back two weeks before then, and there was nothing out of the ordinary. Several calls to and from the people you'd expect."

Des thanked Jessie for the thorough update and asked her to look into Jamie Nelson's background more. She also asked her to bring in the horticulture student for a more thorough interview; maybe she was more involved than she had admitted to Des in the back yard. "One more thing. Have you heard anything from Jimmy? I sent him to track down Melissa Campbell."

"Not a word," said Jessie, and headed off to find out about Maryanne Creamer.

The door closed behind Jessie, and Des leaned back in her chair and closed her eyes so she could focus. The case had appeared to be heading towards a conclusion. Russell Bronoski was the obvious suspect. He had threatened Robbins with a note at the banquet. He had access to the house, and Robbins probably wouldn't have been surprised if he had turned up. Judith Heinz had heard a vehicle that sounded like Bronoski's driving away in the early morning.

The research fraud also pointed to Bronoski. Or to both Bronoski and Robbins. If Bronoski had acted alone, and Robbins had discovered the fraud and threatened to blow the whistle, Bronoski would have a strong motive. If both of them were in on the fraud, maybe Robbins had decided to stop doing it and told Bronoski. Gina had heard Robbins saying that "it all ends tonight." Maybe the research fraud was ending, and Bronoski didn't want it to end. Perhaps Bronoski thought with Robbins out of the way, he would get to take over the research—and nothing would have to end.

The Maasai spear bothered her, obviously. Someone wanted to make a point by shoving a Maasai spear into Robbins' back. Whoever did this must have really hated Robbins. And it must have something to do with Africa, otherwise why make it look like his own precious spear had killed him.

Certainly Russell Bronoski could have wanted to make such a point. They had worked together in Africa. But Robbins had always been in the spotlight, with Bronoski in the shadows, doing the work and not getting the credit. And Bronoski already had a doctorate when he was an assistant to Robbins, who was still a graduate student. Perhaps this was a chance for Bronoski to prove that he had been the alpha dog all along, just waiting for the right time to take over. And he took over by using Africa, in the form of the spear, to stab Robbins in the back, literally and figuratively.

But Des thought Bronoski didn't have that dramatic flair in him. He would probably like Robbins' death to be put down to a burglary gone wrong or a crime of passion by one of Robbins' old flames, someone still in love with him and dismayed by the engagement announced at the banquet. Sheila Cummins could be one of those, and so could Maryanne Creamer.

Des' most likely candidate for "murder with theater," however, was Jamie Nelson. He had cause to hate Robbins, and their connection had been through Africa. Maybe Nelson wanted to show he was still the top man when it came to African wild-life programs. He was enough of a showman to want to create a scene.

And then there was Aaron Schmidt, Robbins' enemy from the Department of Renewable Resources. To hear Ted Graham describe the pair's relationship, they were bitter enemies. Could they have been "mortal" enemies? Maybe Schmidt had had enough, especially after the grand affair honoring Robbins. A rival academic might just be the sort who would want to make a statement. What better way to prove Robbins' vanity by making it look like he had been killed by his own spear. Poetic justice, that seemed like something Aaron Schmidt might relish.

Well, thought Des, that's the thing about police work. You're always wrong until you are finally right. She just wished she knew where "right" was hiding.

She shut down her computer and prepared to head home for the evening. Just then, her cellphone lit up, showing that Jimmy was calling.

"Hello, Jimmy," she said. "I was wondering where you had gotten to. What's up?"

Jimmy's answer was direct. "Melissa Campbell is dead."

25

The parking lot of the apartment complex where Melissa Campbell lived was filled with emergency vehicles, blue and red lights flashing. A crowd had gathered, and Des had to give a quick blast of her siren to alert the onlookers that another police vehicle needed space to park. She climbed out of her car and spotted Jimmy standing outside the door to the apartment building. Des caught his attention. He walked over to her, his usual puppy-dog eagerness supplanted by a deadly serious look.

"What happened?" Des asked.

"She was murdered," Jimmy answered. "Smashed over the skull with a brick."

"A brick?"

Jimmy shook his head. "Yeah, a brick from the book shelves in her living room."

"Jesus," said Des. "When did it happen?"

"Not sure. But she's been dead for a while, several days at least. That's what the doctor says now, but he can't pin it down yet. He'll need an autopsy."

"Is Frank here?" Des asked, referring to the Stone Valley Police Chief.

"Yeah, he got here right after I called it in."

"Wait," Des said and put her hand on Jimmy's shoulder. "You called it in? You found the body?"

Jimmy nodded again. "I did. Me and her neighbor." Jimmy was about to continue when the medical staff emerged from the doorway wheeling a body covered in a plastic sheath. Jimmy and Des watched in silence as they rolled the gurney to the waiting ambulance and then drove away.

"Does Frank know that she's a student at the university?" Des asked.

"Yeah, I told him. As soon as he knew she was from VWU and was someone we were trying to track down, he told me to call you right away."

"Is it okay if we go in?" Des asked.

"Yeah, Frank said to bring you up as soon as you arrived."

She followed Jimmy into the apartment building and then up the stairwell to the second floor. The door to Melissa Campbell's apartment was open, with technicians taking fingerprints and other samples from the doorknobs and other surfaces.

Des spotted the police chief staring out the window. "Hello, Frank."

"Hey, Des," he answered, turning back to face the room. "We've got quite a mess here, I'm afraid."

He was right. The apartment had been trashed, with books and papers tossed everywhere. There wasn't much furniture, typical for a student apartment. A folding table and two chairs sat near the window where Frank stood, overlooking the parking lot. A set of bookshelves, made of bricks and boards, was on the opposite wall, filled with scores of books, notebooks and papers. A small television was in one corner. That was it. Melissa Campbell obviously lived on the shoestring budget of a typical graduate student.

"Can you share some details?" Des asked.

"Sure," Frank said. "It looks pretty clear-cut. She was hit over the head with one of the bricks from the end of the bookshelves." He pointed first to the end of one shelf where the books on the end had tumbled over and then back to the table, where a brick was wrapped in a plastic evidence bag, one end covered in blood. "Looks like a couple of blows, pretty savage."

"Robbery gone wrong, do you think?"

"I don't know," Frank answered, "but probably not. This room is trashed, but the rest of the place hasn't been messed with much. If it were a robbery, you'd think they would have looked through the closet and bedroom drawers for jewelry or other valuables. It looks liked whoever did this was looking for something in this room only."

"Do you think they found what they were looking for?" Des asked.

"Beats me. From the looks of it, I'm guessing that it has something to do with her work at the university. All these papers seem to be scientific things. In fact, if you'd like to take over this part of the investigation, that would be great." Because the crime hadn't taken place on university property, Des' department didn't have jurisdiction. But she and Frank worked together whenever possible, and the possible connection of this murder with that of Drew Robbins made cooperation a good strategy for both cases.

"We'd be glad to do that, Frank," Des said. "Are you aware

that the victim was a student and co-worker with the faculty member who was murdered on campus last week?"

"Yeah, Jimmy told me that. So, you think these deaths are connected?"

"Of course I don't know," Des said, "but my instinct tells me that two murders of people who knew each other and worked together are too much of a coincidence. And you know how police feel about coincidences."

"Right," Frank said, "there are no such things."

"Okay, Jimmy," Des said. "Fill me in." They had moved to a coffee shop down the street where they could talk quietly and out of the way.

Jimmy described that he had first looked into Melissa Campbell's records at the university. There was nothing in her background that was unusual. She had an undergraduate degree in biology from a public school out west and a Masters' degree in wildlife management from a midwestern university. She'd worked for a few years for a wildlife rehabilitation center that focused on saving "big cats" that had been abandoned or mistreated by pet owners or circuses or roadside zoos.

She was in her third year at the university as a doctoral student. She had been working as a teaching assistant since she arrived, mostly for Drew Robbins. She had several awards for her teaching work, and her student evaluations were excellent.

But when Jimmy talked with her department head, Ted Graham, it looked like she might have been struggling with her research. By their third year, Graham told him, most doctoral students had made a lot of progress—had passed their comprehensive exams, formed an advisory committee, filed an approved research plan for their dissertations, and completed several required semi-annual progress reports. But Campbell didn't have any of those steps completed.

"That happens sometimes," Jimmy told Des, "according to Graham. A student gets overly involved in teaching, is good at it and cares about the students, cares too much Ted said. So their research gets stalled. Then advisors get antsy and things might get messy."

Graham had told Jimmy that there wasn't any mess yet with Melissa, at least officially. There was nothing in the university records—and all of that was now in digital form, even down to regular reviews by advisors—to show a problem. The only problem, it seemed, was that there wasn't much in the records at all.

Jimmy had gone to her office to interview her. But she wasn't there, and the other students he talked to in adjacent offices and in Robbins' lab hadn't seen her for several days. They hadn't thought much about it, because graduate students didn't follow routine schedules and wildlife students often were in the field for long periods. He didn't find anyone who claimed to be a close friend. The other students said she was nice, but that she didn't join in social activities much. Kind of a loner, they said.

But there were a couple of undergraduate students in the lab who overheard Jimmy talking with the graduate students and asked to talk with him. They told Jimmy that they were a little concerned because Melissa had missed their seminar class the previous week, something she never did. That was the day of the big award ceremony, though, so the students thought she had just gotten caught up in all that and had forgotten about class.

But then, they said, she hadn't been returning their emails. They told Jimmy she always answered emails within a day—that was a promise she made to them, and no one could remember when it had even taken more than an hour or two to get an answer. But for the past week or so, she hadn't been answering any emails. And no one had seen her, either.

So, Jimmy's next stop was her apartment. He had gotten there in the late afternoon. He knocked on the door, and got no answer. Then he called her cellphone number, and it went immediately to voicemail.

He knocked on the neighbor's doors and found a young woman at home. Ara Sun was her name. She was also a graduate student at VWU and said she and Melissa were friends. No, she hadn't seen her in a bit, but that wasn't all that unusual. They both had busy schedules and worked all hours, so they could go for several days without crossing paths.

But she did have a spare key to the apartment, because the two women took care of each other's plants when one of them was out of town. She let Jimmy into the apartment, and then all hell broke loose. The neighbor screamed when she saw Melissa lying on the floor in a pool of dried blood, and Jimmy had to hold her to keep her from collapsing. He moved her to the chair closest to the door. Jimmy quickly determined that Campbell was dead, and had been for some time. He called 911 and then took Ara back to her apartment to settle her down.

The police and ambulance arrived in a few minutes and Jimmy got involved in helping them with the initial inspection of the scene. Then the medical examiner and forensics crew showed up and began their work. It was quite a while before Jimmy could break away to call Des.

"Wow," said Des. "Good work, Jimmy. Are you doing okay?"

"Sure," said Jimmy, the coffee and a chance to tell the story bringing his old spirit back to life. "Two murder scenes in a week! I was just operating on instinct for a while."

"Well, you did good. I'm proud of you. But now the hard work starts."

"Right, boss," Jimmy said. "What's next."

"You need to sort through that mess in the apartment and try to figure out what the killer was looking for."

"And what am I looking for?" he asked. He wasn't comfortable with the idea of working through those technical papers. "I'm not a scientist, you know."

"Yeah, I know" said Des, "Neither am I. Just look for items that might connect Campbell with Robbins, or any of the other characters we're interested in."

"Bronoski, you mean?"

"Well, yes, Bronoski," she said. Then she realized that Jimmy didn't know about the fingerprints and different murder weapon and Sheila Cummings. She filled him in, expanding the group of people who might be involved. "Get yourself some dinner and then get back to Campbell's apartment. As soon as the forensics crew say it's okay, start the grunt work."

"I'm on it, boss!" She smiled. Jimmy was back.

26

The interview with the police had unnerved Sheila Cummings. She made it through the rest of the day with difficulty, mostly by hiding in her office with the door closed. Now she sat at her kitchen table, desperately trying to hold onto her sanity.

Drew loved her. She knew that in her heart. If he hadn't, he wouldn't have come back to her over and over again. He had run through many infatuations, just ways to satisfy his unbelievably high passion for life. But he always came back to her. He told her time and again that she was the one constant in his life, the one thing he could always count on.

And of course she had looked out for him in the university. He was her man, and she hadn't allowed any of the petty checks and balances meant for lesser people to stand in the way of his accomplishments and recognition. She hadn't done anything wrong, she'd just helped him dodge delays and unnecessary reviews. Drew Robbins was a great man, and she just allowed his greatness to flourish.

But now the police were asking questions that made Sheila doubt her own actions. She was a stickler for rules and proper procedure, everyone knew that and she was proud of her stain-free reputation. By inserting herself into Drew's affairs had she done something wrong? She had routinely granted exceptions for his lack of receipts on travel reimbursements. She had justified her actions because he worked in distant lands, places where restaurants and stores probably never heard of receipts.

Over the years, they had talked about his continuing use of that one company, International Bio-telemetry Services, as his research sub-contractor. Drew had assured her that it was the best, and in many situations, the only company that could be trusted to do the highly specialized work with the accuracy and precision he needed. She had always arranged for non-competitive contracts based on that rationale. But that Dr. Bertoni had unnerved her when she asked about how those contracts had been awarded. Had she trusted Drew when she shouldn't have?

And that made her wonder about other things. Was the pillow talk he shared while they lay in bed together the truth, or had he been lying to her? When he held her hand—at this very table—and looked in her eyes and told her to trust him, that everything was all right, had he been using her?

And then he had betrayed her by asking that slut Gina Rahim to marry him. Drew had always told her that marriage was not for him. He was married to his work, he often said, and spending months in the field every year was a bad formula for a marriage. He would make love to her and then tell her that this, what they had just shared, was better than marriage because it came from their hearts and not some silly societal convention. She had longed to be Mrs. Drew Robbins, but she had learned to be content with just having him in secrecy.

Then Gina came along. Sheila resented everything about her. Gina was beautiful and exotic. The best Sheila could hope for was "pleasant looking." Gina was sophisticated, having lived all over the world. Sheila had only left Virginia a few times and then just to visit relatives. Gina shared Drew's world of wildlife and conservation, while all Sheila contributed was a smooth path through the university bureaucracy. My god, she thought, I hate that woman.

Sheila was sure Gina had manipulated Drew into falling for her, using their common interest in saving animals to trap him. That was something Sheila could never manage. She didn't dislike animals, but she couldn't care less about being around them. She remembered having to help butcher hogs every fall. Her father would hand her the old army knife that her grandfather had gotten as a souvenir of the war, sharpened on both sides to a razor's edge, and make her slit the animals' throats. Then he would laugh as she vomited. A girl needs to be able to defend herself, he would say, and sticking pigs is good practice. When she thought back on it now, she could still feel the bile rising in her throat.

She shook off that feeling, but another, just as nauseating, replaced it. If Gina found it so easy to manipulate Drew, maybe Drew had found Sheila an equally simple target. She was horrified at the thought that Drew might have been deceiving her all along, that he was using her the way he had used others.

She decided she had to find out.

Sheila went to her home computer and logged into her university account. She looked up the file on International Biotelemetry Services. The company was headquartered in Atlanta, Georgia. The contact listed was the company's chief financial officer, named Trevor Henry. She then opened the university's human resources website, which had a link to the service they used to check on the details of prospective employees. She shouldn't be using the service for her personal needs, she knew that, but she was desperate.

Sheila entered Trevor Henry into the system. There were many Trevor Henrys in the country, but when she added a filter for Atlanta, only one was left. She called up his data. As she read, she gave an audible gasp. Trevor Henry's mother was a woman named Angela Bronoski.

With trembling fingers, she keyed in Angela Bronoski. The woman had three children, two from her first marriage—a daughter named Amy and a son named Russell. Her second husband was named William Henry; together they had a son, named Trevor.

Sheila could hardly breathe. The company that did all that work for Drew was run by Russell Bronoski's half-brother. Oh, God, she thought, what have I done?

After staring at the screen for what seemed like hours, her thoughts running in all directions, another fear arose. She knew what she had to do.

Elena picked up her phone, and before she could get out a full greeting she heard Sheila Cummings begin talking. Sheila was trying to act calm, but Elena could tell something was wrong. "Of course, Sheila," Elena said. "If you need me to come over, I will. I'll be right there." Sheila gave her the address and then quickly hung up.

The call puzzled Elena. She had only met Sheila that afternoon, and her reaching out to Elena for help was the last thing she expected. She took a few minutes to change out of her exercise clothes into a casual dress and comb her hair. Sheila had a reputation for being immaculately turned out, and Elena didn't want to look like a slob when she arrived. The drive to Sheila's house took only a few minutes, but Elena also stopped along the way at a local coffee shop for two iced teas and two slices of pound cake.

When she arrived, the Sheila that answered the door was anything but well turned out. She had been crying, and her hair was a mess. Sheila had a look of despair in her eyes, and her hands shook as she invited Elena in.

Elena tried to soften the situation. "I've brought some tea and cake. I hope you like your tea sweet."

Sheila's manners took over automatically. "Oh, how kind of you. Yes, I do love sweet tea. Let's sit in the kitchen, if you don't mind." She laid out plates, forks and napkins, her hands shaking the whole time. Elena worried that Sheila might fall over from the effort.

As soon as they sat down at the table, Sheila blurted out, "I think I've done a terrible thing."

"I'm sure you haven't," said Elena, but she was far from sure, and she was a bit frightened by the situation. After all, she knew very little about Sheila Cummings. Perhaps she was sharing tea and cake with a killer.

"Oh, yes," said Sheila, "I have." Then she described to Elena what she had learned about International Bio-telemetry Services. "The whole company may be a fraud, and Russell Bronoski may have been cheating the university for years by submitting fake invoices."

"Sheila, I am wondering about one thing," Elena said. "Why did you call me instead of calling Des, I mean Chief White?"

Sheila stood up. "Wait here a minute, and I'll show you." She left the kitchen and went into a hallway toward the back of the small house. Going to her bedroom, Elena thought. She came back out with a wooden box, about two-feet square. "Drew gave this to me, years ago. He said I should never mention it or show it to anyone. He was giving it to me for safe-keeping, he said."

"What's inside?" Elena asked.

"I never knew. It was enough that Drew trusted me to look after it. I actually forgot that I had it. It was in the back of my bedroom closet, behind several other storage boxes. But after his murder, I remembered I had it. And after what I learned about International Bio-telemetry, I got worried that the box might have something to do with that. So I took it out and opened it up. It contains a lot of file folders and notebooks. I looked at a couple of them, and it looks like data and notes about hyenas and other animals."

"The box looks really old," Elena said. "It must have been something that Robbins got in Africa awhile ago. I've seen boxes like this when I've been researching old collections in museums, but I've never used one myself. Field researchers these days use plastic boxes to store their data in, something that will keep out water and bugs and mold."

Sheila went on. "I thought that, since you are taking over from Drew, you should have it. I don't think there's any reason for me to keep it, now that Drew is dead."

"What I don't understand," Elena said, "is why Robbins gave it to you, instead of putting it in his office or laboratory. It would have been safe there. I know you were friends, but that's a pretty big imposition on a friend."

Sheila sat back in her chair and began to cry again, big uncontrolled sobs. It took several minutes before she could speak again. "We weren't just friends, Dr. Bertoni. We were in love. We've been in love since we first met."

Elena began to put things together in her mind. Drew Robbins was known to be a skirt-chaser, and his good looks and charm gave him access to just about any woman he wanted. He had used that charm to seduce Sheila Cummings so he would have a protector in the university administration. But keeping an affair like this quiet for years would have been virtually impossible in a gossip-mill like a university. "And you never let anyone know? "

Sheila shook her head. "No. Drew always worried that others would start to ask questions, you know, about inappropriate relationships and favoritism and that sort of thing. He didn't trust people very much. That's why we were so important to each other." That's why he was important to you, Elena thought, but not the other way around.

"And forgive me for saying it, but Drew Robbins had quite a reputation as a lady's man, to put it politely. Yet you two were in a long-term relationship?"

"Oh, yes," said Sheila, a bit of pride showing through her tension. "I understood that those were just flings. Drew had a lot of energy and passion, and he needed ways to expend it. But he loved me, he always loved me and came back to me. And I loved him."

Elena looked at her watch. It was after eleven, but she knew this couldn't wait. "I'm calling Chief White, okay?"

Sheila stared woodenly at Elena but eventually nodded her head yes.

When Des answered, Elena said, "Des, this is Elena. I'm with Sheila Cummings. I hope we didn't wake you."

"No problem, Elena," Des said, "after all we've learned today, I'm having trouble settling down. I need to fill you in on what's been happening."

"Sure, but I'm at Sheila Cummings house, and we've got something to tell you that can't wait." Elena switched the phone to speaker, and Sheila told her story.

Des listened quietly. Indeed, what Sheila was saying was making the situation more complex. Fudging data was one thing, the kind of thing that the research office on campus handled. But stealing money from the university was a crime, and fell directly in Des' lap. First Robbins' murder, then Campbell's, and now this. And she had no idea what that wooden box was about.

When she had finished her story, Sheila said, "I'm so sorry, Desdemona. I've let the university down. I'm so sorry."

"I know, Sheila," Des said, "I know that your heart is really heavy right now. But we can deal with all this, I promise. Try not to worry. Will you be okay tonight, or do we need to send someone to stay with you?"

"I think I'll be okay," said Sheila. In fact, confessing to the police had the effect of lessening her stress. "I don't need to bother you anymore."

"Alright, but it isn't a bother. If you need me, just call. Elena, now I'd like to talk with just you for a minute."

Elena switched off the speaker. "Okay, Des, it's just me now."

"Don't tell Sheila, but we're going to station an officer outside her house, just to make sure nothing bad happens."

"Understood."

"Right. Now I want you to take that box home with you, and we'll deal with it later. Tomorrow morning, I'm going to pick you up at seven and we'll go to see Russell Bronoski. I'd like to do it tonight, but I'm at the end of my rope, and I suspect you're the same."

"You're right, I'm really tired," Elena said.

"Okay, go home and try to get some sleep."

Elena took the box and headed home.

27

Tuesday

Des picked Elena up at seven, as planned. They sat in the police cruiser for a few minutes as Des filled Elena in on the murder of Melissa Campbell.

Elena's head was spinning. She hadn't been close to Melissa, but they had shared coffee on many occasions over the years Melissa had been at the university, discussing teaching and research. It had seemed to Elena that Melissa was looking for a mentor because Robbins wasn't helping her much. Now Elena felt guilty that she hadn't been more proactive. The young woman had been reaching out for help, and Elena hadn't seen the need.

"I feel so bad for Mel," Elena told Des. "What can I do to help?"

"Nothing right now," said Des, "at least on that case. The local police have primary jurisdiction, but they've asked us to help figure out what the killer might have been looking for. Jimmy is going to sort through her papers as soon as the police release them, and we might need you later to help us make sense of what he finds. But now you and I need to concentrate on the mess with the research that Robbins was doing. You okay with that?"

Elena was relieved that the immediate task in front of them was about research, not murder. "Sure," she said. "What do you want me to do?"

She told Elena to drive separately because they might have to go different ways after they met with Russell Bronoski. Elena followed Des to his house, a trip that took them a few miles out of town. His house was small but neatly kept, the opposite of his messy office.

They rang the bell and waited. They could hear sounds of morning activity inside, but it took a moment before Russell came to the door. His initial surprise when he saw the two women turned quickly to concern.

"What are you doing here?" he asked.

"We need to talk," Des said, "and we wanted to do it here, not at the office."

Russell looked back over his shoulder to the kitchen. "Can you wait a few minutes? I have to get my sister ready to leave."

"Sure," Des said. "We'll wait in the car."

They returned to Des' police car and spent time going over the details of the case. They talked most about the wooden box of materials, and they agreed that Elena would take the lead in examining the box's contents.

After about fifteen minutes, a short bus pulled up to the house and the driver gave a friendly beep. Soon after, Russell led a small adult woman out of the house to the bus. They could see that she suffered from Down Syndrome. She and Russell hugged, and she walked up the ramp into the bus. Russell smiled and waved as the bus drove away, his sister smiling and waving back from her seat.

He walked over to the police car. "Okay, come in."

They sat down around the kitchen table as Russell cleared away the breakfast things. "That was my older sister, Amy. She lives here with me. As you could see, she is special. I'm her caregiver."

"It's wonderful that you do that for her, Russell," said Elena. "Do you have any other family who can help?"

Russell shook his head. "No, our parents are both gone now. It's just me."

"It must be hard when you're in the field doing research."

"It is. It's really hard to leave her, especially for long periods of time. But we have a wonderful lady who has been watching her for years. She and Amy are good friends, so it's really like having another sister around. But that's not why you are here, to ask about my sister."

"No," Des said. "It's much more serious than that. Have you been listening to the news?"

"No," Russell said. "In the mornings, Amy gets all my attention. What's up?"

Des studied him closely as she told him the news about Melissa Campbell's murder. He blanched, but acted neither evasive or dismissive. "Oh my god," he said. "She was a nice young woman. I can't imagine any reason why someone would want to harm her."

"What was your relation to her?" Des asked.

"I didn't have one, really. She was Drew's student, of course, so I knew her. She taught his classes for him, and he sometimes mentioned how good she was at teaching and how glad he was she was there to spare him from teaching duties. He wasn't much for teaching."

Elena broke in. "Weren't you helping her with her research? Isn't that what you did with his students?"

"That's right, but she hadn't gotten going on her research yet, so I wasn't involved."

"Three years is a long time without a dissertation topic," questioned Elena, "isn't it?"

"Yes, it is. Drew and I talked about her lack of progress on occasion, but he brushed it off. As long as she's covering my teaching, he used to say, she can stay as long as she wants. And she didn't push him on it, either. She wasn't the type to assert herself, especially with someone as dominant as Drew."

Des was satisfied for the moment that they had heard enough from him about Melissa Campbell. "Okay, we can talk more about that later. We're here to talk to you about International Bio-telemetry Systems."

Now Russell became wary. "What about them?"

"No sense in beating around the bush," Des said. "We know the company is a sham, and that you've been stealing from the university through the fake company. Sheila Cummings has told us how she protected you and Drew Robbins from university oversight. We know that the company is registered to your half-brother, Trevor Henry. We had the Atlanta police check on him overnight. When they talked to him very early this morning, he admitted everything."

Russell's face fell. He started to speak several times, but couldn't find any words.

Elena took over. "I've also examined the data from several of your studies. I know that you fabricated the data, Russell."

He finally found his voice. "Right, you're right. I wondered with Drew being killed, the other things might come out, too. You're right. We've been doing this forever."

"Care to explain how it all happened?" Des said.

"Yeah, okay." Russell said. He took a few moments to gather his thoughts and his courage. "It goes back a long way, at least ten years. Drew was so ambitious, so impatient. I think he meant well, you know, to save the wildlife, but he truly believed that he needed to get a big name quickly so he could then start forcing policies to change, that sort of thing."

"So you came up with a scheme to fake the data?" asked Elena.

"Yes," Russell said. "You're a population modeler, Elena, so you know it can be done. Once you get a little real data, you can back-track and make up other data. I'm sure you've done it to make up data sets for students to use in class."

Elena nodded. "Yes, I have. But I have never tried to pass the data off as real. How could you do such a thing?"

Russell became defensive. "You saw Amy just now. How much do you think it costs to provide her with the care she needs? I've been her source of support for a long time, ever since our parents died. I needed the money for her, not for myself. I couldn't care less about anything for me. I needed money to take care of Amy."

"And you used your step-brother to pull it off?" asked Des.

Russell scoffed. "Yeah, he's good for nothing. Never has been. He'll do just about anything for cash for beer and gambling. All he had to do was collect the checks and deposit them in the bank account I set up."

Des continued. "So, why kill Robbins?"

"I didn't kill him," Russell said, "I told you that before, and it's true. I didn't kill him. You're right, why would I? He was my gravy-train. Now that it is over, I don't mind that he's dead. He was mean and selfish and he didn't care about anyone but himself. But I didn't kill him."

"Time to go, Russell," Des said.

"What about Amy?" he asked.

"We can handle that later," Des answered. "You can call your lawyer, and we'll let you out on bond. But now we need to go to the station. You're under arrest, Russell."

Des led him to the police car, and they drove off. Elena stood on the sidewalk for a moment, trying to grasp what had happened. Two colleagues were dead, another had just been arrested for fraud. One of the university's head accountants had been looking the other way while her boyfriend acted criminally and unethically.

And now Elena had a wooden box of mysteries on her coffee table. She got in and drove home.

28

Des brought Russell Bronoski into the police station for a second time in less than a week. She processed him for the multiple financial crimes he had confessed to doing. Then she turned him over to the duty officers to await his attorney. She left instructions that he should be released on his own recognizance. It was only nine in the morning, but a long day remained ahead.

Jimmy was there already, sitting behind several stacks of papers, notebooks and computer printouts. He had been to Melissa Campbell's apartment and collected the papers that had been strewn around her living room. That was the easy part. The hard part was going to be making sense of it all. It would be a long day for him, too.

She called Jimmy and Jessie into the office and motioned for them to sit down in the two chairs across from her desk. She brought them up to speed on events since the previous night, including the mysterious box that Sheila Cummings had given to Elena and Russell Bronoski's admission of research and financial mis-deeds.

"It's looking worse and worse for Bronoski," said Jimmy, "isn't it?'

"Well, for sure he's in big trouble about stealing money and publishing fake research," Des said, "but I'm just not sure about him being a murderer. Of either Drew Robbins or Melissa Campbell."

"So who's at the top of the list now," Jessie asked. "Sheila Cummings?"

Des shook her head. "Too many people, Jessie. And there's one more suspect that we need to add to the list."

"Who?" asked Jimmy.

"Gina Rahim."

Jimmy looked shocked. "Aw, c'mon, boss, Gina didn't do it. She was in love with the guy. Heck, she accepted his proposal just the night before, in front of hundreds of people."

"I know," said Des. "It doesn't make sense from a motive point of view, but think about the facts. Gina lived with the victim and was in the house when the murder happened. She discovered the body, but she could have easily been the murderer as well. Her fingerprints are on the murder weapon, well, on the thing we thought was the murder weapon. And if you wanted to throw us off-track, what better way than getting engaged to your potential victim."

"Yeah, but, she's your friend," Jessie said. "You know her well. Do you really think she could do something like this?"

"I wish I knew. Believe me, I've been through this over and over in my mind, trying to make sense of it all, and I can't. I've watched her happiness since she moved in with Robbins. She got engaged to him the night before the murder. She just completed her Ph.D. It certainly isn't in her interest to murder someone right now."

Now Jimmy became the devil's advocate. "How do we know it isn't in her interest?" he asked. "Maybe his will leaves everything to her. Robbins got a check for three million dollars that night, too. Maybe she wanted it for herself."

Des shrugged. "She was going to get the benefit of it for herself anyhow. Believe me, she could get anything she wanted from Drew Robbins. She had him wrapped around her little finger." Des gave a rueful smile. "And now she has a beautiful ring on another finger, but she lost the man who gave it to her."

Des shook her head to clear those thoughts. "So here's what I want you to do, Jessie. While Jimmy is sorting through Melissa Campbell's things, I want you to take a deeper look at Jamie Nelson's background. Okay?"

"Of course," said Jessie, " the mysterious life of Jamie Nelson revealed!"

"Sounds like a true-crime podcast," Des laughed, "but, yeah, that's the idea." Jessie left to get started. She wasn't the eager puppy that Jimmy was, but she still liked to please the boss.

"Now I'm going to go see Gina. She's still in a pretty bad way," Des said.

Jimmy looked concerned. "Are you sure you don't want me to come with, so we have two people who can verify what you discuss?"

"No, Jimmy, I'm just going to see her as a friend. I need you to work on your own pile of mysteries." Jimmy frowned, but Des smiled. "Don't worry, kiddo, I'll be the perfect model of a modern major-general."

"What?" said Jimmy, "the what of a what?"

Musical theater obviously wasn't Jimmy's thing. "Never mind. Later."

She grabbed her jacket and left Jimmy sitting in her office. He didn't get up right away, instead thinking about his boss. Desdemona White was his mentor and his idol. She was always so calm, so competent, and so instinctive about people. Jimmy hoped he'd get there someday, but he couldn't compare his experience with hers. He studied the three photos on the credenza behind her desk. One showed her in full combat dress in Afghanistan. He knew she had earned both a Bronze Star and Purple Heart during her service, but those honors weren't on display. Just the working uniform of a soldier. That was Des White, a professional who didn't seek the spotlight.

Another photo pictured her surrounded by a group of young children, playing some sort of ring-game in a playground. Des was heavily involved in programs for the disadvantaged youth in town, and when things were quiet, she spent a few hours each week at the after-school center playing with the kids. Jimmy knew she came from one of the poorer neighborhoods in Richmond, and she was committed to helping others achieve the same success she had.

The third photo showed her with her family—mother, father and two older brothers. She didn't talk much about them, but Jimmy knew that they meant the world to her. Every time she took a few days off, she went to see them. No trips to the beach or mountains, just to her family in Richmond.

"Why are you still in there, Jimmy?" Jessie peaked in from around the corner, and her question startled him from his thoughts. "Imagining when you'll get to sit behind that desk instead of in front of it?"

"Give it a rest, Jessie," he said. "We've got a pretty great boss, you know?"

Jessie nodded enthusiastically in agreement. "Yeah, she rocks. It's nice to have a role model like her to look up to. Sometimes, though, I wish she weren't so dedicated so we could all let up a bit. She needs a boyfriend." Jimmy and Jessie occasionally speculated if there was a man in her life, but they were pretty sure there wasn't. Des never dropped any hints, never brought a companion to university events, never got deliveries of flowers that made her blush.

A faraway look and a subtle grin filled Jimmy's face. "Yeah, she does need a boyfriend."

Jessie laughed out loud. "In your dreams, lover boy."

29

Elena drove home and walked through the back door into the kitchen. As she set a kettle on to make tea, she looked into the adjoining room. The wooden box sat on the coffee table, beckoning. She was itching to open the box and start working through the contents. It was Tuesday, and on Tuesdays Elena blocked out time to prepare for class the next day. So no meetings or appointments were stopping her from getting right to it. Just the tea kettle, which like a watched pot, seemed to refuse to boil.

Just as she set down on the couch with a cup of English breakfast tea, her cellphone buzzed. The screen showed that Sanjay Smythe was calling. It was very early in Idaho. "Hello, Dr. Smythe" she said. "How nice to hear from you."

"Hello, Dr. Bertoni," he said. "I'm sorry to be calling so early."

"It isn't that early here," Elena said, "but it certainly is in Idaho. What's up?"

"I have something I need to tell you."

"About your work with Drew Robbins?" What else could it be, Elena thought.

"Perhaps," said Sanjay. "You know I was away for two weeks and had just returned when we talked on Saturday."

"Yes, I remember."

"On Monday morning, yesterday, I met with my administrative assistant. Among the messages he told me about was a call from another person at your university. The person asked that I call as soon as possible, because she had a question about my doctoral research. I thought it was strange that I'd gotten two calls from Virginia Western so close together. So, I thought I should let you know, in case the two of you were looking at the same thing. No sense to duplicate the effort, right?"

"Of course," Elena said, "good thinking. Who was the call from?"

"A woman named Melissa Campbell."

Elena managed to hold herself together until she ended her call with Sanjay. With shaky hands she called Des and told her the news—Melissa Campbell had been following the same trail as Elena, and now she was dead.

Des heard the fear in Elena's voice, and it matched her own concern. "We need to be on our toes, Elena, because you're right, this does change things. I want you to stay in touch with me regularly, and don't go anywhere without letting me know."

"Okay," Elena said, "I think I'm just beginning to understand how serious this all is."

"Deadly serious," Des said, "but we'll all be okay if we stick together and stay in contact. Now, how are you coming with the old box of files?"

"I was just sitting down to start when Sanjay called."

"Well," Des said, "that's what you need to concentrate on

right now. Stay home and dig into the files. You are the only one who can really make sense of them."

30

Gina's face lit up when she answered the door and found Des standing there.

"Hello, Gina. Got a glass of iced tea for the police chief?"

Gina hugged her friend. "You bet. It's so good to see you. Even if you are here as the police chief!"

They took their teas onto the back patio and sat in the sunshine. The spring sun on her face and a friend by her side brightened Gina's mood. Almost a week had passed since Drew's death, so the immediate impact was starting to wear off.

"Have you been listening to the news?" Des asked.

"No, " Gina answered, "I'm not much interested in the rest of the world right now."

Des went over the news of Melissa Campbell's death. Just as Russell did, Gina expressed shock and concern. But then she got a different look on her face.

"What's wrong, Gina?" Des asked.

"I just remembered," she said, "that Mel left a message on my phone a week or so ago. She said she wanted to discuss research with me."

"What did she want to know?"

Gina shook her head. "I don't know. I never got back to her. With all the fuss about the award ceremony and such, it just slipped my mind."

Des followed up. "You know, Gina, we talked about Melissa a couple of days ago. Why didn't you tell me about her call then?"

"It just slipped my mind," Gina said. "Besides, I don't know I would have mentioned it anyhow. It didn't relate to Drew's death. It wasn't important."

"Do you still have the message?"

Gina shook her head again. "No, I'm sure not. I delete routine messages as soon as I read them usually. I hate the clutter of left over messages and texts and such."

As with Bronoski, Des decided to leave Melissa Campbell's death for now. She was really just here as a big sister, to check on her friend. She took a sip of the tea and changed the subject. "Enough about that. I'm just here to see how you're doing. And let me say that for a girl from England, you sure do make a good glass of sweet tea. I was in London once for a conference, and I couldn't understand how a country so committed to drinking tea had no concept of iced tea. Iced coffee was everywhere, but iced tea was about as rare as cold beer."

Gina actually giggled. "Just another one of my unexpected skills. But I want to talk to the Police Chief for another minute. Do you have any news for me about Drew?"

"Yes and no," admitted Des. She wasn't about to reveal what they had learned about the murder weapon or other details of the investigation. But she did tell her about the research fraud and theft that they had uncovered.

Gina looked horrified, but she immediately defended her dead fiancée. "I'm sure that Drew had nothing to do with it. He was such a dedicated scientist, I can't imagine him doing anything that would discredit his work, or conservation in general." For a moment, Gina seemed to drift off into her memories. Des thought the defense of Robbins was a little shallow, but she let it pass.

The sound of Des setting her glass on the patio table snapped Gina back to the conversation. "But," said Gina, "I guess I'm not that surprised if Russki did something like that. I remember when I was starting my fieldwork, I wanted to do more of the sampling myself, collecting more data. It's a rush when you are actually watching a predator experience its environment. But Russki told me that wasn't their research protocol. It seemed odd at the time, but several of their other students told me that they had had the same experience, so I accepted it. Now it makes sense, if Russki was fudging the data."

Des gradually worked their conversation away from the case. She wanted to get Gina talking about something other than the murders, so she prodded her about her childhood.

"You know, Gina, I don't know much about your life before you got here. All I remember is that you went to boarding school in England. As a kid from the wrong side of the tracks in Richmond, I never knew anyone who did that. How'd it happen?"

Gina shrugged. "Seems like everyone I knew went to boarding school. My grandfather was Saudi and a government diplomat. That's how my mother met my father. My grandfather was stationed in Johannesburg, and my mother met this dashing young Englishman at an embassy event. That's what my mother says, anyhow, because I don't remember my father at all. They got married, against my grandfather's wishes, I think, and I came along soon after."

"Sounds like Meryl Streep and Robert Redford in *Out of Africa*. How romantic!"

"Well, it started out that way," said Gina, "but apparently it didn't last. My mother said my father abandoned us, and that made her realize her natural habitat was dinner parties and opera premieres in evening dress. So, we went to live with my grandfather, who had moved on to the Saudi embassy in London. And then, like most children of the upper classes in England, I was shipped off to boarding school."

"Where did you go?"

"The Chetlenham Preparatory School for Girls in Exeter, in the south of England."

"Sound impressive," Des said, "What was it like?"

"It wasn't like all those novels and television shows about cat-fights and cruel head-mistresses. I had a jolly time." Gina laughed. "See, who else but an English school girl would say 'jolly'? I learned all sorts of 'jolly' things that nice English girls need to know and have no value in society. I can play the piano pretty well, and I can do all the standard ballroom dances. I can arrange flowers, and I can walk gracefully in heels with a book on my head. I'm trained in fencing and calligraphy—how's that for contrast? So, in case you need some invitations nicely printed, call me. And I usually starred in our school plays. Want to see my Lady MacBeth?"

Des joined in the joke. "No, I'd rather see you do Meryl Streep."

"Anyway," Gina continued, "I eventually got interested in science, especially biology. And I became quite an eco-freak, pushing our school to start recycling and grow our own veggies and make a compost heap. Great fun. I went on to the University of Surrey and got a degree in animal behavior. And then I came here."

"I'd guess you could have gone about anywhere you wanted," Des said, "so why come to VWU, out in the middle of nowhere?"

"At the University of Surrey, we're encouraged to take a year off to do an internship somewhere outside England. I spent my time at the North Carolina Zoo in Asheboro. I got to work with the big cats, and I knew that was my mission in life, to help conserve those beautiful, magnificent animals."

"And then you came here to study with Drew?"

"Well, no," Gina said. "Competition to get into Drew's program was really stiff, so I needed to get more experience. After I graduated, my grandfather used his influence to get me a position working for a conservation group in Scotland. I worked on all sorts of projects. It was great. Eventually I got assigned to help on a Scottish wildcat project. It was a species that Drew was interested in, and what I did my dissertation on."

"That was a fortunate coincidence," Des said.

"Not really. I loved working in North Carolina, and while I was there, I learned that a world famous wildlife professor was just a few hundred miles north, at VWU. I decided that someday I'd work for him."

Gina sighed and looked like she were about to start sobbing. Des quickly deflected the conversation away from Gina's dead fiancé. "So, if you had an English father, how'd you get a last name like Rahim? That doesn't sound very English to me."

"It isn't. When we moved to England with my grandfather, he changed our last name back to his. He didn't want us to have any association with my father. I don't even know what my father's name was, to be honest. He was never discussed by my grandfather or my mother. I guess his name is on my birth certificate, but I've never seen it."

"You must have been pretty young when you went to England."

"Oh, yes. My mother told me I was only three at the time. It's kind of strange, isn't it—I was born in Africa but have never been back, have an English father whom I can't remember, but I grew up in London as a Saudi diplomat's grand-daughter."

Strange indeed, Des thought. She couldn't even imagine a young life that privileged and interesting. She was just happy she figured out how to cross the tracks.

31

Elena pried the lid loose from the old wooden box that Sheila Cummings had given her and emptied all the contents onto her coffee table. She quickly scanned the materials, an organizational skill common to most field researchers—get the big picture of the habitat and then go back for the details. There was nothing inside except file folders and notebooks dated from the late 1980s and early 1990s. The cover of each described the data inside and when the data had been collected. Most were about hyenas in Mazarie National Park, the same topic and location that had earned Drew Robbins his doctorate and made him famous. Others were about a number of other predatory species —the black-backed jackal, serval, and banded mongoose. Each cover also listed the name of the researcher who had collected the data, always Thomas Hyde-Martin.

She walked to her desk and punched her computer to life. She entered the name Thomas Hyde-Martin in the library's search function. Several papers showed up that he had written in the 1980s and early 1990s, all about hyenas in Tanzania. But nothing new had been published by him since then. Then she performed a citation analysis that allowed her to follow which

222

later authors had referred back to Hyde-Martin's papers. There it was. Drew Robbins cited his papers frequently in his early publications, including his dissertation.

For the second time that morning, the ringing of her cell-phone startled her. The screen showed that Timor Madras was calling. In all that had happened since yesterday afternoon, she had forgotten that she had drafted him to help her.

"Hello, Timor."

"Hello, Dr. Bertoni," he said, "I hope I'm not disturbing you too early."

Elena looked at the clock. It was just after ten. She could hear excitement in his voice. She imagined that he had been sitting with his phone in his hand, waiting until a respectable time to call her. "No, Timor, I've been up for quite a while. What's up?"

"I finished the analysis you wanted me to do," he said, "and I wanted to tell you the results as soon as I could."

"That's great, Timor. You must have worked all night."

He let out a small laugh. "Yes, of course, I did. Once I got started, I just couldn't stop. I love doing this."

"Okay," Elena said, wishing all her students were this focused. "What have you learned?"

"It's just like the other study, the one about India plains wolves," he said. "When I broke the Scottish wildcat data down to monthly samples, all the standard deviations were basically identical for each study animal. And the same was true for the study of Namibian hyenas, also."

"My god," Elena mused, "it has been going on for years."

"What has been going on?" asked Timor. "Have there been problems in the model for all that time?"

His question snapped Elena out of her thoughts. She couldn't tell him what she thought had happened. "I don't know, Timor," she lied. "I just meant that the same data patterns have been happening for a long time."

"What would you like me to do now, Dr. Bertoni?" he asked.

"You've done very well, Timor. Thank you. What I want you to do next is get some rest. Go to sleep."

"Ok, Dr. Bertoni. Call anytime if you need me. Good-bye."

Timor had just confirmed what Russell Bronoski had confessed to Des and her earlier. The pieces were coming together in Elena's mind. When Robbins got a grant to study the behavior of a new animal, he would recruit a graduate student familiar with the species and where the study would occur. Bronoski would train the student to follow their research protocol: the student captured and tagged animals and then followed them for a short time; after that, International Bio-telemetry Services took over. Bronoski would generate fake data, report that it had come from International Bio-telemetry Services and submit invoices for their work. Robbins would keep seducing Sheila Cummings so she would keep approving the company to do the work and then shepherd the fake invoices through the university.

The massiveness of the scheme amazed her. The two of them had fooled the university and the conservation community for years. At the same time, they had been stealing money from their research funders and the university. Elena knew that researchers sometimes tampered with their results to make the outcomes look more convincing, but this was a daring con carried out over and over.

She walked back to her couch and sat down. She looked at

the stack of Thomas Hyde-Martin's files on the table in front of her, and a very troublesome thought began to take over her focus. Robbins and Bronoski had faked the data for at least three projects and probably many more. What if Robbins had been doing that all the way back to his dissertation research? What if he had taken the data from Hyde-Martin's files—the files now arrayed on her coffee table—changed the dates, and then presented them as his own work?

She arranged Hyde-Martin's files in chronological order. The work covered more than a decade, ending in the early 1990s. If she were going to steal some of these data, where would she start? She reasoned that Hyde-Martin would have gotten better at the work over the years, and that the hyenas he studied would have gotten more comfortable with him as time passed, so she decided to look at the last three years of data.

She carried the three files back to her computer. She again accessed the university library, where copies of all university dissertations were stored digitally. She searched for and found the dissertation of Andrew Robbins, completed in 2005. In an appendix were three years of raw data on which he had based his doctoral research. She began comparing Robbins' data to those of Hyde-Martin.

It didn't take her long to discover what she feared. She stared at the data tables in disbelief. Three years of Robbins' work corresponded exactly to the last three years of data from the wooden box, data collected by Thomas Hyde-Martin. Robbins had not even tried to disguise his theft by switching around the years or shuffling the sampling seasons. The last three years of data from the files in the wooden box corresponded date by date, number by number, to the three years of data that Robbins used for his dissertation. The only thing he had changed were the years the data were collected. Not only was he a cheat, Elena thought, but an outrageously arrogant one.

She now understood why Robbins hadn't stored the box in his office or laboratory, or even his home. He never wanted anyone to stumble on the box and discover his secret. He had lured a naïve Sheila Cummings to his bed and convinced her that she was his true love, so he had been sure she would never violate his trust. And she never did, right up to the moment he proposed to another woman in front of the whole world.

She wondered why he kept that box of files rather than destroying it. He liked souvenirs of his projects and achievements—his den was full of them—so maybe the box was another memento of one of his conquests. Maybe he figured that it was a connection with Sheila Cummings that would keep her believing his big love lies. But what she really thought was he had saved the files for future use. There were files about species other than hyenas, more of Hyde-Martin's data that Robbins could steal and publish himself when his output needed a boost.

Elena returned to her living room with the three files. She realized that the box and its contents were critical evidence, and she had to get them to Des White. By force of habit, she neatly stacked all the material on the coffee table alongside the wooden box. She noticed that the stack was a few inches shorter than the height of the box. She was sure the box had been full to the top when she opened it, and she worried that she had misplaced some of the contents. She found nothing misplaced around or under the couch or table, then went back to her computer. No, she had not left anything there either.

Elena shrugged off the discrepancy as an artifact of yesterday's late night and today's early morning. She loaded all the material back into the box and then furrowed her brow. The box was full. Impossible, she thought. She took everything back out and stacked the files beside the box. Just like before, the stack was now a few inches shorter than the height of the box.

Elena examined the empty box. Perhaps the wooden bottom of the box was so thick it made up the difference in height. She turned the box over and heard a faint clunk. She turned the box upright and heard the sound again. She thumped on the inside bottom of the box and heard a hollow sound. Good lord, she thought, it has a false bottom.

She retrieved a letter-opener from her desk and wedged it between an inside wall of the box and the false bottom. It took several tries before she found a gap that allowed the opener to slip down below the false bottom. She pried gently, moving the letter-opener along the wall as the gap became larger. Slowly the false bottom came loose, eventually popping open.

The shallow compartment below the false bottom held one more notebook. When Elena opened it, however, she realized that it wasn't a data notebook at all. It was a journal, and just like every other file and notebook, it held the name of its owner: Thomas Hyde-Martin.

Elena sat down to read, forgetting all about Des White.

32

As soon as Des returned from visiting Gina, Jessie knocked on her office door. "I think we should move Jamie Nelson to the top of the suspect list," Jessie said.

"Hm, interesting. Find something 'mysterious' in Nelson's past?"

"I accessed the usual law enforcement databases here, but I also checked in Canada," said Jessie. "Seems like our favorite television producer has had problems all over the world. He got busted for bringing pills into Canada from Thailand back when he was a college student during an internship on a travel show."

Des smirked. "I'd hate to see the list of all the show-business people who had something like that on their records."

"Yeah, I know. He's also got a couple of misdemeanor arrests for fights, always disagreements with people he worked with. It looks like he doesn't take constructive criticism very well. But listen to this, Des. He had a restraining order not to bother a young woman who accused him of stalking her. I tracked her down in Orlando, where she works now. I called her and, wow, what a story. She is an animal trainer, and she worked on Nelson's *Africa Wild* series for a couple of years. She said

Nelson pulled all sorts of terrible stunts with animals in order to get the shots he needed for his shows. Like staking prey so they couldn't get away from predators, and taking new-born animals from their mothers to get the kinds of "aw, cute" shots every-one loves."

"Not a nice guy," said Des. "Where does the restraining order come in?"

"She said that Nelson kept trying to make advances on her while they were working in Africa. But she wouldn't have any-thing to do with a man who was cruel to animals. Then, once they were back in Toronto, Nelson kept coming to her apart-ment. So, she got the restraining order."

Jessie wasn't done. "But here's the real kicker. Nelson got caught bringing unregistered antique weapons into Canada from Germany. He claimed that they were gifts from people he worked with, but the Canadian customs people thought differently. Customs confiscated most of the loot, but they let him keep a couple, you know, the number that a normal tourist might have bought as souvenirs."

"So let me guess," Des said, "one was a Maasai spear?"

"No, but one was a World War II military dagger."

"Bring him in, Jessie. Bring him in right now."

Jamie Nelson wasn't in a good mood when he arrived at the police station with Jessie and a uniformed police officer an hour later. He'd been read his rights on the drive to the station, making him both worried and angry. "I hope you have a good reason for this," he growled. "Otherwise you are going to be sued for everything you're worth."

"Sit down, Mr. Nelson," Des said, "and I'd suggest refraining from the threats. You're in no position to threaten anyone."

Nelson sat down, but his threatening mood didn't soften at all.

"Now, Mr. Nelson, we checked into your background," continued Des. "Looks like you don't have much respect for the law."

Nelson growled some more. "Yeah, well, who does? Everyone breaks the speed limit."

"But not everyone gets busted for smuggling drugs."

"I wasn't smuggling. Those pills were for me, for a nervous condition. I bought them legally in Thailand. I didn't know they were illegal at home."

"How about the antique weapons you tried to bring back to Canada from Germany?"

"Yeah, well, that was a mistake, too. Who knows all those rules, for god's sake?"

Des wasn't about to let up. "Mr. Nelson, do you own a World War II dagger?"

He didn't like all this "Mr. Nelson" stuff. This was much more formal than the last time they talked. "Jeez, how do you know all this? Big brother really is watching. Yeah, I own one. It's my good luck charm."

"And where is it now?"

"It's in my car. I always carry it with me. For good luck, and in case one of you violent Americans gets too excited. Why do you care? It's not a Maasai spear, if that's where you're going."

"I've got bad news for you, Mr. Nelson. We know that a dagger—just like the one you own—killed Drew Robbins, not a Maasai spear."

Nelson recoiled. "What do you mean? He had a Maasai spear in his back. I saw it."

The room got silent. Des and Jessie stared at Nelson. Nelson stared back defiantly until he realized what he had just said.

"You saw it?" asked Des. "When did you see it?"

Nelson shook his head. "No, no, I didn't mean that. I meant that I heard he was stabbed with the spear. You told me. Everyone knows that."

"No, everyone doesn't know that. And we didn't tell you, either. So, here's the situation. You were going to get dropped from producing Robbins' new show, so you had a good motive for confronting him. You had a nasty argument with him on the afternoon before the award banquet. You have a history of violence with people—and animals, for that matter. You admit owning a weapon that could be the real murder weapon and that you have the weapon with you. And now you say you saw a spear in the dead man's back. It's time for you to tell the truth."

Nelson's hands were shaking and his voice was cracking. "Okay, okay. I'll tell you the truth. Can I have a cigarette?" he asked.

"No you cannot," answered Des. "But we'll get you a bottle of water. Jessie, please."

When Jessie returned with the water, Nelson drank like a man who just reached a desert oasis. Then he started talking like a wind-up doll. "You're right, I was furious with Robbins for what he was going to do to my career. I didn't know this was happening until I went to see him on the afternoon before his big night. He showed me the contract, and then he laughed at me. That's when we started yelling at each other. And then the banquet. I sat there all evening at the head table, watching all those people making a hero out of the guy who was ruining me. I was so mad I could have ...."

"Could have what, Mr. Nelson?" Des asked. "Kill him?"

"No, no, I didn't mean to say that. I didn't kill him."

"Funny, we think you did."

"No, no, no," Jamie said, "no, I didn't kill him. He was already dead."

"Keep explaining, Mr. Nelson, because so far you aren't convincing us of anything."

"I couldn't sleep that night, I was so upset. You can ask Misty. She kept telling me to stop fidgeting in bed. She finally took a pill so she could get some sleep. About dawn, I couldn't stand it any longer. I got up and drove to Robbins' house. I parked out front and went around to the back of the house. I knew all about his habits from the profiles we did on him to promote his episode on my show—rising early to work in his stupid explorer's study. I wanted to have it out with him one more time. I saw the light was on at his desk, and I knocked on the patio door. When he didn't answer, I leaned on the door so I could look in better. Then, as my eyes adjusted, I saw him hunched over the desk, with the spear in his back. I could see the blood running down his side and onto the floor. I didn't really know if he was dead or not, but I wasn't going to stick around to see if he was. I couldn't care less what happened to the guy. I crept back around to the front and drove back to the hotel."

"What kind of car do you drive?" Des asked.

"A 1980 Mercedes. Why do you care what kind of car I drive?"

"I'll ask the questions," Des responded. "Is it a diesel?"

"Yes," Nelson said. "You'd know that if you ever heard it. The 300D has a turbodiesel but it still sounds like it should, clanking down the highway, making everyone look your way."

Des returned to the main line of questions. "Why didn't you call the police when you saw Robbins' body?"

Nelson scoffed. "Are you kidding? So you could do to me what you're doing now? No offense, but I don't trust police any more than I trust television executives."

"Your knife is in your car, is that right?" asked Des.

"Well, I think so. I haven't checked on this trip."

"We're going to need to see it and test it for traces of blood. If there is blood on that knife, Mr. Nelson, and it matches Drew Robbins', we will charge you with murder. Do you understand?"

"Yeah, I get it," he said, "but you won't find his blood on my knife because I didn't kill him. I told you."

As much as she didn't want to, Des did believe him. He might be a petty criminal, but she thought people who mistreated animals were generally cowards. And what possible connection could he have to the other murder, of Melissa Campbell? His explanation of his movements also explained the noisy car that Judith Heinz had heard and thought was Bronoski's.

"One more thing before Jessie takes you back to get the knife. Did you see Russell Bronoski give a note to Drew Robbins during the award banquet?"

Nelson thought for a moment and then nodded his head. "Yeah, I did. It was before all the speeches and such. I even remember watching him write the note—on the back of the program, I'm pretty sure. He folded it and walked up and gave it to Robbins."

"Do you recall Robbins' reaction?"

"Yeah, sure," said Nelson. "Robbins opened the note and read it. He sat for a brief minute and then a smile crossed his face, the same smile he'd given me that afternoon. 'Never,' he said to Bronoski, 'never in a million years.' Something like that. Then he folded the note back up and put it in his pocket. And Bronoski looked like he'd been punched in the gut. I'm pretty sure everyone at the head table heard it. Gina must have heard it, she was sitting right next to him."

Des stood up. "Go get the knife, Jessie, and get it to the team for analysis. And, Mr. Nelson, for the second time, don't leave town."

Jamie Nelson looked very unhappy, but it wasn't the murder charge that upset him. It was how Misty would react when he told her they were still stuck in podunk.

33

Elena opened the journal and began to read.

"March 17, 1985. Arrived in Arusha today to start my adventure. It will be my practice to record each day's events so that my family—if I ever have one—will be able to look back on their father's and grandfather's great adventure studying the wildlife of Africa. Who knows where this will lead, but we'll get there together."

Well, I'm neither daughter nor granddaughter, Elena thought, but let's take this journey together, Dr. Thomas Hyde-Martin. She read steadily for an hour, listening to Tom (she had taken to thinking of him as Tom) tell his story. He had been sent by the London Natural History Museum to Tanzania to study hyenas, and his work with them filled most of his days. He described how he used local guides to show him where hyenas lived, then how he spent day after day letting the animals get used to his presence. Gradually the animals started ignoring him, so he could observe their natural behavior. He learned what the animals would accept and what would scare them off. Elena could sense the spirit of adventure in Tom's words, and his love of the

235

animals and the landscape they, the hyenas and their observer, now shared.

The journal contained mostly short entries about his work for the first few years, and they became shorter and less frequent as time passed. Life and research become routine, Elena thought, even for a scientist studying such fascinating creatures. Elena skimmed through most of those, but occasionally an entry was charged with awe and wonder.

"I watched the female I call Harriet give birth today. She had three pups in quick succession. Just like dogs on our farm at home, Harriet licked each one clean as soon as it was born. Then she lay down so they could suckle. Other members of the clan came to smell the newborns and nuzzle Harriet's face. I know a scientist should not feel this way, but the look of contentment and joy on her face was so human-like that I wanted to hold those hyena cubs in my arms and hum them Brahms' lullaby. It was a lovely domestic scene in the midst of this mostly survive-at-all-costs wildness. Like all new mothers, Harriet was glowing and beautiful."

The journal took another turn when Tom went to Johannesburg for a conference on predator behavior in 1988. He had been invited to a reception at the home of the British Ambassador to South Africa, along with other scientists sponsored by the museum. Among the other guests were the Saudi ambassador and his family.

"I saw her as soon as she entered the room. I had never seen anyone

so beautiful in my life. I was enthralled. Using the same skills by which I approach wild animals, I maneuvered closer and closer until I could speak to her. Her name is Alesandra, a name as beautiful as she. Once we began to talk, everyone else in the room disappeared. My life will never be the same again."

The journal now told two stories. One was the continuing description of Tom's research on hyenas, becoming a smaller part of the entries. The other story was the romance between Tom and Alesandra. Tom found reasons to travel back to Johannesburg as often as possible, spending most of his time with her. Elena could imagine Alesandra's side of the story, although her words weren't present. She was attracted to the difference between Tom and her father, Elena imagined. Her father was refined and diplomatic, Tom was rugged and garrulous, ready with a story and a joke, so full of life it surrounded him like an aura. Alesandra wanted adventure. Elena read about Tom's pursuit of Alesandra, despite her father's objection. After two years of courtship, they snuck off and married in Dar es Salaam.

Within a year the journal was telling the story of Alesandra's pregnancy and then the birth of their daughter. They named her Ngorojine, a Maasai word for hyena. Tom thought the name as beautiful as his "little hyena." He called her Jine for short.

"Jine took her first steps today, at just seven months old. She's a cracker-jack, just like her old man. She'll be running in no time. I can't wait to take her out with me to watch her namesake hyenas.

She'll be just like them—strong, fearless and cunning. My wonderful little Jine."

Fatherly love jumped from the pages of the journal. Little Jine had replaced wildlife as the center of Tom's life. And he had been correct. Jine was like a little hyena, full of energy and curiosity, ready to stick her nose into everything. She loved the animals her father studied and went with him whenever he allowed her to go.

Unfortunately, Alesandra was finding the life in the little research camp less romantic and more repressive every day. Her father had been transferred to London, and Tom wrote in his journal that he could feel the draw of her old life.

"I fear that Alesandra is losing her enthusiasm for me and our grubby little home. She's had about enough of this adventure. Four years in the field is a long time for a woman used to the finer things in life. I'm not sure how long this will all last."

It didn't last much longer. Tom's journal entries told the story of quarrels, bouts of depression, and disagreements about Ngorojine's future. Elena cried as she read Tom's words the day that Alesandra left, taking Jine with her.

"I drove Alesandra and Ngorojine to Arusha today. I could hardly breathe as I watched them board the plane that took them away from me. My Alesandra was gone, but, oh, so was my darling Jine. My little hyena, my treasure. God help me. My life is over."

Tom's journal entries then focused on losing his wife and daughter, as he tried to reconcile what had happened. He understood that Alesandra needed more in her life than he could offer. The loss that devastated him was being separated from his daughter. He wrote that he knew she should be with her mother, in a place where Jine could go to a good school, learn about the whole, wide world and become whatever she wanted to be. But the pain of her leaving was all-consuming.

And it did consume him. His journal entries became fewer as time went on, and they mostly expressed his loneliness. He wrote that he couldn't manage to return to the field to conduct his research. Instead, he sought the company of the one friend he still had—the gin bottle.

"The notice came today that the museum was suspending my funding. They're right. I wonder what took so long. I haven't done anything in months except sit in this godforsaken bar and drink until the pain went away. I don't care anymore. Nothing matters. Nothing."

With the loss of his funding, his income also dried up. The park told him he had to leave, so he moved into a small hut behind The Hyena Bar. Tom had saved most of his salary while working in Africa, especially after his research pals had moved on, so he had enough to pay Markall, the bar owner, for his one-room hut. When those funds ran out, Markall let Tom stay on in exchange for doing odd-jobs.

Markall has taken pity on me. I do whatever he needs doing, and he lets me stay in his hovel and feeds me and gives me gin. His little son, another Markall, runs around the bar all day long, and just reminds me that my own daughter is gone, and that I am alone. I have to take whatever I can find, just like the hyena. How ironic—I'm acting like a hyena in a place called The Hyena Bar.

Tom had begun several other entries as time went on, but they never got farther than a few words. Elena felt his despair through the blank pages just as strongly as if they had been filled with words. The empty pages screamed the emptiness of his life.

She flipped through the blank pages, expecting to find nothing else. She was surprised to see that Tom had started writing again, farther back in the journal. Perhaps, she thought, he left those pages as a symbol of lost time. The new entries started in 2003.

"A young man came up to me at the bar yesterday. Claims he was sent by Milky Burns to find me. Says that Milky wants me to repay an old debit I owe him. That was when Milky and I reported rhinoceros poachers to the police in Akagera National Park in Rwanda. The police brought in the poachers, and we identified them. Then they all started laughing, because the police had been bribed by the poachers to look the other way. Instead, the police locked us up. But good old Milky always kept a 100-pound note in his shoe for just such an emergency. We bribed the guard and then stole a boat and floated down the Akagera River until we knew we were back in Tanzania. I guess I owe Milky my life. He wants me to help this kid study hyenas.

As if I were still capable of that. What a cruel joke. Maybe I'll help him, who knows."

A few days later, Tom made another entry.

"I decided to help the kid. He doesn't know a hyena from his ass, or any other ass, but maybe he can learn. I've been thinking about Milky. We did a lot of good together, our research and such. And we had some great times. Milky Burns and Tommy Tonic. It'll be good for me to get out of the bar for a change. The kid's name is Andrew Robbins. I call him Andy. He doesn't like that. Too bad. I'm the alpha dog around here."

Elena sat straight up on the couch. Andrew Robbins had been tutored in Africa by this old man, this Thomas Hyde-Martin. Robbins had cited Hyde-Martin's earlier work, but hadn't made him a co-author or even acknowledged him in Robbins' own papers. So, Robbins learned all he could from the old man and then stole his data. She was shocked that even Robbins could be so ruthless.

She read on. Tom's entries were never as frequent or complete as they had been in his early years, but Elena sensed a revival in his words.

"My god, it's great to be back out in the field. Seeing the country-side and watching the animals. Seems I do have a lot to teach young Andy. He's a quick study, but he sure is impatient. Not a good quality in an animal behaviorist. But he's learning. And I'm feeling some

of the juices flowing that I thought had dried up completely. That deserves a little gin and tonic, eh?"

The positive entries continued infrequently for three years. During the field season, Tom told about their excursions and how Robbins was getting better with the hyenas. During the times when Robbins was back in the university in Virginia, Tom wrote less frequently. The most interesting entries were about contacting his daughter. He had done some digging and learned that his daughter was in boarding school in England, and he had begun to write her letters. His joy when she responded almost leaped from the journal.

"She wrote to me! My little Jine wrote to me, after all these years. I never thought she'd answer my letter. She doesn't even know me, really. She was so young when she left. But she wrote back! I love her, my little Jine. I still have my daughter. I still have her."

The happy tone took over the journal, as Tom described his communication with his daughter. Then the happy entries abruptly ended. The last few pages of the journal were again filled with bitterness and disappointment.

"I never should have trusted that arrogant, selfish bastard. I taught him. I gave him my hyenas. And then he publishes our work himself. Him as the author, not the two of us. Never so much as a mention of me. If he was here, I'd kill him. I swear I'd kill him. And then I'd kill

myself. Should have done it a long time ago. The gin will do it this time, by god. The gin is all I've got left."

Elena was exhausted from reading the emotional journey of Thomas Hyde-Martin's life. She was relieved to be finished with this task, but flipped through the final blank pages of the journal, just to be thorough. Taped to the back cover she found a small photograph. The photograph was a teen-aged girl in a school uniform. Elena thought she looked familiar, but couldn't place her. She pulled the tape loose so she could look if there was a message on the back. She turned the picture over and saw an inscription: "To Dad, from 'Jine,' Your Little Hyena".

A terrifying thought began to form in Elena's mind. She couldn't put off talking with Des White any longer.

34

Jimmy Nesbitt wasn't the studious type. He preferred the more active parts of police work, even if that only meant keeping the lid on football tailgate parties or chasing down a squirrel that joined the spin class at the gym. But if Des wanted him to spend his day organizing someone's jumbled files, well, then, that's what he was going to do.

Still, he wished there was something interesting in the mess of papers from Melissa Campbell's apartment. Ransom letters, maybe, or love letters. Heck, letters of any kind would be welcome. Instead all he had were computer printouts, tables of numbers and an occasional set of notes—about those printouts and numbers.

He managed to sort them all into three categories. One was a pile of papers that were all about something abbreviated as IPW. A second set was all the papers labelled SWC. The third was everything else. He labelled that pile MISC. Clever, he told himself, pretty clever.

Among the sheets of numbers, though, he found some text that helped him identify the stacks further. IPW, he concluded, stood for "India Plains Wolf," and SWC stood for "Scottish

Wild Cat." He searched on the web and found that both were real animals, and that recent postings about both had come from Drew Robbins' Carnivore Research Center. That makes sense, he thought, since Melissa Campbell worked with Robbins. Nothing to raise any suspicions in that.

And there was nothing much in the MISC pile, either. Mostly the pile held general personal items, like receipts from last month's bills, and students papers she was grading. Most of the papers had a few comments written on them, but Jimmy noticed one that Melissa must have spent a lot of time on. It was covered in comments, and it looked as though it had been read repeatedly—corners of the pages were bent, some math had been done on the back of one page, and Melissa had written comments with different colored pens. Several pages had coffee stains, as though Melissa had spent long enough to set her cup down and think. The paper had been written by a student named Timor Madras, and the subject was the India plains wolf. Jimmy put it on top of the pile.

The crackle of the intercom got his attention. "Call for Officer Nesbitt on the non-emergency number." He picked up the handset and punched the button next to the blinking light.

"This is Officer Nesbitt."

"Oh, Jimmy, hey. This is Frank Marin. I was hoping to talk to Des."

Jimmy knew the voice of the Stone Valley police chief. "She's not here, Frank. Can I help?"

"I guess," Frank said. "I've got news about the murder of Melissa Campbell."

"At the moment, I'm the one working on that. Been sorting

through her papers all day. So give me the details and I'll pass them along to Des."

"Great," Frank agreed. "First off, she was killed at least a week ago, but not much earlier than that."

"That squares with what we've been learning," Jimmy said. "No one had seen her since at least last Wednesday." Jimmy counted to himself. Seven days since last Wednesday.

"Right," Frank said, "but there's more. The woman next door, the one with the key who let you in, she has some interesting stuff to say about Campbell and some of her co-workers. Seems like all might not have been going well."

"Like what?" Jimmy asked.

"You know, I'd rather have her tell you herself. Rather than hearing it second-hand from me. I'm not familiar with all the names and such from your other investigation, and you know how the university works a lot better than me." Jimmy wasn't so sure about that. "She's home now, so I think you should go talk with her."

"I'll head right over," Jimmy said. "Thanks for the heads up." He hung up and headed out the door, happy to abandon the three stacks of paper on his desk.

Jimmy knocked, and the same woman who had let him into Melissa Campbell's apartment opened the door a crack. "Hello, Miss Sun, I hope you remember me. Jimmy Nesbitt from the university police."

"Oh, yes," she said, opening the door wider. "Sorry, I didn't recognize you at first. Please come in."

Jimmy understood her caution. "I'm sure you've been getting some unwelcome attention from reporters and such, right?"

"Yes," she said, "and I don't like it. I'm a pretty private person." Pretty, that's for sure, thought Jimmy. She pointed to a chair by the front window. "Please sit down. The policeman told me someone from the university might be coming to see me. Can I make you some tea?" Jimmy didn't drink tea, except sweet and iced, but he found himself nodding yes.

She returned with the tea, and Jimmy took a tentative sip. "Thank you. This is delicious. I didn't expect it to be sweet."

Ara Sun smiled. "I've learned that Americans like their tea sweet, whether it is hot or cold."

"You aren't from here, then, Miss Sun?"

"Please call me Ara," she said. "No, I am from South Korea, but I came here to attend college." She smiled again, and Jimmy found himself losing focus, listening to her soft, lilting voice. "That was five years ago, and I'm still here."

"I'm so glad that you're still here," Jimmy said.

"Pardon me?" Ara asked.

Jimmy colored a bit, and back-tracked. "I just meant that, uh, the university is always glad that students like their experience and want to continue. May I ask what you're studying, Miss, I mean, Ara?"

"Conservation," she said and frowned, "just like Mel, Melissa."

The mention of the murder victim brought Jimmy back to the purpose of his visit. "So you two worked together?"

Ara tilted her head, considering her answer, and Jimmy drifted off again. "Sort of, but not that directly. We were in the same department, but it is large, and we studied different things. I work on protected areas, like parks and nature preserves, but Mel was working on predator behavior."

"But you were friends?"

"Oh, yes," Ara said, nodding, "we got along well. That's how I came to live next to her. She told me that this apartment was going to be available, and I moved in about a year ago. It's great to have a friend nearby."

Jimmy could drink tea and listen to Ara talk all day long, but he knew he needed to get back to business. "The town police said you had some important information to help our investigation. Of course, you're aware that Drew Robbins, one of the faculty members in your department, was also killed?"

"Of course," Ara said, "that's what I wanted to tell you about." Jimmy nodded, encouraging her to continue. "Mel has been telling me for a while that she hadn't been getting along with her advisor. That was Dr. Robbins. She was way behind on her dissertation research, but she wasn't getting any help or encouragement from him."

"But she worked closely with him on his teaching, right?" Jimmy asked.

"Not closely, no. Mel did almost all the work on his courses. That was one of the reasons she was behind on her research, spending so much time on the teaching. Mel was so nice, and she cared so much about the students."

"I can see how that would be a problem," Jimmy said, but he wasn't sure that he did understand. Wasn't teaching the reason they were all here?

"But there's more," Ara continued. "Mel and I talked several times recently that she was looking at a couple of Robbins' other studies and found things she couldn't explain." Again, Jimmy nodded, but didn't interrupt. "She said that some data about the movements of animals they had tracked were much too similar to be real. Nature didn't work that precisely, she said."

Jimmy was starting to make connections. "Do you know what projects she had been looking at?"

Ara nodded. "Yes. She told me that a student had done a paper on one of them that raised her curiosity. It was about the India plains wolf." Bingo, thought Jimmy, our friend the IPW.

"And the other one?" Jimmy asked.

"That was interesting," Ara said. "Mel had decided to look at the most recent study, the one being done by another student, Gina Rahim. She said Gina was about to graduate, and Mel wanted to catch a problem if there was one. To warn Gina before she published something that wasn't right."

"What was Gina studying?"

"The Scottish Wildcat," Ara said.

That's pile two, thought Jimmy, SWC. "Thank you, Ara, that's very useful." Jimmy was thinking what this all might mean, and he voiced his thoughts. "I wonder if she had talked with Robbins or Gina Rahim about this."

"Yes, she had," Ara said. "The last time we talked, Mel told me that she had let both of them know about her concerns. That's when things started to get worse with her advisor, she said, because he hadn't been happy about what Mel had been doing. Mel said he accused her of trying to sabotage him. And Gina wasn't happy about it, either."

It was time that Jimmy got back to the office so he could fill in Des and the others working on the case. He finished his tea and thanked Ara. He handed her his card. "If you think of anything else, Ara, please give me a call. Or if anyone, like reporters or other neighbors, bother you about this, just call."

"Thank you, Officer Nesbitt," she said and smiled.

"Oh, please, call me Jimmy."

35

Elena called Des at the police station as soon as she finished reading. But it was Jimmy who answered the phone. He had just returned from his interview with Ara Sun.

""Hey, Jimmy, this is Elena. Is Des around? It's important."

"Sorry, Elena, but she's not here. She's in the with the university's leadership team, briefing them on the state of the investigation and on a big event we have this evening."

"I guess that means no interruptions, right?"

"Unless it is life or death, no," said Jimmy. "I haven't even been able to talk with her this afternoon, and I've got a lot to share." He quickly filled Elena in on what he had learned from examining Melissa Campbell's papers and from his talk with Ara Sun.

She needed to talk with Timor again, to confirm that he had told Melissa Campbell about his concern with the wolf data. If so, and she was pretty sure it was so, then Melissa had been following the same trail about fake data that she had been following. The big difference was that Melissa had confronted both Drew Robbins and Gina Rahim about it.

"When will Des be free?" Elena asked Jimmy. "I need to talk with her."

"I don't think she can get back to you later today at all," Jimmy said. "We have a controversial environmental activist coming to give a big lecture and hold a rally this evening. We're scheduled to provide security the whole evening."

Elena had forgotten about the speaker, given what she had been focusing on for the last few days. She remembered now that the university was hosting a climate change expert from Denmark who had been campaigning worldwide to make beef production illegal because cows generated greenhouse gases. Elena had even forgotten that she had assigned her class to attend and that she was scheduled to be there as well. Even more, because the speaker was from Denmark, Hans had arranged to hold a reception for her after the talk at the Scandia Café. Elena was supposed to be there, too.

"I forgot all about this, Jimmy," Elena said. "We've been a little pre-occupied, haven't we?"

"That's an understatement," Jimmy said.

"Well, I've just spent the whole day reviewing the files in that wooden box," said Elena, "and I've got some new ideas about what might be behind Robbins' murder. But before we go there, I need your help with something."

"Sure, Elena. Des is going to be out for a while still, and the thought of looking through those stacks of papers more is making me ill. What's up?"

"I need you to find out what Gina Rahim's name was when she was born. Des told me that Gina's mother had changed her name and that Gina didn't even know what it was. I think Gina was lying about that. I've got a hunch that there is another connection between Gina and Drew Robbins that goes back a long way."

Jimmy hesitated. "How would I do that? Because I'm way out of my depth here."

Elena thought for a moment. "Well, Gina is a British citizen, so I'd start by calling the British Embassy in Washington. That's what I was going to do, but I can't imagine they'd give information like that to me. But you're a police officer working on a murder investigation. They ought to help the cops, don't you think?"

"Beats me, but I'll try," said Jimmy.

"Thanks, Jimmy." She looked at her watch. "Now I've got to get ready for class tomorrow. I'll see you at the lecture tonight."

The task wasn't as bad as Jimmy had expected. He went a few rounds with the staff at the British Embassy to prove who he was and that his enquiry was legitimate. Eventually he was transferred to an office in London, at a place called Somerset House. Apparently, Jimmy learned from the web while he was on hold, Somerset House was where all the official records of births and deaths and such were kept.

The records weren't actually kept there anymore, of course. They were all computerized. All the better for Jimmy, because the nice woman who sounded like Emily Blunt could help him, even though it was now late evening in London. She had no trouble finding the name-change certificate for one Gina Rahim. The nice British woman attached it to an email and sent it on in a matter of seconds. The whole transaction took only a few minutes. Sometimes, Jimmy thought, all this modern technology actually works.

Jimmy opened the email and accessed the attachment. Because the name change was for a minor, the parents were listed: Thomas Hyde-Martin, father, and Alesandra Rahim, mother. The child's original name: Ngorojine Hyde-Martin. The child's new name: Gina Rahim. He printed the certificate so he could show Des later.

The name of the parents didn't mean anything to Jimmy, but he thought that Gina's original name was pretty unusual. Ngorojine. People often chided him about being named Jimmy. They said grown men weren't called Jimmy, they were called James or maybe Jim, but not Jimmy. Yeah, well, that's what his name was on his birth certificate. Jimmy. And no one was going to call him anything else. But Ngorojine, that was a new one.

He started typing the name in his web browser. As soon as he got to Ngoro, the autofill feature completed the subject field with "Ngorongoro Crater." Jimmy knew he had recognized something about that. Ngorongoro Crater was the famous wildlife park in Tanzania; he'd watched a television special about it, narrated by that guy with the British accent, David something. David Beckham, maybe.

He read a bit about the crater, including that its name was a Maasai word. He went back to the search line and completed typing Ngorojine into the browser. Bingo, there it was. Ngorojine was one of the words that Maasai people used for the hyena.

When Des picked him up to head to their evening on the security detail, he filled her in on his work with Melissa Campbell's papers and his visit with her neighbor.

"So, while I was beating my gums with a bunch of

administrators," Des said, "you were doing real police work. Good job, kiddo."

Jimmy beamed. "So, maybe Drew Robbins killed Melissa because she was going to expose him as a fraud."

"That's a possibility, for sure," Des said, "but the town police are going to have to connect a lot of dots before reaching that conclusion. And that doesn't help us much, unless someone who cared a lot about Melissa and thought Drew killed her went ahead and killed him. What about the neighbor?"

"No, I don't think so," Jimmy said. "Ara seems as sweet and gentle as, uh,… I don't know. Real sweet and gentle."

Des looked over to see Jimmy blushing slightly. "Ara, huh? You two on a first-name basis?"

Jimmy changed the subject, quickly. "While you were gone, Elena called and asked me to find out what Gina Rahim's original name was. It took a little negotiating with the British folks, but here is her name-change certificate." He held it up to show her as she drove. "Her birth name was Ngorojine Hyde-Martin."

"I wonder why Elena wanted you to dig that up. But whatever the reason, it'll have to wait until tomorrow. Now let's go make sure our young environmental superstar is treated hospitably."

36

The evening's events came off without a hitch. The young activist gave a spell-binding talk that brought the audience, most of which were vegetarians, to its feet in a standing ovation. The crowd of meat-loving protestors outside had remained peaceful. Elena sat with Hans near the aisle of the auditorium. She spotted Des near the back of the room along with Jimmy and Jessie. After the talk, Elena looked for Des so they could review what Elena had learned from the wooden box, but Des was occupied keeping the speaker's well-wishers in order and her detractors at arms length.

The reception at Hans' café also went well. But once again, Elena couldn't find a time with Des when they could talk.

After the reception, Hans beamed with the success. He suggested that Elena spend the night with him, but got a brisk rebuff. "What's going on?" he asked her. "Your head has been somewhere else all night."

Elena knew better than to talk about her worries. "It's nothing," she lied. "I'm just not ready for tomorrow's class and it's already late. I've got to get home so I can finish preparing and get some sleep." She gave Hans a quick kiss and headed home. "I'll make it up to you, I promise."

Elena taught her class the next morning, but her students noticed that she seemed to be distracted. She even ended class a few minutes early, something she had never done before, and raced out of the room waving off their attempts to talk with her. The same suspicious student from Monday's class told his friend, "She's up to something."

Elena pulled out her cellphone as soon as she got outside the classroom building. But there was no message from either Des or Jimmy about Gina's given name.

She double-timed across campus, back to her department. As she passed the departmental library, she saw Timor sitting at a study table.

"Timor," she said, louder than she planned. Others in the room looked up in surprise, and Timor looked worried. "Come into the hall."

He followed her out, and she continued. "Did you talk with Melissa Campbell about your problem with the India plains wolf data?"

He nodded. "Yes. Well, no. Not really."

Elena was impatient. "What do you mean, Timor? I don't have time for games."

Timor blanched. "That's the topic I had chosen for my term paper. We had to turn in an outline, along with introduction and methods sections a couple of weeks ago. So, she knew about it I guess, if she had reviewed the paper yet, but I never actually talked to her about it. I don't know if she had even read it before...well, you know, before she died."

"Oh, she read it alright. She read it." Elena headed straight to Ted Graham's office. Ted was talking with Aaron Schmidt, and both looked up in surprise as she burst through the door.

"Oh, sorry," Elena said. "I didn't know you were talking to someone, Ted."

Ted smiled. "No big deal, Elena. Aaron and I were just going over some ideas about revising the curriculum. I'm sure we'd both like to talk about anything else but that!"

Elena didn't return the smile. "Yeah, well, you're not going to be happy with what I have to say. Arguing about the curriculum is going to seem like fun compared to this."

"Sit down, Elena," Ted said, sensing that Elena was deadly serious. "Is it okay if Aaron listens in?"

Elena looked at Aaron, who nodded reassuringly. His presence started to calm her down. "Please, yes. I'd like him to hear this. Besides, it's all going to come out soon anyhow."

Ted hated bad news, and he'd been getting nothing but bad news lately. It was bad enough that Aaron Schmidt wanted all new students to take a wood anatomy course—a bedrock of conservation, Aaron liked to say—but Elena's nearly frantic demeanor was making him very nervous.

"I'll get straight to it," said Elena. "I've discovered that Drew Robbins stole the data he used for his dissertation from another researcher."

"Not more of this," moaned Ted. "The last time we talked, you told me that he dend Russell had been fudging their recent data. Then Mel Campbell was killed. And now you're saying Robbins faked his dissertation, too? How do you know this?"

Elena quickly explained getting the wooden box of files from Sheila Cummings and how she compared the data in the box with Robbins' raw data from his dissertation. And then she told them about finding the journal and the revelations in it. She finished by relating what Timor had learned about Robbins' other projects and the probable connection between Melissa's death and the research misconduct.

Ted was furious. He looked like he might explode. "Melissa Campbell died over this? How could anyone be so corrupt and evil? And someone we all knew. I guess the only good thing about all this is that Drew Robbins ended up with one of his own precious spears buried in his back."

The three sat quietly for a moment as they let Ted's comment sink in.

"I didn't really mean that," he said softly, "you know I didn't mean it."

Aaron tried to deflect the conversation. "Those spears," he said, "I find them curious."

Elena encouraged him to continue talking. "What's curious about them?"

"Open your copy of the new departmental brochure, Ted," said Aaron. "Turn to the page with Robbins' and Bronoski's pictures."

Ted looked at him like he had lost his mind, but flipped through the brochure until he got to the right page. There stood Drew Robbins and Russell Bronoski, each holding a Maasai spear. Aaron tapped the picture with his finger. "See, look at that. It's very curious."

"Come on, Aaron," said Ted, "all I see is two guys holding their spears, indicating that they worked in Africa. Just like you in the next picture." He pointed to the facing page, in which

Aaron stood in front of the giant cross-cut of a tree trunk. "You're holding your tree cookie. They're holding their spears."

"Not exactly," said Aaron. "They aren't holding their own spears, they're holding each other's."

Elena looked more closely at the picture. "How do you know, Aaron? Those spears look exactly the same to me."

Aaron shook his head. "But they aren't, believe me. You can't see it very well in the picture, but I was there when the picture was taken. Remember, our times with the photographer were scheduled in alphabetical order. Schmidt is next," he pointed to his picture, "right after Robbins. So, I was waiting my turn, watching the photographer set up and take their pictures."

"Gina Rahim was there also," he continued, "just like always, tagging after Robbins like a love-sick puppy. Disgusting."

"We don't care about your opinions of young love," said Elena, "but what about the spears?"

"If you know anything about wood anatomy," Aaron said, "and you should if you claim to be a natural resources professional, you'd recognize immediately that the shafts of the two spears are different. One of them—Robbins' spear—has a handle made from the umbrella thorn acacia and Russell's is made from yellow fever acacia."

"You've got to be kidding," Ted said. "You can tell that just from looking at them?"

"I've been looking at wood longer than you've been alive, Ted," said Aaron. "So, yes, I could easily see the shafts were different."

"How do you know whose spear is whose?" asked Elena.

"I've seen them. Russell keeps his in his office, and he showed it to me once. I also saw it on Sunday when he was cleaning out his office. I love that yellow fever acacia wood. The tree is called yellow fever acacia because early European colonists thought camping near those trees caused yellow fever. But, of course, it is the mosquitos that live in the damper sections of forest that cause the disease. The yellow fever tree likes wet environments, so the tree and mosquitoes often occur together. Look carefully and you'll see the grain swirls around, like a fingerprint."

Ted and Elena looked again at the photo, but still weren't convinced. "What about Robbins' spear?" Elena asked.

"Remember that stupid retreat we had last year?" Aaron said. "The one where we were listing the strengths and weaknesses of the department? We had it at Robbins' house, and he showed everyone his precious spears, above his precious fireplace. His are just ordinary umbrella thorn acacia wood. The grain on that is a lot straighter, like an oak."

Ted grimaced. He didn't like retreats either, but the dean made them do one every year. "So you're saying that Gina got the spears mixed up?"

"No," said Aaron, "she wasn't mixed up. She seemed very purposeful about which spear she gave to which man. They weren't paying any attention, but she was. She gave Russell's spear, made of yellow fever acacia, to Drew, and she gave Drew's spear, made of umbrella acacia, to Russell. And she took the spears back from the men right after the picture was snapped and hurried away with them"

Elena stood up. "Which means the spear that ended up in Robbins' back was the one that Russell was holding in the picture. Gina made sure that his fingerprints would be on the murder weapon."

"Whoa, whoa, whoa," said Ted. "Are you saying that she switched the spears to frame Russell with the murder? Are you crazy?"

"No, I'm not crazy," Elena said as she headed out the door, "but someone is. Crazy and dangerous."

Elena was on her phone as she hurried from Ted's office and down the stairs to the parking lot. Des was in her office with Jimmy, and she answered on the second ring. She put the phone on speaker so Jimmy could join in. "I was just about to call you. Have you looked at that box of files yet?"

"Yes, Des," Elena said, almost breathless as she reached her car. "But that's not important right now. I think that Gina has been trying to frame Russell for the murder."

She explained Aaron's revelation about Gina switching the spears for the photograph of Robbins and Bronoski. The obvious conclusion, which had been unthinkable, was that Gina had murdered her fiancee. But why?

"Incredible," said Des. "So Aaron Schmidt broke the case for us based on identifying the wood in the spear handles? Just incredible."

"Jimmy," Elena asked, "did you find out Gina's real name?"

"Yes, I did. I did what you suggested and it worked great. Her original name was really strange, Ngorojine. It means hyena in the Maasai language."

Elena's hands were shaking as she held the phone. "What was her last name?"

"Hyde-Martin. Ngorojine Hyde-Martin."

"Oh, my god," Elena cried. "She's the daughter of the man whose research Robbins stole for his dissertation."

"Slow down, Elena," said Des. "What are you talking about?"

Elena sat in the car and quickly summarized what she had learned from reading the contents of the wooden box. Des could hardly believe her ears. "Okay, Elena, here's what I want you to do. Go home, lock your doors and keep that box safe. Jimmy and I are going to pick up Gina."

37

Gina was roused from her thoughts by the sound of the doorbell. She answered the door and found Judith Heinz on her porch holding a basket.

"Hello, dear," said Judith, "I made us some blueberry muffins. May I come in and share one with you?"

Gina wasn't in a mood for company but didn't know how to get rid of her neighbor graciously. Instead she turned on the charm. "Sure, that would be great. The muffins smell delicious. It's so nice this morning, let's sit on the patio."

Gina poured coffee for them both and led the way to the back patio.

"So how are you doing?" asked Judith. Judith thought she knew the answer, as the house was a mess as they walked through, and Gina didn't look much better.

"I'm okay. I'm sleeping a little better every day," answered Gina. "I'm just worried because Drew's killer is still on the loose. I don't know why they haven't arrested Russell yet."

"My goodness," said Judith, "do the police think he did it?"

"They should," said Gina. "All the evidence points to him. He threatened Drew at the award banquet. He had been making up data and stealing from the university. His fingerprints were on the spear that killed Drew. And he had a key to the house." Gina was getting more and more agitated as she talked. "What more do they need?"

Most of this was news to Judith who hadn't spoken to the police since the day of the murder.

"Well, I suppose the police have to be very careful before they make an arrest," said Judith, trying to calm Gina down. But then another thought occurred to her. "Do you think you are in danger, Gina?"

Instead of calming down, Gina was getting more agitated. "No, I don't think so. At heart Russell is a coward, a parasite without a backbone. That's why he kept working as Drew's assistant for all these years, sucking off a bit of Drew's success. He didn't have the courage to set out on his own. If anything, he should be afraid of me."

"Oh, my dear, don't say such things," warned Judith. "I know you want this all to be settled, but you can't take matters in your own hands. That's the police's job."

"Don't make me laugh," said Gina. "The police are running all over looking for a killer when the truth is right under their noses. They need to arrest Russki."

Gina was getting more excited, and Judith wondered if she should leave her alone. But Gina kept on talking.

"Russki has something of mine," Gina said. "I mean something of Drew's, and I need to get it back. But I know he won't give it to me."

"What is it, dear?"

Gina thought about the wooden box. Her father had written to her about the box in his last letter, the one she received from his friend, Markall. Markall had included a note saying that her father had died and wanted her to have this last letter. The letter was short and the handwriting was nearly illegible. Her father told Gina that Andrew Robbins had stolen his work and that he had taken a wooden box that contained all his research files and journals. He begged Gina to find the box and expose Drew Robbins as a thief and a fraud. And I could add a murderer, Gina thought, as she imagined how Robbins had charmed her father into helping him and had then left him to die. Her father's heart had been broken twice, once by her mother and again by that snake Drew Robbins.

"Is it valuable?" Judith asked, jarring Gina back to the present.

"It is to me," Gina said. She stood up and began pacing around the patio. Judith thought she looked like a vicious animal, a lion or tiger, prowling for something to attack. The look in Gina's eyes terrified Judith.

"Sit down, my dear," said Judith. She was frightened that Gina might do something silly, or dangerous. Judith needed to settle her back down. "Shall I get us another cup of coffee?"

Gina growled back at her. "No, I can't sit down, and I don't need coffee. I need action. I need to get what belongs to me."

"But the police..." began Judith.

Gina cut her off, her agitation growing. "The police had their chance. Now it's my turn. You need to go, Judith."

"But, Gina..."

"Now, Judith. You need to go home, now."

The venom in Gina's voice left Judith no option. She stood and watched Gina head back into the house. "What are you going to do, Gina?"

"I'm going to get what's mine from Russell Bronoski."

Judith was in her studio trying to paint when she heard the police car drive up and park in front of her neighbor's house. She watched from the window as Des and Jimmy got out of the car and talked for a moment before approaching the house. Des went to the front door, but Jimmy walked around to the back. Judith had seen Des visit Gina several times since the murder, but she realized now that this was no courtesy call. Des rang the front door bell, but got no answer. She tried again, several times. Eventually, the front door opened, and Jimmy walked out. Judith remembered that the back door had been open when she and Gina were on the patio. Judith decided she needed to talk with the police and went out to meet them.

They were still on the front steps talking when Judith came across the lawn. "Hello, Des. I'm afraid Gina isn't home."

They turned to see the neighbor approaching. "Hello, Judith," Des said. "Yes, we've determined that she isn't here. Do you know where she might be?"

"Oh yes," said Judith, "I'm afraid I do. She went to find Russell Bronoski. I'm worried that she might do something foolish."

"What's going on?"

"Gina told me that Russell has something of hers, or Drew's. I'm not sure which. Anyway she said she was going to find Russell to get it from him. She was very upset. She's convinced Russell killed Drew, and if she confronts him, I'm worried that he might get violent with her."

"So am I, Judith," Des said, "but the other way around. Russell is the one in danger, not Gina. Let's go, Jimmy."

This time they ran to the car and sped off with the lights flashing and siren blasting.

Des called Russell at his office as Jimmy drove. When he didn't answer, she called his home. This time he answered, but Des broke in on his greeting.

"This is Des White, Russell. Gina is on her way to see you. She might be dangerous. We're on the way."

"Hold on," said Russell, "you're too late. Gina's already been here and left."

"Are you okay? What happened?"

"She barged in without even knocking," Russell said. "She was in a frantic state. She asked me about a wooden crate that Drew had brought back from Africa a long time ago. I remember him having it when we came back from Africa, but I haven't seen it since then. It took me a long time to convince her that I didn't have it. She said she had looked everywhere in their house and in Drew's office, but couldn't find it. She was getting more and more upset as we talked. I couldn't figure out what the big deal was. She kept pressing me, getting really angry. Finally I suggested she check with Sheila Cummings. As you know, Drew was pretty close to Sheila."

"Then what?" asked Des.

"Then Gina said, 'Of course, that bitch has it.' And she went running to her car."

Des hung up on Russell. "New directions, Jimmy. Head to the admin building. She's going after Sheila."

38

The sound of breaking glass startled Sheila as she lay on her bed. She had called in sick again, still overcome by Drew's murder. It was after noon, but she had no interest in eating or getting dressed or doing anything.

Then she heard the back door open. She reached into her bedside table and pulled out the handgun her father had given her. He had warned her that someone might break into her house. Now some intruder was doing just that, unaware that she had stayed home from work.

She crept into the kitchen, her hand shaking slightly as she pointed the gun ahead of her.

"Stop right there," Sheila said.

The intruder looked up from the opposite side of the kitchen table. Sheila gasped aloud when she realized she was looking into the face of Gina Rahim. "What are you doing here?"

Gina smiled and her eyes gleamed. "I came for what is mine, Sheila. But I didn't expect to find you here. Why aren't you at work?" Gina walked slowly around the table toward Sheila.

"Stop," Sheila said. "Stop, or I swear I'll shoot you."

Gina laughed. "You won't shoot me. You don't have the nerve. You should have done it the first time you had a chance."

"What do you mean?" asked Sheila.

Gina continued walking toward Sheila. "I saw you hiding in the bushes at Drew's house after the banquet. You stood out like a flashing neon sign to someone trained to spot wild animals in nature. Why do you think I stayed so close to him all the way into the house?" Sheila started to protest, but Gina cut her off. "Who were you intending to shoot anyhow? Me, because I stole Drew from you? Or Drew because you finally realized how he had been using you? Or both of us?"

Sheila's arm had begun to drop as Gina talked, but now she aimed directly at her again. "You, of course, you little tramp! I was going to shoot you!"

"Oh, I'm the tramp, am I?" Gina snorted. "At least once I got into Drew's bed no one else ever climbed in. You stayed with him while he screwed everything in a skirt. You're the tramp, Sheila, not me."

Gina took another step toward Sheila. "Stay where you are, Gina, or I swear I'll shoot."

"Don't make me laugh," said Gina. "You're a coward, and that's why Drew could never be satisfied with you. He was a predator, and you were just his prey, his weak, vulnerable prey. He played with you like a cat plays with a mouse before eating it. He wanted me for his mate, a predator just like he was." Now Gina did laugh out loud. "You know, Sheila, if I hadn't set up Russell so carefully to take the blame for killing Drew, I would have framed you for his murder."

Sheila shrieked, "You killed Drew?"

"Of course I did," said Gina. "And now I'm here to finish the job."

Sheila put both hands on the gun, trying to stop it from shaking. She stared into Gina's eyes and began to squeeze the trigger. At that instant, Gina lunged, knocking Sheila off balance. Sheila hit the floor, her head smashing against the hard tile. The last thing she remembered was the sound of the gun going off and Gina's voice crying out in pain.

When Sheila regained consciousness, she was sitting in a chair. Her head throbbed so loudly it felt like a jackhammer inside her skull. She tried to move, but couldn't. She looked down and saw that each of her hands was bound in duct tape to an arm of the chair and each ankle was taped to a leg. She slowly remembered what had happened, and a cold shudder ran through her body. The kitchen was turned upside down, and most of the contents of the pantry were thrown in the middle of the room. The roll of duct tape that she kept in a drawer by the sink was on the table.

She could hear loud noises coming from another room in the house, probably her bedroom. From where she was taped onto the chair, she could see into the living room. Her belongings were strewn across the floor. She realized that Gina was ransacking her home. She scraped her chair towards the front of the house, but lost her balance and crashed to the floor still taped into the chair.

The noise stopped abruptly, and Gina walked back to the kitchen. "I thought I heard something," said Gina. "It's about time you came to,"

The left sleeve of Gina's blouse was soaked in blood. Sheila gasped when she saw it. "That's right," said Gina, gingerly feeling her arm and wincing, "you shot me. Don't worry, I'll live. You might not, though, if you don't give me what I want."

Sheila stared at her in terror. Gina stepped close to Sheila and whispered in her ear. "So listen, Sheila, tell me where my father's files are. I know you have them."

"I don't know what you're talking about," whimpered Sheila. "I don't know who your father is."

"Don't play games with me," Gina said and slapped Sheila across the face. Sheila recoiled in pain and fear. "I've torn your house apart looking for it, but I know it's here. Drew stole a wooden box full of my father's files and brought them back from Africa. I want them back."

Gina saw the look of recognition that flashed across Sheila's face. "So you do know what I'm talking about, don't you, Sheila? Drew gave it to you to keep, didn't he?"

Sheila shook her head and started to deny the truth, but Gina slapped her again. "Do we have to keep doing this all day, Sheila, or are you going to tell me where the box is?"

Sheila managed to spit out a few words. "Okay, yes, Drew did give me an old wooden box, years ago. I didn't know what was in it."

"So where is it then, Sheila?"

"It's not here."

Gina's eyes glowed with rage. "Tell me where it is, or you'll never take another breath. I killed your lover boy and Mel Campbell. I won't hesitate to kill you."

Sheila cringed as Gina prepared to slap her again. "I gave it to Elena Bertoni."

"Good girl, Sheila, good girl." Gina laughed and patted her

cheek this time, rather than slapping it. Nonetheless, Sheila recoiled at the touch. "Today is your lucky day. You told me the truth, so I'm not going to kill you. She ripped a new piece of duct tape from the roll and pressed it across Sheila's mouth. "Elena Bertoni might not be so lucky."

Jimmy drove with his foot to the floor. Des called Sheila's office from the passenger seat.

A receptionist answered and said that Sheila had called in sick and wasn't at work.

"Head to Sheila's house, Jimmy."

The speed they were moving made the drive hazardous, but they managed to arrive safely within a few minutes. They rang the doorbell, but got no answer. They knocked loudly, but still got no answer. Just as they had done earlier, Des stayed on the doorstep and Jimmy went around the back of the house. In a few seconds, Jimmy quietly opened the front door. She saw that he had drawn his weapon. He whispered, "Sheila's in the kitchen. She's been attacked, but I think she's stable."

"Where's Gina?" Des asked.

"I don't know," Jimmy answered. "She could still be in the house." They searched the house room by room until they were certain Gina was not around. The house was in shambles, with Sheila's belongings scattered everywhere.

They went back to the kitchen. Sheila was strapped to a chair, her mouth covered with a piece of duct tape. They gently removed the tape from her mouth.

"Oh, thank god," she cried. "I thought she was coming back to kill me."

"Who was going to kill you?" Des asked.

"Gina," Sheila gasped, "Gina Rahim."

"You're safe now, Sheila," Des said, as Jimmy cut her loose from the tape bindings. "Can you tell us what happened?"

Sheila spoke between her sobs. "I called in sick; I couldn't go to work. I was resting in bed when Gina broke into the house. I confronted her with the gun I keep by my bed. We struggled, and I shot her."

"My god," Des said. "Where is she? Is she dead?"

Sheila shook her head. "No, no, I just shot her arm. We struggled, and I must have hit my head and passed out. When I woke up, Gina had tied me in the chair. She wanted me to give her the box that Drew had given me. I told her I didn't have it, and then she started hitting me." Sheila began sobbing, unable to speak any longer.

A new fear now gripped Des. "Sheila, did you tell her that Elena has the box?"

Sheila began to cry again. "I didn't mean to, but I was so scared. I knew she would kill me if I didn't tell her. Yes, yes, I told her that I had given the box to Elena. I'm so sorry."

"How long ago did Gina leave?"

Sheila tried to focus. "About an hour ago, maybe."

Des spoke quickly to Jimmy. "Call an ambulance for her and stay with her until the EMT's take over. Then meet me."

"Where?" he said.

"At Elena's house. I hope we're not too late."

39

Elena heard the siren as the police car approached her home. Her heart beat faster. Now was the moment of truth. "I think I should let them in," she said, "don't you?"

Gina seemed conflicted. What will the next few minutes mean to me, she thought, and to my future. But the thought that she might have a violent confrontation with the police—and especially if Des was with them—terrified her. She trembled at the thought of harming Des. The idea that this would not go as planned also haunted her.

She nodded her head and answered Elena. "Yes, go let them in."

Des was running up the walk when the front door opened. She stopped and crouched, gripping her pistol in case Gina came out intending violence. But it was Elena who opened the door.

"Are you alright?" Des yelled to Elena. She expected that Gina might be right behind Elena, with a weapon at her back. "Where is Gina?"

"I'm fine," said Elena, "and Gina is fine, too. She's in here with me."

A confused Des responded, "You're not in danger?"

"Oh, no," said Elena, "I'm not in danger. Gina and I are just talking. No problem. Everything is good, isn't it, Gina?"

Gina now appeared in the doorway, moving from behind Elena. Des leveled her pistol at Gina. "Don't move, Gina, and put your arms up where I can see them."

Gina did as she was asked, and Elena interceded on her behalf. "It's okay, Des," Elena said. "It's really okay. You can put that gun away. Please come in."

At that moment another police car pulled to the curb, and Jimmy jumped out. He knelt behind the front of the car as he drew his weapon. "I'm here, Des," he yelled to her, "and more are on the way."

Des put her weapon in its holster and spoke quietly to Jimmy through her radio. "Stand down, Jimmy. I'm going to go in the house with Elena and Gina, but I want you to stay on alert out here, and when the next unit comes, post them around the back. Stay in radio contact with me, but don't take any action unless I order it."

Jimmy was bewildered. "But, Des, there's a killer in there, with a hostage."

"I don't think that's the case, Jimmy. We need to keep the situation under control. So, I say again, do nothing until I tell you to. Understand?"

"I understand," said Jimmy, but he didn't understand. Des was going into a volatile situation with a suspected murderer, alone and without her weapon at the ready.

The three women walked into the house together. Elena led the way to the living room, where the wooden box and its contents were arrayed on the coffee table. Elena and Gina sat on the couch next to each other. Des chose a chair opposite, where she could watch Gina. She kept a calm demeanor, but inside she remained on high alert.

Des didn't know what to make of the arrangement. The scene looked like two colleagues had been working on a project together. Several files lay open, and Elena had been making notes on a pad of paper. They both had cups of coffee in front of them.

"What's going on?" asked Des.

Gina looked at Elena and nodded for Elena to answer. "We've just been talking about the research that Gina's father had done on hyenas in Tanzania. The research that Drew Robbins stole for his dissertation. Gina's father—Dr. Thomas Hyde-Martin— did wonderful work back then. I've been looking at it over the past couple of days. It was ground-breaking work in animal be-havior. I'm so glad that we're going to get all this straightened out. Right, Gina?"

"Yes, that's right," Gina said, smiling at Des. "Elena has promised to make sure that my father gets credit for his original work, and that the university will retract everything that Drew Robbins has gotten credit for. Drew Robbins will be destroyed as a scientist. He'll be known as a fake and a thief. He will be despised by everyone he wanted to worship him. Just like I despised him."

"Gina, I'm glad you've worked this out with Elena," said Des. "But you know why I'm here, don't you?"

Gina smiled again. "Of course. You're here to arrest me for killing Drew."

"So you did kill him?" asked Des.

Gina nodded. "Yes, I did. And I'd do it again if I could.

I killed him so many times in my dreams, it is sort of anti-climactic to have it over with."

"But, why, Gina?" asked Des. "You loved him so much. You had just agreed to marry him."

"I told you I was a good actress, didn't I? I didn't love him. I hated him, hated him with all my heart. Drew had killed my father by betraying him. It was my destiny to avenge what happened to him. What better way than to convince him that I was in love with him?"

"Good lord," said Des. "This whole thing—from the time you came as a graduate student to right now—was a charade?"

Gina was now happy to tell the story. "Yes, it was. But it started much earlier. My father's final letter told me what Robbins had done and begged me to stop him. I was still in boarding school, but from that moment, I began my plot to end up here. I read everything I could find about Drew Robbins, and then I did everything possible to duplicate his path. I became a biologist, I studied animal behavior, I did research projects on predators. I played every part necessary so that I'd end up as Drew Robbins' graduate student. Once I got here, I resisted his advances until he was consumed by the need to have me. Then I became his lover. He thought he was the predator, but he wasn't. He was the prey, trapped from the day I decided to destroy him."

A single tear ran down Gina's face as she continued. "My only real regret was that I had to deceive you, Des. You were my first friend, and you've always been someone I could count on to keep me going when my determination started to falter. I hated to use you, but nothing was going to deter me from my destiny."

Des thought back to the many times when she and Gina

talked together about Gina's frame of mind. Des had always thought Gina was discouraged about her research, the kind of feelings that most graduate students have from time to time. She shuddered now to realize that what she had been doing was giving Gina the confidence to destroy Drew Robbins.

It was Elena's turn to ask the questions. "If killing Robbins was your destiny, then why did you try to frame Russell for the murder?"

"He was Drew's partner," said Gina, the venom in her voice rising. "Whatever Drew was doing, Russell was doing, too. That arrangement about how we took data—I took the first sample and then some company did the rest—was so contrary to normal procedures, the two of them had to be in it together."

"You did a good job of convincing us that Russell was the murderer," said Elena.

Gina relaxed again and smiled. "That was the fun part, you know. Getting it all right."

"We figured out how you switched the spears," said Elena. "You made sure that Russell's fingerprints were all over Drew's spear when their photograph was taken."

"Easy," said Gina. "Drew just did whatever I wanted. And Russell did whatever Drew wanted."

"But what about the note that Russell gave to Drew at the banquet?" asked Des.

"That was just as easy," Gina said. "Russell did pass Drew a note. I took it out of his pocket later. He just asked Drew to share a little credit. What a fool. Drew would never share the credit, with Russell or anyone else, including my father. When the banquet was ending, I asked Russell to bring me a clean copy of the program from his table so I could have a souvenir. There was an extra at the seat where Mel should have been. When he handed it to me, I asked him to slip it in the folder that the award came in. So I never touched it then. That night at home, I put on gloves and printed the fake message, using the block printing that Russell always taught us in the field." Gina looked at Des. "Remember, Des, I told you that I was good at calligraphy? Another of those boarding school skills that came in handy."

Des shook her head in amazement. "One last question. Why stab him with the knife and then plant the spear?"

Gina frowned. "Well, that was a mistake. I never thought you would discover that there were two wounds. I wanted to kill Drew with my father's knife. When my father's friend, the man who ran the bar where he lived, sent me his final letter, he also sent me my father's other belongings. There wasn't much, but the dagger was in there. He also said that my father had a big wooden box full of files and other things, but that it wasn't there anymore."

"And now we know what was in the box," Elena explained to Des. "And I've told Gina that I will make sure her father's story gets told."

"Yes, thank you, Elena," said Gina. "Since I got my father's dying letter in boarding school, I've only wanted to accomplish two things in my life. One was to track down and kill Drew Robbins. The other was to restore my father's reputation as a great scientist."

Des wasn't finished. "Did you kill Melissa Campbell, too?"

Gina nodded. "Yes, I had to. I didn't want to. I had nothing against Mel. But she called me and wanted to talk about my dissertation. She said there were problems with the data and she wanted to discuss them before I published the results. So I went to her apartment and we talked. She had discovered that Drew had been faking data, including mine. I asked her to let it go for a while, but she was adamant that she had to tell the university right away. I couldn't let her do that. She was going to ruin my plan."

"So you hit her?"

"That's right, Des," Gina said. "I hadn't planned to kill her. When I knew she had to be silenced, I grabbed a brick from the bookshelves and hit her. I messed up the room to make it look like a robbery."

Des stood up. "Okay, Gina, now you need to come with me."

"Before that, can I show you one more thing?" Gina asked.

"Sure," said Des, "but then it's over."

Gina reached into her large purse that was on the floor next to the couch. She pulled out her father's dagger. "I thought you might want the murder weapon."

Instinctively, Des reached for her holster. "Yes, I do want it. Give me the knife, Gina. Don't do anything stupid."

"You can have the knife in a minute" said Gina, a fierce fire burning in her eyes. "But I'm not going anywhere with you."

"Don't be a fool, Gina," said Des. "You won't get away with harming us. Jimmy is right outside the door, and more police are on the way. And you don't want to hurt Elena. She is going to bring back your father's good name."

Gina's face took on a different aura. "I wouldn't hurt either of you. You are my friends. But now I go to be with my father." She turned the knife toward herself and thrust it deep into her heart.

40

Within a few weeks after Gina Rahim's suicide, life had begun to return to normal at Virginia Western University.

Robbins' will left everything that he owned to the university for the Carnivore Research Center, stipulating that it be named after him. The university, however, disavowed the gift; the disposition of it would take a court to determine. The Wallace Foundation retracted the award it had given Robbins, and the university, now the owner of the prize money, returned the funds to the foundation.

Russell Bronoski resigned his position at the university and pled guilty to a number of financial crimes. His lawyer asked for leniency so that he could care for his sister, and the university agreed that they did not wish to see Bronoski go to jail.

Sheila Cummings also resigned. An initial review of her actions showed that she had been negligent but not criminal. The university put new protocols into place that added several bureaucratic layers of review for all financial decisions. Faculty, as usual, complained.

Jamie Nelson finally got back to Toronto, with Misty Stanhope in tow. It didn't work out well between the two. Jamie got hired as a production assistant for a show about cave exploring in the Antarctic. Misty declined the opportunity to accompany him. Instead, emboldened by her recent experience, she instructed her agent to find her roles playing a tough police detective.

The university issued a statement regarding Drew Robbins' research fraud and re-assigned Elena Bertoni for one year to review all his work and determine what retractions and other actions were necessary. She hired Timor Madras to help her.

Elena Bertoni and Des White shared coffee one afternoon as the buzz surrounding the case was settling down.

"I want to thank you for all your help," Des said. "I'm not sure we would have ever figured all this out without you."

"I was very happy to help. Life for an academic is pretty boring compared to what I've been doing since I met you. And now I have this new assignment to continue being a sleuth." Elena smiled and asked, "Guess what they're calling me around the department?"

"I can't imagine," Des said.

"Miss Marple."

"Well, Miss Marple," Des laughed, "If you're not busy solving a mystery in St. Mary Mead, I wouldn't mind a sidekick for the police charity triathlon on Memorial Day. Care to join me?"

Acknowledgments

This is a work of fiction. All aspects of the book—characters, places, events and situations—are fiction and any resemblance to real individuals, places or events is coincidence.

I would like to thank my family members and friends, who encouraged me to take on this project and kept me moving forward. Successful mystery writer Katy Munger gave me needed advice and Paul Gaffney provided essential feedback on an earlier draft. All their help was valuable, but errors and weaknesses in the book are entirely of my making.

About the Author

Larry A. Nielsen is emeritus professor of natural resources at North Carolina State University. He retired as an Alumni Distinguished Undergraduate Professor in 2017. Along with more than 100 academic and professional articles, he is co-editor or co-author of three text-books (*Introduction to Fisheries Science, Fisheries Techniques, Ecosystem Management*). He is author of three recent non-fiction books, *Provost—Experiences, Reflections, and Advice From a Former "Number Two" on Campus* (2013), *Nature's Allies—Eight Conservationists Who Changed Our World* (2017), and *Wolfpack Ramblings—A Thousand-Mile Walk Across NC State's Campus* (2021). He hosts the website *Today in Conservation* (todayinconservation.com), which includes stories from the history of conservation and the environment for every date of the year. Larry lives with Sharon, his wife of more than fifty years, in Cary, North Carolina. HIs grandchildren like to remind him that although he writes murder mysteries, he has never won a game of Clue in his life.